SHIM

Books by Reuben Davis

Butcher Bird
Shim

SHIM

A Novel by
Reuben Davis

With an introduction
by Bertram Wyatt-Brown

Banner Books
University Press of Mississippi / Jackson

First published in 1953 by The Bobbs-Merrill Company, Inc.
Copyright © 1995 by the University Press of Mississippi
All rights reserved
Manufactured in the United States of America

98 97 96 95   4 3 2 1

The paper in this book meets the guidelines for permanence and durability of the Committee on Production Guidelines for Book Longevity of the Council on Library Resources.

Library of Congress Cataloging-in-Publication Data

Davis, Reuben.
    Shim : a novel / by Reuben Davis ; with an introduction by Bertram Wyatt-Brown.
        p.   cm.
    ISBN 0-87805-773-0 (cloth : alk. paper).—ISBN 0-87805-774-9 (paper : alk. paper)
    I. Title.
PS1519.D42S54   1995
813'.52—dc20   95-15741
                                    CIP

British Library Cataloging-in-Publication data available

To Louvica and Nick

Inside the crescent-shaped boundary of hills that leave the Mississippi River at Memphis, swing in an arc eastward and southward and rejoin the river at Vicksburg, lie the thousands of acres of flat bottomlands known as the Mississippi Delta.

Many years ago these fertile acres were covered with virgin woods—giant cypresses, oaks, elms, gums, maples and hickories—only nibbled at here and there by a small town, a little lonely farm, a big plantation.

Scattered through this wilderness were swamps, lakes and bayous, thickets of bushes and briers and occasional immense canebrakes, unpenetrated by man. But by skirting these a man could ride at a swift gallop for miles under big trees whose towering tops shut out the sunlight from ground almost bare of undergrowth.

Introduction

One of the most persistent themes in southern literature is that of a boy's search for a surrogate father. Reuben Davis's *Shim*, a novel with unusual power and hidden complexity, belongs to this venerable tradition. Mark Twain, creator of the orphaned Huckleberry Finn, was the first to adopt the genre. In his deepening relationship with the runaway slave Jim, Huck becomes the child in us all who pursues safe adventure under the affectionate regard of an undemanding elder. William Faulkner mined the topic to grand effect as well. Chick Mallison in *Intruder in the Dust*, Bayard Sartoris in *The Unvanquished*, Isaac McCaslin in "The Bear," Sarty Snopes in "Barn Burning," and, more tragically, Quentin Compson in *The Sound and the Fury* each in a singular way seeks his manhood by hunting for a father, a fatherlike figure, or an exceptional woman whom he can worship and who will guide him into the mysteries of adult life. Disillusioned by the literal or figurative absence of the natural father, each searches for a substitute who will teach and love him.

The southern youth in aggrieved pursuit of a caring senior appears in works of more popular fiction as well, including some that have been translated into film, such as Pat Conroy's *Prince of Tides* and John Grisham's *The Client*. In these stories, cinematic and otherwise, common themes appear: violence, sometimes racial outrage, wildwood hardship, and close ties that bind some family members against a hostile world. For some, these fictional elements may have become threadbare; yet such narratives have such special meaning for those who cherish southern culture with its patriarchal traits and love of the outdoors. Reuben Davis's *Shim* contains all the familiar characteristics. It is as vivid, moving, and distinctive as any of the American classics mentioned above. Moreover, it has the kind of qualities that at once suggest transcription to the screen: a fast-paced plot, dramatic turns, and visual and aural authenticity—the lights and shadows and sounds of the forest setting.

Based upon Davis's own background, *Shim*, like Faulkner's "The Bear," reflects on life in a past both physically and emotionally primitive and mythic. The Delta landscape in *Shim* recreates a world no longer with us. It was a primeval South of impenetrable thickets, swamps, canebrakes, wild beasts, unbearable heat, and wintry cold. With a huntsman's heightened senses, Davis conjures up the fragrance of wood smoke, the caw of the birds, the terror of seeing a panther's burning eyes in the night. Born on December 22, 1888, in sparsely populated Tallahatchie County, Davis grew up in a Mississippi Delta that no one today would recognize. Automobiles had not yet arrived, and paved roads did not exist. Drinking water from uncontaminated artesian wells was a rarity. Even rich folks in Greenville and Greenwood had yet to install screens to keep out the relentless assaults of mosquitoes and flies. Set like an oasis in the dark of surrounding woods, the Davises' settlement more closely resembled the early southwestern frontier than the coming era of small towns and bustling commerce. In a short memoir Davis recalled, "The nearest white family lived a mile away, and the school and post office were two miles away. The nearest railroad station was fifteen miles away, and our cotton and provisions had to be hauled by wagon through that fifteen miles of woods and cane brakes if from the west, and through woods and small farms if from the east."

As if to match the elemental character of the land, the people of Tallahatchie made storytelling a way to entertain and to instruct themselves in enduring values. Davis's narrative abilities had deep roots in his native soil. Memories of the Civil War were as vibrant for the county oldsters as those of the Second World War have been for the fast-disappearing veterans today. They told their exciting tales of heroism and daring to awestruck boys like Davis himself in a manner that the late Peter Taylor so effectively captured in his short story "In the Miro District." Although the great war does not figure in *Shim,* its shadow lies across the novel as a subject simply to be taken for granted. Davis's father, another Reuben, had served as a captain under the renowned cavalry warrior Nathan Bedford Forrest, and, in the novel, the father of the boy-hero Shim is one Capt'n Govan.

Reuben Davis was only nine years old when his father died, a crushing loss for the youngest child in the family. In a manuscript recollection, he connects the death with his misery and loneliness in school and recalls that his mother and older brothers were hard-pressed to keep him at his studies when he preferred to roam the forest alone. He remembered that "they got me as far as entering Mississippi College." Spending most of his time perfecting his boxing, he was enrolled for only one term. After some years of bumming across the country, he joined the 20th Engineers in 1917 and served in France. Davis apparently received severe wounds in the war and spent several years in government and private hospitals, not marrying until he was thirty-eight in 1926. His wife, Helen Dick from Memphis, was a brilliant graduate of the University of Wisconsin. While rearing two children, she helped her husband immeasurably with his novels and short stories until his death in 1966 in Yazoo County, Mississippi, where he had retired.

Davis was not prolific, a factor that has contributed to his current—and unmerited—obscurity. In what was a customarily small edition for a first-time author, Davis's novel, *Butcher Bird*, was published by Little, Brown in 1936. The work centers on a botched insurance fraud that leads to murder. Its chief purpose, however, was to depict the routines, rustic pleasures, and lives of black sharecroppers at the beginning of the twentieth century. It was a subject he knew well. "By the time I was seven," Davis once wrote, "the little negroes [*sic*] on the farm who were my chief playmates, had taught me how to hunt rabbits with a tap stick, and at nine I learned to shoot. At twelve years old I was a steady hunter, shooting coons out of trees at night wearing a headlight, hunting deer and bear and panthers with the men, both black and white."

Davis's understanding of African-American humanity sets him apart from all but a handful of other white southern writers of his time. A close observer of language and gesture, he caught the subtleties and intriguing patterns of vernacular speech in the black Delta. His remarkable sensitivity to linguistic habits and economy of expression—he was a practiced short-story writer— enhance the verisimilitude of *Butcher Bird*. With the novel's favorable reviews, the publishers were doubtless encouraged to expect other works to follow in quick succession. Davis, however, had none ready until he completed *Shim*, published by Bobbs Merrill, seventeen years later in 1953.

When *Shim* reached the reviewers' desks, they uniformly praised it as a thrilling, "irresistible" boy's story. At the *New York Times*, Orville Prescott hailed the novel as the peer of Marjorie Kinnan Rawlings's *The Yearling* and Mary O'Hara's *My Friend Flicka*. Lewis Gannett in the *New York Herald Tribune* aligned it with the best of the fall season's selections: Alan Paton's *Too Late the Phalarope* and Nadine Gordimer's *The Lying Days*, both enduring classics. In the *Washington Star*, Thomas J. Kelley struck a chord that other critics echoed when he declared that a reading of *Shim* "will make young boys dream of adventure and old men dream of their boyhood." Uniformly the journalists stressed its winning nostalgia for a bygone day before the encroaching timber companies began felling the almost human-seeming oaks, cypresses and pines. They also admired the innocent decency, conforming temperament, and keen intelligence of the fourteen-year-old hero, unaware that such a representation would become all too rare in the fiction of the latter half of the twentieth century. The alienated Holden Caulfield in J. D. Salinger's *Catcher in the Rye*, published just two years earlier than Davis's novel, set the model for more brittle, urbane, and self-conscious young fictional heroes.

The critical praise lavished on *Shim* forty-odd years ago still happily rings true, even if the journalists' remarks seem hackneyed. Three features, however, escaped the notice of Davis's contemporary reviewers: first, the curious autobiographical subtext to the novel; second, the racial aspect of the story; and finally, the psychological complexity of the white characters who are representations of the author's own deeply human needs. All three factors were intimately bound together but must be dealt with separately.

Consciously rejecting an openly autobiographical approach, Davis had subtler purposes in mind than we are likely to suspect at first. Yet his method of handling them revealed a common but seldom recognized scheme of repression in southern letters. Adopting the regional pose of leisurely indifference to hard work, intellectual or otherwise, Davis claimed that he wrote fiction with the most modest of intentions. "It seems to me these people and things I remember have a meaning. I do not pretend to tell you what it is, simply to recall them; for the pleasure of those who have similar memories, and for the curiosity—and I can hope, greater understanding—of those who never knew those old days of both peace and violence."

How simple Davis has made his task appear to be. He would not engage in narcissistic and soul-baring autobiography—an undertaking, he claimed, much more perilous than fiction writing. "So I've hatched up a lazy idea: Play it straight," he proposed. Actually he was throwing dust in readers' eyes. There was nothing at all "straight" about the matter. Instead, he showed that he adhered to the old code of southern honor. That sensibility did not permit self-revelation—no public display of one's inner thoughts or personal affairs. By longstanding convention, the confessional road was supposed to lead to ruin. An enemy might use any vulnerabilities disclosed to destroy the reputation of the ill-advised confessor. Davis admits to a nagging fear: he might inadvertently "reveal his personal thoughts and experiences." The tell-it-all mode went against the grain of this southern writer, who said that "revealing yourself is the one thing you can't do, no matter how hard you try. I'll be as unknown to you as your wife, your husband, your child, your parents—or for that matter, yourself—at the end of the book as at the beginning." The tone is defensive, the issuing of a challenge to the reader: probe no further.

By identifying his narrator with the thoughts of the boy, Shim, Davis limits the range of those psychological insights that might draw attention to the author's own emotional life. Gentlemen, particularly ones from the South, were intractably determined to conceal their private lives. In the rarified domain of literary criticism, contemporary thinkers like Robert Penn Warren, Cleanth Brooks, Allen Tate, and Caroline Gordon—southerners all—were setting the criteria by which works of art were supposed to be judged. These New Critics, as the school was called, insisted on the sovereignty of the text, and they proscribed a scholar's intrusive questions about a writer's private motives or processes in its creation. As a member of the old school of regional gentility, Reuben Davis would have approved of any application of New Criticism to the examination of his work. Yet, protected from keen scrutiny, such writers as he often become unreliable guides for the entering of their fictional world. Although Davis refused to acknowledge it, he was filtering his own past through the present, providing a story rich with possibilities but denying any relationship to his own development as a writer. A close reading is required, however, to make such connections between author and work. In a sense the adventurous elements in the narrative are there partly to restrict the reader's curiosity. Yet it does not matter at all that we cannot completely break the author's code and enter his personal world: it is the very tension between revelation and reticence that places *Shim* among the jewels of southern literary art. Far from being a handicap, the ambiguity enriches the portrait of Davis's fictional world. The work can be read and enjoyed as pure adventure. But on reflection we become aware that the lineaments of the narrative reveal an anguish and a mourning not just for a vanished rural existence but for the artist's own powers of creativity.

The problem of authorial repression arises with regard to the second element that contemporary critics overlooked—the racial factor. Not once do we learn directly that Henry, the boy-hero Shim's surrogate father and the chief adult in the story, is black. The narrator says, "Most of the important things Shim knew—things about the woods around the plantation—he's learned from following Henry around since he was big enough to keep up with him" (p. 38). Henry's color must be inferred, since the narrator, adopting the perspective of the child, makes no distinction. Yet what really was the relationship between white owners and black tenants in the story—and by extension in Davis's own neighborhood so many years before? We are not told very much, only that Henry, Capt'n Govan's plantation manager, is almost the same age as Govan himself, Shim's distant and formidable father. We get the impression that the old plantation owner does not quite approve of his son's regard for a field Negro like Henry. At the same time, the absence of racial cruelties is not just a matter of romantic denial in the fictional tradition of the loveable and unthreatening Mammy and Ole Black Joe. Reuben

Davis's purpose is to strengthen the individuality of the aging sharecropper, not to fulfill the stereotype of an avuncular Remus or Pompey. Henry is the natural leader of the young Govans—Shim and his always-teasing brother Dave, age seventeen, and their uncle Ben—and all the others who join Henry's hunting expeditions.

The independence of Henry's spirit comes through as Davis brilliantly reveals the nature of two unequal relationships in which Henry is the key figure. Shim loves Henry without reservation. The old plantation major domo, however, does not entirely return that affection. He likes the boy and teaches him what he can about the woods, but he is an adult with other pressing concerns. Although the author never says so, Henry knows that the tie binding the white boy to himself is transitory: in a few weeks or months, Shim will take up other matters—particularly the pursuit of girls, as the closing pages reveal. And at some point, by the imperatives of southern society, the racial wall will have to rise as well, though the author makes no hint of such a turn.

Apart from his role as woodland tutor to Shim, Henry is involved in another unequal relationship, one in which he is the secondary figure. Filled with parental solicitude, Henry dotes on Kiz, his wife's niece and the expert cook for the plantation household. He loves her as intensely as Shim loves him. But, on the threshold of physical maturity, she seeks independence from her elders and falls for a young stranger who turns out to be insane. The sequence of events leads to tragedy and then to the stunning and poignant ending of the story.

Critics writing in 1953 were unable to see that Henry is a masterful artistic creation, another representation like Lucas Beauchamps in Faulkner's *Intruder in the Dust*. Though doubtless born a slave, Henry is a solitary oak, a proud black, confident of his woodlore and his secret ability to read and write. Few of his fellow croppers can do so. In a sensitive scene, Shim asks Henry, "How come you don't buy some land of your own to work?" Henry gives him an answer appropriate to white folks' questions, saying that he once had a farm but "owning land ain't nothing but trouble" and unending anxiety. After a crop failure, he continues, "there'd be debts to pester me, taxes to get up" (p. 43). In actuality, thousands of enterprising Delta freedmen like Henry had rented and then bought lands from former slaveowners. Until the 1890s depression, most made progress, but ever-lower cotton prices raked them down to ruin. Bankers and storekeepers were unwilling to lend them the money to carry on. Disfranchised, poor, and unorganized, Delta blacks like Henry had to remain quiet and sell out. Like the Govans' plantation overseer, they reluctantly swallowed their pride and bowed under the yoke of the reigning planter class. True to the racial circumstances of the time, Henry says, "I sold them hundred and sixty acres and thanks the Lord for the day I done it. I moved here with the Captain and lets him do the worrying" (p. 44). When Henry decamps at the end of the story, he at last expresses his hidden feelings in words addressed to the son of his white employer, carving into the wooden step of his now-deserted cabin a four-word sentence that speaks more eloquently than a paragraph of explanation. According to Shim's narrator in the story, the prospective loss of the forests to the sawmill owners drives Henry from the Govans' plantation. Much more important—if we can go beyond the author's presentation of an inexperienced boy's thoughts—was Henry's unslaked grief for the loss of his surrogate daughter, Kiz. Perhaps, too, we can imagine that the old Negro had nursed his grievances long enough and was determined once again to seek independence from white control.

If further conjecture is allowed, was not the departure of Henry from Shim's life a symbol of Reuben Davis's inarticulate sense of parental loss in his own childhood? The author would take offense at such speculations, but out of the depths of his sorrow he had created an unforgettable character. Henry's unwillingness to reveal himself to Shim parallels the author's silence about his own agenda. If white folks failed to open themselves to others, blacks, for even better reasons, behaved the same way in the presence of whites. Davis's Henry, like the African Americans among whom the writer grew up, nourishes his own secret longings beyond white people's ken. Like the writer W. J. Cash, in *The Mind of the South*, Davis recognized that, for all their boasting, whites could not read their black neighbors' minds at all. And, as mentioned earlier, Reuben Davis also marveled at how little we know each other, even ourselves.

With regard to the psychology of whites in the story, Reuben Davis is equally masterful and his storytelling richly textured. Yet, being a part of the society about which he writes, he again conceals as much as he explains. The Govans live in a community where the principles of honor are gradually disappearing but not so much that primordial outbreaks of passion do not erupt unexpectedly in clashes engendered by class antagonisms. Four killings in which both whites and blacks are involved occur in the story. The senselessness of violence begins to dawn on the young hero, reminding the reader of Bayard Sartoris, who bravely confronts but refuses to shoot his father's killer in *The Unvanquished*. Yet, like Faulkner's Bayard and his other young heroes, Shim understands violence as part of the ethic in which he is being reared. The boy carries his own "pepperbox" and, on more than one occasion, finds comfort in having the firearm stuck in the back of his pants. In the wilderness setting, bravery was the chief virtue for men and boys, and nothing was more insulting than a taunt of cowardice. Men demanded respect from their associates because without it they felt incomplete, debased, desolate, unmanned. Sometimes such a sense of emptiness prompted them to test their prowess against rivals as a means of self-reassurance. So it is in *Shim* for the would-be aristocrat, J. Ney Ward, jealous enemy of Shim's uncle Ben. Yet what are we ultimately to make of the incidents that lead to Ward's death and the near murder of Ben? Readers will have to judge the episodes on their own, but the narrative implies that Ward hates himself for his sexual attraction to his enemy and tries to destroy the object of his uncontrolled feelings. Like so many other southern writers, Davis merely hints about matters that cross the "normal" sexual boundaries.

Undoubtedly much of the strength of Davis's fiction arises from the inner turmoil that his own ambiguities about self-revelation engendered. Having lost his father, Captain Reuben Davis, when he was so young, he had joined the army of poets and writers whose creativity had much to do with the expression of early grief. Over 70 percent of the poets in the *Oxford Book of English Verse* experienced the death of one or both parents before they were fourteen. The translation of pain and an angry sense of abandonment into imaginary re-creations of family life seems to be a hallmark of southern writers as well. Shim's uncomplicated and happily boyish attitude toward his parents—Capt'n Govan and Miss Cherry—reflected less what Davis himself, reclusive and troubled, may have experienced than what, at some level, he would like to have felt. The brisk, compelling stories of fights with bears, panthers, alligators, snakes—and murderers, white and black—keep the reader quickly turning the pages until the last line. But a deep sadness pervades the novel, too. Perhaps that emotion is conveyed because Reuben Davis realized that this was the last novel he would write. Nevertheless he has left us with a most lyrical and evocative account of a southern boy's search for maturity and parental love, among the best ever written. Given the high competition in that genre, from Twain to Faulkner, that is no mean achievement.

Bertram Wyatt-Brown
University of Florida, Gainesville

chapter one

DARKNESS WAS CROWDING twilight in the Mississippi Delta.

A flock of bronze turkeys rose, one and two at a time, from the ground in a pin-oak flat and flew up to roost in the big trees bordering a shallow brake.

In a thicket of cane and vines a doe stroked her fawn with her tongue a couple of times to quiet him before leaving him to go down to the bayou and drink.

A farmer fastened the gate to the high paling fence that protected his livestock and stood a moment looking across his twenty-acre field at woods where a panther had been squalling at short intervals since before sundown. He went inside, for supper and to close the door and windows in the two-room log house against the night air and varmints.

Somewhere to the south a plantation owner led his saddle horse from the lot where wolves had played havoc with his calves and sheep last night. On the turnrow he mounted, whistled for his dogs and, resting his shotgun across the saddle, rode toward his young corn to run the bears back over the rail fence they had climbed, prematurely hunting roasting ears.

At the edge of Beaver Lake, Shim Govan dipped his rusty tin bucket into the dark dreggy water and raised little ripples that flashed a silvery light. Motionless, he watched them, wondering, as he often had before, where they got their brightness. Many times, duckhunting, he'd watched ducks drop down out of the night sky and be completely lost to sight on the dark water, until silvery ripples, flashing back from their breasts as they swam, would show him where they were. Where did the light come from that made the ripples bright on the dark water?

Straightening, he rested one shoulder against a big cypress knee and looked across to the other bank, where the sun had just dropped behind the tall trees. He saw a gray squirrel high on a cypress at the water's edge disappear into a den hole in the trunk. Farther over, a pair of hawks circled slowly among the tops of big oak trees, searching the ground in thickets of briers, in bushes and in vines for a last tasty snack of rabbit or bird before going to roost. The bucket in his hand forgotten, Shim drank in the sights and sounds of sundown.

"Quit gawking at nothing and put that fire out, Shim."

His brother Dave's voice brought him to himself, and he headed toward the campfire higher up on the bank. Slowly, hating to exchange the rich, sweet smell of wood smoke for the flat, steamy smell of wet ashes and charred wood that meant the day was over, he trickled the water onto the fire.

Dave had the mules about hitched to the wagon, and Shim could hear Ben Caulfield and Wick Beckham crashing through the brush along the lake bank, talking in the short, quick sentences men used when toting a heavy load. Ben, Mama's youngest brother, was Shim's and Dave's uncle. He and Wick had ridden over to the Govan place this morning, and the four of them had hatched up this fishing trip. But Ben, always too restless to stick at any one thing for long, had got tired of fishing early in the afternoon. Borrowing Dave's rifle, he'd gone off into the woods. Just about the time Dave and Wick and Shim had their fish cooked and were ready to eat, Ben had lucked up on a deer and killed it, and hallooed for some of them to come help bring it in. Instead of going, they'd hollered him in to eat with them, and then he and Wick had gone back to get the deer.

They came out from among the trees, heading toward the wagon, the feet of an eight-point buck tied together and swung over a pole on their shoulders. Ben's broad shoulders were stooped a little to keep from throwing most of the weight back onto the shorter Wick.

Shim reached down absent-mindedly for a well-fried perch he'd just spied on the piece of newspaper they'd used for a platter. He was already full as a tick, but he stripped the meat off with his teeth and tossed the bones toward the lake.

"Doesn't your hand fit anything?" Dave called.

Shim saw they had lowered the buck at the wagon and were all looking at him. Ben, a good six feet tall, Wick, stocky and strong as a mule, and Dave, at seventeen nearly as stout as a man—all stood there waiting for him to come help lift. Any two of them could load that deer without the help of his fourteen-year-old strength, but older folks always got fun out of joking younger ones. They'd be ragging him about one thing or another all the way home. He broke the cord off his fishing pole, pushed the hook into the cork and walked toward them, taking his time and wrapping the cord around the cork as he went. Helping lift the deer would be a pleasure if he was really needed, but he didn't see any sense in hurrying when he wasn't.

"The only boy I ever saw who could sleep on his feet," Dave

said. Shim stood over the buck, still fiddling with the fishing cord.

"To his way of thinking," Ben said, "there's nothing else on the map but these woods and lakes."

This gave Shim a chance to delay leaving the woods a little longer. "Well," he said slowly, "like the crow flies, Memphis is about a hundred and thirty miles north. If you go south far enough you'll hit Vicksburg. Go west far enough through those woods across the lake and you'll come to the Mississippi River."

"And east about seventeen miles is the depot," Wick said. "Did you see the old Mississippi when you went to Memphis with the Captain?"

"I wasn't blind," Shim said. Dropping his cork and line inside the wagon, he stooped with the others to do his share of hoisting the unwieldy carcass. It fell with a thump into the wagon bed, antlered head against the endgate, legs sticking stiffly out.

"Everything ready?" Ben said, checking with his eyes a shotgun, Dave's rifle and the ax on the bottom of the wagon.

From force of habit Shim passed a hand over the right front pocket of his short cottonade pants to feel his own pistol, a four-barrel derringer that everybody called a pepperbox. Dave, when he got his first good pistol a couple of years ago, had discarded the derringer. He'd made fun of Shim when he found him carrying it around, said it wouldn't hit anything over ten feet away. Shim didn't care. It kept him from feeling half dressed. Just about all the men and older boys carried pistols, and he could hit with it a whole lot farther than any ten feet, too. Until he was old enough to have a better one, he made out just fine with this one.

He climbed up and sat down beside Wick on a plank laid

SHIM 15

across the shallow wagon bed. Dave and Ben sat on the front plank. Dave tightened on the lines and whistled, and the mules pulled into the narrow winding woods trail.

Shim was tired but contented. The wagon bumping over exposed tree roots and low-cut stumps rested him. He hadn't caught but four goggle-eyes and a bream, but he'd had all he could eat, because Dave and Wick had caught plenty. And he'd been all day on the lake.

"Well, boys," Ben said, "it's been a good day."

"Good for everybody but Shim," Dave said.

"What ails Shim?" Ben asked.

"Nothing, yet. But something's fixing to. Papa's going to get home and miss these mules."

Shim squirmed a little on the plank. Dave was just joreeing him, but there was truth in what he said. The Captain, their father, wasn't going to like it about the mules being out this way in worktime. It was better than four miles to the house, and night was closing down on the thick woods much faster than the full, contented mules were walking.

"You're in it as much as I am," Shim said, and gave a backward kick to the handle of the frying pan jostling against his foot in the bottom of the wagon.

"You crazy boys didn't take these mules away from the plow just to bring us over here and fish?" Ben said.

"Shim's idea," Dave said. "He outtalked Henry for them. Promised Henry he'd have them back by sundown."

"Why didn't you say so before now?" Ben said, like he was really worried.

Dave shrugged. "Shim made the deal. It's his trouble."

Shim let them have their fun. He was usually the youngest one in a crowd of older men and boys, and he reckoned if they ever quit joreeing him he'd miss it. Dave would take his share of the blame when the time came, and the Captain wouldn't be too hard on them anyhow with school just out. It was May, and this was the first time they'd been to Beaver Lake since last fall.

Shim had quit trying to figure out why everybody was always so anxious to keep work going on all the time anyhow. He believed mules were like folks—glad to take a trip and see new places now and then. Today, instead of just going up and down cotton rows all day, these mules had smelled the good smell of woods, eaten a lot of tender green mutton cane and drunk good lake water. If they were tired, let them rest tomorrow. One day not pulling a plow wouldn't matter. Folks raised too much of everything, anyway. Every spring when breaking time came for the new crop, they plowed under cotton they hadn't got around to pick the fall before. They always had a crib of corn they didn't need, and more hay than the stock could eat, more hogs and cows to worry with than they needed—more of everything.

"Shim—" Ben was looking at him over his shoulder—"I swear I'll wear you teetotally out if you've riled the Captain by taking these mules. I came to ask a favor of him, and I want him in a good humor."

The unnatural seriousness on Ben's lively, good-natured face tickled Shim. "I'll tell him it was you who was so dead set on taking the mules and coming to Beaver Lake," he said, and ducked Ben's backhand swipe at his head.

Ben laughed. "You little devil. Your mammy should have broken your neck when a sewing thread would have done the job."

Ben fell into a silence like he was studying mighty hard about something, and they jogged along the road saying nothing. Shim began wondering what favor Uncle Ben wanted from the Captain. It was sure to be something exciting, not the everyday kind of favors kinfolks and neighbors asked of each other—the loan of a couple of horses, a ton or two of cotton seed or a few dollars from the money sack the Captain kept in the big wardrobe in his bedroom. Uncle Ben had big, wonderful ideas, the kind nobody else ever thought of.

When he'd come to the Captain boiling over with some big new scheme, Miss Cherry, Shim's mother, would always take up for Ben. The Captain would tell her Ben was like all the Caulfields, not a lick of plain common sense in the whole kit and caboodle of them. Then Miss Cherry would laugh and say it took venturesome folks like hers, the Caulfields, to keep folks like the Captain from getting stale. All except the time two or three years ago when Ben ran off to fight in the Spanish-American War. Then it was the Captain who had taken up for Ben, telling Miss Cherry it was the very thing to take the wildness out of him. Uncle Ben had been back from the war almost a year now, and Shim had heard the Captain say not long ago that he was more harebrained than ever, that it looked like he never was going to settle down to serious farming like the rest of his folks. Shim couldn't imagine Uncle Ben any different from what he was, always joking and keeping folks laughing, and always with some big money-making deal in his head.

The trees they passed were fast becoming blurs, and when an overhanging limb he'd failed to see raked Shim's face, he knew full dark was here. Ben's wide shoulders in front of him had been quiet for as long as he could keep them still. He straightened them with a deep breath, threw back his head and heisted a song in his deep baritone. "Come where my love—"

"—lies dreaming." Wick came in with a bass, Dave with a second tenor and a backjab of his elbow at Shim's knee for him to join them. Shim's voice wasn't long enough out of the gosling stage to be trusted every time, but, warmed at Dave's encouragement, he sang the next couple of lines with them, then dropped out, the better to enjoy listening to the harmonizing of the others.

They were well into the second verse of the song when he felt the wagon lurch forward and knew they were starting the downgrade into Rabbit Bayou, already dry here where the road crossed it. The mules, feeling slack run into the traces, raised their heads to hold their collars in place and scotched back against the breast chains to slow the wagon. They were topping the other bank when a pause by the singers to catch their breaths came at the same moment as an instant's break in the clucking sound of the wagon hubs on thimbles. In the second of silence Shim heard something, jerked upright and cocked his head, listening.

The singers, their lungs full of air, began again, and Shim said loudly, "Hush, you all." The singing stopped short, and he heard the sound again, this time clearly. They all heard it. Wolves. Five, six, maybe more, badly stirred up, howling, and not very far away.

Everybody moved. Shim hadn't aimed to, but the plank he was sitting on was knocked catawampus as Ben whirled and dived past him to get to the shooting irons. Wick was down there with him. Shim, having lost his seat, was on his knees. Dave, still holding the reins, stood backed up against the high front endgate, swaying with the bumping wagon and staring, big-eyed like the rest of them, into the darkness thick as a wall behind them.

"The deer," Ben said. "They smell it and are coming after it."

"They'll have to get me first," Wick said.

SHIM

"If there's enough of them, they wouldn't mind doing that," Ben said.

"Shim, take these lines and give me your pepperbox," Dave said in a tight, dry voice. "I'm going out on the tongue and keep them off the mules."

Shim knew exactly how he felt. Wick had the shotgun, Ben had Dave's rifle, and Dave wanted mighty bad to get his hands on some kind of hardware. But Shim didn't want to be unarmed himself. In a pinch Dave could use the ax. "They won't tackle mules," he said. "Besides, they're behind us."

"They can get in front of us mighty easy, and if they scare these mules and make them run away . . . Give it here," Dave said.

"You're driving," Shim said. "I'll walk out there on the tongue."

"You couldn't hit a bear with a spade. Give me that pepperbox," Dave ordered.

"You nor nobody else could hit a flock of elephants in this dark," Shim retorted, keeping his hand tight on his pistol.

Dave stopped arguing. The wolves were closing in. Their howls were shorter and a lot of yipping and growling was going on. Their stomachs were hurting for some of that deer meat, and they were mad.

"I'm going to open up with the shotgun," Wick said, and his voice sounded different than when he'd bragged a minute ago that they'd have to take him first.

"I'll join you," Ben said, raising the rifle. "If we can kill or wound one, they'll stop to eat him."

"Save your cartridges," Wick said. "You can't hit anything with that rifle out there in this black dark. I've got a chance with this spatter-gun."

He let fly one barrel right after the other, and the roar of the gun sounded good. Shim felt the hairs standing at the back of his head lower to normal, and the cold shivers running up and down his back stopped. But only for an instant. The silence following the shot wasn't right. If any of those small shot had found wolf flesh at that distance, there'd have been some yelping.

A ragged chorus of "missed" came from lips that sounded as dry as his own felt. The woods around them, the wolves and the ground were all black dark, and no telling which was which. The silence was worse than the howls had been. The wolves might be slinking closer from anywhere, on both sides, behind or ahead.

"Hey," Shim said, his voice a dry croak, "there's a lantern here somewhere. I saw it this morning."

"Light it, quick," Ben said.

Dave shoved the lines into Shim's hands and went down on his knees, fumbling at an old crokersack in the corner. No use for anybody to hold the lines, for only the mules could see the road. Shim stiffened. Much closer and in full cry the wolves opened up behind them. They were overtaking them fast.

He checked a panicky desire to put the mules to a fast trot. It wouldn't do. On this narrow winding road the wagon would be slammed against a tree or a stump in no time. There was nothing to do but let the mules go on picking their own slow way. He tried to guess the number of wolves. There weren't more than half a dozen howling at a time, but you couldn't always tell by that.

Dave had fished the lantern out from under the crokersack, but he wasn't getting it lighted. The matches he struck kept going out.

"Hand it here," Wick said impatiently.

"If we can get the leader," Ben said.

Dave's match caught, he lowered the chimney into place and a dim light flickered over the wagon bed. Near the back Wick and Ben, down on their knees to keep from being thrown out of the lurching wagon, held their guns ready. Dave scrambled between them with the lantern.

"Lie down so we can shoot over you," Ben said. "Hold the light over the endgate so it'll shine out there and not back in our eyes."

"How long before we'll hit some good road so these mules can trot?" Wick asked.

"Too long," Dave said, flattening himself as well as he could between them and hanging the arm with the lantern outside the wagon. The wolves hushed. There wasn't a sound in the darkness.

"Watch for them up there, Shim," Dave said uneasily. "They may be circling to get ahead of us."

Shim grunted. The pepperbox was in his hand, but since he could hardly see the mules' rumps, all he could watch with was his ears, and they were already straining to their last notch for any sound that wasn't part of the moving wagon.

"Don't you all let one of those varmints bite off my hand that's holding this lantern," Dave said.

"A varmint won't come close to a light," Wick said.

So Shim had heard, but the glow of that one lantern was mighty feeble to bluff animals as powerful and vicious as those wolves. Wick didn't sound like he believed it any too strongly right now himself.

The howling and yipping suddenly broke out where it had left off. Shim flashed his eyes back at the darkness behind them and had just brought them down to focus over the rear endgate when, stiff-legged, dark objects loped into the spot of ground the lantern lighted. He raised his pepperbox, but the other two guns spoke loud and long. The nearest wolf fell and the others vanished.

"Whoa." Shim pulled up on the lines and the mules stopped.

"We got one." Ben and Wick, reloading, spoke together. Dave scrambled to his feet, and the three of them jumped out of the wagon.

Cautiously, their guns ready, their ears straining for any sound, their eyes stretched wide to the farthest limits of the lantern light, they walked the few feet back to the dead wolf and stopped with disappointed grunts.

"A bitch," Ben said. "Get back to the wagon. It won't take them long to eat her and be after us again."

"Wait a minute." Dave held the lantern higher and pointed. "Over there." It was another wolf, dead as a doornail.

"A male, and a whopper." Wick's voice was loud with relief. "The leader, without a sign of a doubt."

Ben and Wick stooped, caught the two hind feet and lit out running with him to the wagon. Shim saw the dark, rangy body swing over the endgate and felt the jar of the wagon as the dead wolf landed. There it lay, beside the buck it had given its life to reach. It looked small beside the deer, but it was the biggest wolf Shim had ever seen. What a prize for them to show!

"Drive on," Dave said. The men scrambled into the moving wagon. Ben and Wick sat down on the back plank, Dave took the lines and Shim sat down beside him.

It was a couple of minutes before anybody spoke. Then Wick said, "Whether you fellows know it or not, that was a close call."

Ben said, "We took care of it all right, though. They'll eat that dead bitch, then spend the rest of the night fighting to decide on a new leader."

"You all talk louder so I can hear you," Dave said. "You about busted my eardrums when you shot over me."

"I'd love to watch that fight over who'll be the new leader," Shim said. "Henry watched a wolk pack fight to choose a new leader once. He was sitting up in a tree."

Nobody made any reply. Shim figured they didn't believe it, but wouldn't hurt his feelings by saying so. He believed it. Henry knew more about the woods than anybody in the world.

The cautious mules picked their way steadily along the winding road toward home, and the men fell silent. Shim began to feel drowsy. One good thing: the Captain would forget to be sore about the mules when he saw that big wolf. Shim was half dozing to the restful jolting of the wagon when dogs, greeting them cheerfully and noisily, roused him.

They were in the lane that ran in front of the house, and all the dogs—the Captain's four hounds, the curly-haired shepherd, the collie, the setter, and Shim's own little feist Gimlet—were barking and prancing around the slow-moving wagon. Leaning sideways, Shim reached a hand down in the darkness and, when he found Gimlet's slick, short-haired little back, lifted him into the wagon.

Through the yard trees, the white of the narrow upper gallery shone pale in the starlight, but the bulk of the house was dark except for a light in the wide hallway. The double front doors stood open, and at the gate, outlined against the light, stood the Captain, his hands on top of the pickets.

Dave reined out of the lane, crossed the outer yard and pulled up at the gate. Everybody jumped down, all talking at once, calling the Captain to come see the buck and the wolf. Dave was holding up the lantern; the rest of them crowded around the wagon bed.

The Captain's tall, supple body never moved fast unless the occasion called for it, and he didn't seem to think this one did. Instead of coming to the wagon bed to look at the carcasses, he stepped first to the mules' heads and ran a hand under their collars. Shim knew he was feeling to see if they were hot, and reckoned he and Dave weren't going to get off scot free after all. But right now was no time to worry about tomorrow.

Crowding up between Ben and Dave, Shim leaned over the endgate, got his first close look at the wolf and caught the Captain's arm. "Look," he said, pointing excitedly to a streak of scar tissue sprinkled with sparse white hairs. It began over the wolf's wicked-looking left eye and ran back beneath the ear. "It's the one you shot coming out of our calf pen last fall."

The Captain leaned to look more closely. The tightness left his face, and he straightened up, talking. "That's him, I bet six bits." They all knew what he was going to tell, and were as eager to hear it again as he was to tell it. Tales of brushes with dangerous animals never lost their flavor.

"When I heard the rookus that night," the Captain said, "I jumped out of bed and grabbed the first thing handy—my forty-five. I climbed the yard fence so the dogs couldn't follow me, and just before I got to the calf pen—there wasn't much light, just a quarter moon—I saw these dark objects coming out through the fence between the top plank and the wire. The last one, bigger than the others, hit the ground when I was still about sixty steps away. I cracked down on him and thought I had him. I knew I'd hit him in the head because he jumped straight up in the air and fell back on the ground. But

SHIM

by the time I got there he was gone. He'd stayed in the shadow of the fence and I hadn't seen him leave. Gentlemen, this is him, sure as a goose goes barefoot."

"If that hide's any 'count, you ought to have it mounted, Captain," Ben said.

"It's the positive truth, sir," Wick said.

The Captain was looking mighty pleased. Now they'd all drive on down below the lot, get Henry to help dress the deer and skin the wolf, and there'd be tales of other wolf battles and good talk of hunting.

Shim could hardly wait. "I'll go wake up Henry," he said eagerly, and knew right straight when the Captain turned slowly to look at him that he'd done the wrong thing by attracting the Captain's attention.

"You go to bed, son," the Captain said thoughtfully. "You'll see Henry in the morning—" he hesitated—"when you go with him to get some white oak for making splits."

Shim turned quickly to the gate and went up the front walk, walking fast but not too fast or the others would guess his disappointment. He should have known the Captain wouldn't overlook their taking the mules out for pleasure in worktime. He'd punish both him and Dave by keeping them mighty busy for a few days. He'd had to think up something right quick was why he'd said splits. They didn't need white oak for splits this time of year any more than a shoat needs a sidesaddle. They had plenty of feed baskets and wouldn't need splits for cotton baskets till just before picking time this fall.

Shim crossed the wide gallery, went down the long hall past the Captain and Miss Cherry's bedroom on the left, and turned in the last door on the right, to his and Dave's room. Undressing without lighting the lamp, he fell into bed. It had been a good day, and he was tireder than he'd thought, but it hurt to be sent off to bed like he was a young'un not old enough to stay up with the men and hear their talk.

He heard the light quick scrape of toenails on the floor, and something landed on his bed and curled up quietly at the foot, close against his bare leg. Shim's disappointment was gone. He had company. Gimlet hadn't gone with the others either. He rubbed the soft head with his toes. Dave, though, would have a fit when he came in if he found Gimlet in the bed.

"Gimlet," Shim said drowsily, "if you make any fuss when Dave comes in here, I'll have to kick a yelp out of you long as a plowline."

Gimlet began licking his toes, and Shim fell asleep.

chapter two

SHIM WOKE NEXT morning to the clinking of trace chains on hames. Day was breaking, and the jingling trace chains that were making such pretty music would hitch the mules again to plows left in the field yesterday wherever sundown had overtaken them. The open window by Shim's bed came clear to the floor, and, without moving, he saw, through darkness that still lingered under the shade trees in the yard, the lighter gray of the field beyond where mules with their riders were following the turnrow to work.

Through half-closed eyes he watched them come into his line of vision one or two at a time, and amused himself sleepily, identifying them by their outlines. Knowing the shape and way of moving of every tenant and mule on the place, he recognized them as fast as they came into sight. The game was too easy; with a yawn, he rolled over onto his back and stretched. When his feet didn't strike a warm, small heaviness anywhere, he sat up and looked around the room.

Gimlet was gone. So was Dave. Shim got out of bed, reaching for the nearest clothes handy, those on the floor that he'd pulled off the night before. He thought better of it. His sister Fanchie would be sure to say they smelled like fish. She used to didn't pay any more attention to clothes than he did, but here lately she was getting powerful prissy and particular. Shim pulled out a clean shirt and pants from the drawer at the bottom of the big wardrobe he and Dave shared. Then his shoes, and he was ready. Starting for the door, he turned back, and from the pocket of the pants he had worn yesterday, he dug out his fishing cork and line.

He went out and down the wide hall to the back. Here the hall swung to the right, narrowed and became a side gallery along the ell that ran back from the main part of the house, forming dining room, kitchen and smokehouse. In the wide curve the gallery made as it narrowed, and in the angle the ell made, Shim stopped at the washstand. Dipping water from the bucket into the bowl, he washed his face and hands. Catching sight of his tousled black hair in a mirror beside the towel, he tugged a comb through its thickness a couple of times. Miss Cherry and Fanchie couldn't say he hadn't combed his hair this morning.

He pulled his fishing line from his pocket and laid it on a narrow shelf nailed between two of the gallery posts opposite the washstand, carefully shaking the line loose from the cork so it would dry. He was moving leisurely down the gallery toward the open dining-room door when his eyes caught a movement on the ground over by the black-gum tree. It was a mockingbird and a thrasher, cutting queer capers. Breakfast forgotten, he stopped to watch them.

The mockingbird kept maneuvering to get behind the thrasher, and when he did would dart angrily at him. Each time, just as he started his attack, the thrasher would whirl and face him. The mockingbird would put on a great show of innocence, hop busily around as if hunting for bugs and not studying the thrasher at all. But Shim saw that every hop he made was planned to get once more behind the thrasher. The third time the mockingbird's rush was too well under way to be hidden when the thrasher whirled, and they joined battle. A reddish-brown streak darted out from under the house. Shim's sharp cry "Gimlet" was too late. The thrasher flew to the holly tree by the ash hopper, the mockingbird to the pole where the black washpot hung, and Gimlet bounced up the steps and began jumping around Shim's feet.

"What you want to break up a good fight for?" Shim scolded, but his fussing at Gimlet was cut short.

"There you is, dragging around like you is still half asleep." Kiz's voice came from the narrow railed walkway that connected the outdoor kitchen to the gallery. "Other folks gets half a day's work done whilst you stands around watching varmints and birds and things. You'd stand there and starve to death watching them two little old birds fighting. Henry been here looking for you twice already."

Kiz was Henry's niece he'd raised from a baby—that is, she was his wife's, Aggie's, niece—and Henry, who was a bigger fool about her than he was about his own boys, had talked Miss Cherry into trying her in the kitchen. She'd been cooking for Miss Cherry all winter, and Shim was used to her bantering him. She made a heap of fun of him, but there wasn't anything she wouldn't do for him—skin his squirrels, clean his fish, put his dinner up for him in the warming oven when he was late.

Her friendly joreeing brought him wide awake to the day

and its demands on him. He felt his face drawing into a half grin, acknowledging she might be right, but it wasn't going to change him any.

He reached the dining-room door just ahead of her and, as he passed her, sniffed hungrily at the plate of hot biscuits she was bringing from the kitchen to the table.

Inside the high-ceilinged dining room the smell from a platter of venison suddenly made him as hungry for it as that wolf had been last night. The Captain sat at the head of the table, with Dave at his left and Fanchie at his right. Miss Cherry sat at the foot. Shim slid into his chair at Miss Cherry's left, beside his sister Fanchie. Everything looked extra good—the ham and eggs, the muscadine preserves, the fresh mold of butter with the shape of an acorn on top, the sorghum molasses—and the biscuits Kiz was passing were brown and flaky like he liked them.

Miss Cherry smiled good morning at him but was speaking to the Captain. "I thought Ben and Wick would spend the night." The way she said it, it was a question.

The Captain kept stirring his coffee and didn't answer till Kiz left the room. There was a little frown on his face. He took a drink of coffee, set his cup carefully back in the saucer and wiped his lips with his napkin. Its crumpled whiteness hid his mouth and his black beard, and when he took it down the frown was gone.

"Miss Cherry," he said, "I sometimes think I married the only one of the Caulfield's that's got bat sense."

He was trying to hide something that was bothering him behind his familiar teasing of Miss Cherry about her folks. Shim remembered the favor Ben had mentioned wanting to ask the Captain. Whatever it was, it had riled the Captain more than usual. He took an awful lot of time buttering a hot biscuit just right, and then, instead of taking a bite, he laid it down on his plate.

"Your brother Ben," he said, and Shim saw his lips tighten, "has gone hog-wild over these sawmill men in Mulberry."

"That again." Miss Cherry laughed like she was relieved. She had a soft, chuckling laugh that always made Shim feel good. He spooned some preserves onto his plate and reached for another biscuit.

"You know Ben," Miss Cherry went on. "Every time sawmill men come to Mulberry and start stirring folks up with talk of putting in a mill there, Ben is the first one to be carried away by it. These strangers will leave, like the others have, and it will all blow over."

The frown was back now, sure enough, on the Captain's face. "I don't know," he said. "They won't have any trouble getting hold of the state-owned land, but it's a long way back from Mulberry where they want to set their mill. What's kept a sawmill out this long has been that they couldn't get the good will of the townsfolks and of the people close around whose woods they need to buy, both for a right of way to get to the state-owned woods and to offset the expense of that long haul. It looks like this outfit in town now is about to get a toehold."

Fanchie, beside Shim, gave a little jerk like something had stung her, and was staring at the Captain with her mouth partly open like she did when she got excited. Dave was looking down at his plate but he wasn't eating, and Shim could tell by the look on his face that he was all ears. Dave and Fanchie didn't usually pay this kind of attention to talk between the Captain and Miss Cherry; they were busy with their own thoughts like he was. He began to listen himself when the Captain went on.

"Jake Coster and Evans Madder and one or two more have started talking mighty favorable here lately. Jake and Evans and a few more had a mighty short crop last year, and the price they're being offered for their woods is scandalous high. We had quite a round in the barbershop last week. I told them quick where I stood, but they sent Ben out here to talk me over to their way of thinking. He wanted me to agree to sell and to let a couple of men come and stay here with us for a few days while they rode over my woods."

The bite of biscuit and preserves in Shim's mouth got bigger and bigger. Uncle Ben wanted the Captain to let strangers stay in their house and go prowling through their woods. Shim swallowed and half choked, just as Dave's head jerked up and he said, "I feel like Ben does about all that money these rich outsiders are throwing around."

"So do I." Fanchie put in her two bits' worth, and Shim's eyes flew to her. Her face was as white as the curl papers she'd taken to screwing her hair up in lately, but she went on. "Things are so dead and dull around here, and one of those sawmill men is the best-looking thing, and young. Uncle Ben introduced me to him in town the other day."

"In town?" the Captain said sharply. "They been out to Overcup Ridge?"

Fanchie tossed her head. "I don't call Overcup Ridge any town—a little old school and a couple of stores and the post office and three houses. No, I met him in Mulberry."

Fanchie wasn't much more than a year older than Shim, and she didn't need to act so uppity about Overcup Ridge a couple of miles up the road. It was where they went to school and got their mail. Mulberry was the county seat and what grown folks meant when they said "town." Fanchie was getting too grown-y to suit him.

"I thought Miss Cherry has always told you to stay away

from stray folks," Shim said. "Nobody knows who those sawmill folks are nor where they come from."

Fanchie turned to look at him. She had light hazel eyes like the Captain's and, like his, they could look a hole through you. They were doing that now. "They come from way off somewhere, Mr. Smarty, and they're better educated than we are. They talk like writing in books, I'll have you to know. I'd hate to see what they'd think of you—calling your own mama 'Miss Cherry' and your own papa 'Captain,' just because the tenants do, just because Henry does. You stay with Henry so much you act just like him and talk just like him. You make me sick."

Shim had called Mama "Miss Cherry" and Papa "the Captain" all his life, and nobody that he knew of had ever thought there was anything wrong with it. Just about everybody called them that. Fanchie was getting so prissy and strange-acting lately, what she said didn't make sense about half the time. Something was sure eating her this morning. All of them were stirred up by something he couldn't quite get the straight of, nor see why it concerned them.

Miss Cherry was frowning at Fanchie, shaking her head at her for fussing, when Dave, his face red as a turkey gobbler's, looked straight at the Captain and blurted out, "You've got many an oak, sweet gum and cypress, Papa, that will measure six feet through. They'll bring so much money we'll be rich."

Shim's mouth fell open. Trees bring money? *Their* trees bring money? Not squirrels and coons and all the other game; not wild honey, and nuts, and wood for fires, and shade from the sun—but money?

The Captain's voice reached him from a long way off, and what the Captain had said dawned on him only when he saw them all looking at him. "Miss Cherry, do you think you could prevail upon your youngest offspring to sit up to the table and eat like folks?"

Shim realized that his shoulders were pressed hard against the back of his chair and that he was holding a fork loaded with egg halfway to his mouth while he stared at Dave. He laid the fork back on the plate with a hand that felt heavy as lead and, wrapping his feet around his chair legs, hitched himself politely closer to the table. But he couldn't pick up his fork and go on eating. His appetite was gone. His heart was hammering and his throat was too dry to swallow. The woods—— Dave and Fanchie were trying to talk the Captain into selling the woods!

"Ben says——" Dave began, and Shim wanted to fight him, slam his fists into Dave's stubborn mouth. The Captain's chair moved back as his long legs straightened, and with a single movement he was on his feet. The scar on his left cheek, usually not noticeable under his full beard, showed plain as day. When that Yankee bullet had hit him he'd been only about a year older than Shim, but Shim couldn't picture his ever having been so young.

He just stood there, looking from one to the other of them for a minute, then he spoke, in the extra-soft voice that meant he was really stirred up. "Listen to me, every one of you. Easy-got money is the worst possible thing for the peace and decency of this country. You'll probably all live long enough to find it out, but don't let me hear any more talk of sawmill in this house. Dave, the bank of that big ditch in the first northeast corner needs your attention this morning. Shim, you'll go with Henry after some second-growth white oak."

Straight as a poker, he went out the door and down the side

gallery to the back steps where a boy was holding his horse. Not until they saw him through the dining-room window, riding off toward the field, did anybody at the table make a sound. Fanchie burst out crying and went running out of the room. Dave and Shim were shoving back their chairs to leave too, when, from the corner of his eye, Shim caught a quick look pass between Dave and Miss Cherry, and before he knew it he blurted out, "Do you want to cut the trees, too?" He'd never said anything loud or rude to Miss Cherry before, and he hated it. His voice cracked to boot.

"Still in the gosling stage and think you know everything," Dave jeered angrily. Then more calmly: "I'm sorry, Mama. Look, Shim, you don't understand. Those sawmill men will pay big money for the woods, just the trees, and will be clearing up our land for us at the same time. They'll pay big money for trees that are just in our way, on land that will make a bale of cotton to the acre. Instead of us having to spend time and money to clear the land, they'll just about clear it, and pay us besides. For once Uncle Ben has got the right sow by the ear."

There was a strange, glittery shine in Dave's eyes that Shim had seen before only in Uncle Ben's. "We've got plenty of money, and we make plenty of cotton," Shim said slowly. "We don't need any more of either one. But the woods—why, there wouldn't be any place to hunt."

"Hunt, hunt, hunt. That's all you study about. Don't you ever study about getting ahead?"

Shim frowned. "Ahead of what?"

"See, Mama." Dave was now talking too loud to be polite. "He isn't being fresh. He means it. He doesn't know anything but woods. I tell you Henry's ruining him. He'll wind up an old sorry fisherman or trapper, living in a tent somewhere."

Dave stood up. "You ought to talk Papa into selling the woods just to civilize Shim. He hasn't got the sense God gave a monkey wrench except about woods, woods, woods."

"David," Miss Cherry said, and her dark eyes flashed, "your Papa will do what is best."

Dave headed for the door as fast as Fanchie had. Shim had never seen him forget his manners with Miss Cherry before. This bolt-out-of-the-blue threat to woods Shim had always thought of as secure and unchanging as the sky seemed to cut off the air he breathed. Miss Cherry hadn't denied that she too wanted to sell the woods. He had to know. She was sitting quietly, placing her knife and fork at exactly the right angle on her plate. If she'd just look at him . . .

She stood up, and Shim stood too, but she still didn't raise her eyes. She pushed her chair carefully up to the table, brushed a crumb from the cloth with one hand into the other and dropped it onto her plate. She reached over and cupped a hand under Shim's chin, and a smile wiped the seriousness from her face, like the sun coming out after a shower. She ducked her head a little—he was almost as tall as she was, he noticed for the first time—and, giving his nose a quick, affectionate rub with her own, said, "Run along, Punkin, and find Henry. You heard the Captain say he isn't going to sell the woods."

The weight lifted from Shim's chest and he headed for the door. Miss Cherry always straightened things out when they got tangled up. His feet were light again.

chapter three

AT THE woodpile Shim picked up the ax. The earlymorning sun was already sifting down through the leaves of the shade trees. Henry would mouth at him for being a sleepyhead, but he took his time walking down the clean-beaten path that wound through the peach orchard to the barn lot. Going after white oak with Henry would be fun, but there was no reason to hurry.

Dave's talk at the breakfast table had faded to just plain tomfoolery. Why, trees were as different as folks, and all of them friendly, and all of them, in their own season and own way, important. Today they wanted splits, so it was white oak they'd look for. Later on they'd be going after the winter firewood, and then they'd look for trees that split and burned well —oak, sweet gum, bitter pecan, hickory. Hunting, it was the trees you watched. In the spring, squirrel hunting, you looked for red oak and ironwood, because they had the earliest rations on them. In the first of the fall it was in the oaks with their acorns and in the scaly-bark and hickory-nut trees where you'd find the squirrels. Later on they'd be feeding on balls from tupelo gums and cypresses, and way late in the fall you'd find them around the elm trees, where a small sweet sack, dark brown like beggar's-lice, came on the end of each leaf. Just about everything liked acorns—bears and deer as well as squirrels and ducks. And turkeys—well, they were plumb fools about pin-oak acorns.

Shim's eyes followed a pair of redbirds darting among the fruit trees. Henry always said redbirds were the first to know that day was fixing to break, and start singing about it. Most of the important things he knew—things about the woods and the plantation—he'd learned from following Henry around since he was big enough to keep up with him.

The peach trees all around Shim were loaded with fruit. The May peaches were already turning red, but the others, not much bigger than persimmons and hard as rocks, were fine for chunking. Reaching up, he stripped a handful and shoved them into his pants pocket. A few steps farther on he dug them out and dribbled them along in the grass beside the path. Henry would start lecturing him about waste. All grownups, even Henry, fussed at him if he pulled a few green peaches to chunk. It didn't make any sense, when every year the fruit hung so heavy the limbs had to be propped up to keep them from breaking under their load, and the shelves in the smokehouse always had jars and jars of preserves left over from the year before.

Coming out at the barn lot, he saw Henry sitting on the sill of the wagon shed. His broad shoulders were bent over a square-shaped contraption woven out of smooth wire that it looked like he was putting the finishing touches to. Henry's hands always fit whatever he was doing as if they'd been shaped especially for that exact job.

"What's that thing?" Shim asked, resting his ax on the ground.

Henry twisted a wire in place with a pair of pliers and cut his eyes up at him. "Oh, yes, smart aleck, wolves like to got you last night."

"We got them," Shim said, and, leaning over for a closer look: "What are you making?"

"I might could tell you if you'd get your head from betwixt me and it," Henry said.

Shim straightened. Henry cut off a ragged end of wire and turned the object around in his hands. "I'll bet you jumped out of that wagon and went up a tree when them wolves got after you," he bantered.

"You lose," Shim said. Someday he'd have a big time telling Henry all about it, but right now he was still feeling a little swelled up over Henry's hearing the story from the rest of them last night. "What is that you've got there, Henry?" he said again.

Henry stood up and swung the wire box over his shoulder. "Layovers to catch meddlers," he grunted. "Come on with me. I'm glad you took them mules off yesterday, because the Captain has done put you to work for it." He headed for the back gate. Shim, shouldering the ax, followed him. Henry wasn't going to tell him what that wire contraption was till he took a notion to.

Through the gate, they followed a deeply worn path that made almost a straight line among the trees of the woods lot. Halfway across it, Henry in the lead, Shim heard the patter of feet on the leaf mold, and Gimlet, panting with excitement, came running by them.

"Here's that worrisome little old feist," Henry grumbled. "Tail curled over his back so tight it's about to lift his hind feets off the ground. He'll pick a fuss out of an elephant if he gets a chance."

"Many dogs as you've got at your house, how come you're always grumbling about Gimlet?" Shim asked.

"I ain't got no feist dogs," Henry said emphatically. "Hunting hounds is different. They earn their keep. Little dogs ain't good for nothing but to get you into trouble."

"Gimlet never has got me into trouble."

"He just ain't no account to begin with," Henry said. "A man's got no business letting his heart get set on a dog, or a woman, that ain't no account to begin with. Just get you killed someday, and for nothing."

A board fence, topped with three strands of barbed wire, kept varmints from the woods out of the woods lot. Henry was over it before Shim got there. Shoving his ax through a crack, Shim put one hand on top of a post and a foot on the upper plank; he caught hold of the wires with the other hand and swung over, hitting the ground only to hear Gimlet whining and scratching behind him. Reaching back, he caught Gimlet by the neck and hauled him through, while Henry, with a grunt of disgust, walked on.

Now they were in the real woods. The trees were so big the sun hit the ground only in patches, and every bush was still heavy with dew. Hurrying to catch up, Shim saw a grayish, unfilled honeycomb beside a shallow hole—the remains of a yellow-jacket nest dug up last night by a hungry coon. Shim rolled the dry comb around with the toe of his shoe, wishing he could have seen Mr. Coon, all covered with mud he'd rolled in to keep the yellow jackets from stinging him while he scooped out the nest and ate the young.

Gimlet's sudden furious barking roused him. Gimlet and Henry both were out of sight among the trees. The barking came from a thicket of young sweet gums ahead and to the right. Shim pushed through the thickets and found Gimlet barking excitedly into a hole at the root of a tall red oak.

"Henry," he called, and saw Henry right beside him, stooping and looking into the hole.

Henry straightened. "Little no-account dog ain't done nothing but treed an old mammy possum in her den. Come on."

"Let's get her out." Shim whammed his ax into a root.

"Look at you," Henry shamed him, "wanting to kill that old possum and leave her babies to starve. Where's your manners? You know you had better raising than that."

Shim felt his cheeks getting hot. He'd let Gimlet's enthusiasm make him forget that you didn't kill possums this time of year. "That's right," he mumbled, and struck out after Henry. Gimlet, after a few disappointed yips, gave it up and followed them.

They came to a wagon road and followed it to the rail fence that ran on the north side of the field. Here Henry put his wire contraption on the ground beside a cottonwood tree, took the ax from Shim and led the way through the woods toward a little ridge a hundred yards or so away. Shim remembered there was a smattering of white-oak saplings over there. On the ridge he watched Henry cut down two saplings and hack off a four-foot section of each. Henry shouldered one of the sections and Shim the other. Back beside the rutty road, they dropped them.

"Let's see how work's getting along," Henry said, and walked to the high field fence. Henry was tall enough to see over the rails into the field beyond, and Shim stepped up on a stump beside him to look.

In the bright hot sunlight over there, two men, each behind a mule pulling a scraper, were going up one side of a row and down the other, cutting the dirt away from the young cotton plants. Behind them hoe hands followed, cutting out the grass and thinning the cotton to a stand, leaving one or two plants about every twelve inches. Over to their right, four plows, grouped together, were flat-breaking land to be planted in peas for hay.

"Henry," Shim said, "how come you all always say cotton is a child of the sun? All crops need sun."

"Not like cotton do," Henry said. "First off, the cotton seed busts through the ground and comes up just when the sun rises, and later on when the blooms come they opens, too, when the sun rises. Look yonder how them leaves keeps their flat sides facing the sun. They follows it all day that-a-way. Ain't no other crop as big a fool about the sun as cotton is."

Henry shaded his eyes with a hand, and Shim knew he was looking away on over to his own crop. Shim made out the movement of two plows going over there and two figures with hoes following them. That would be Henry's four boys. A fifth figure was hoeing too, but stopping now and then to cut a lot of extra didos.

"That Kiz," Henry said, and his white teeth showed in a slow grin. "She's like the Irishman's flea—one minute at the house, the next way over at the back of the field. Your mama about sent her to my house for something, and she grabbed up a hoe just because it was handy. Look at her, dancing and frolicking and still keeping up with the others. She'll hoe a row and be back at the house before your mama ever miss her."

"Looks like she'd tromp on that cotton," Shim said.

"Not Kiz," Henry said. "She's sure-footed as a goat. Grabs any work that's handy and does it better 'n anybody, but it never stops her from cutting figures with her feets."

You could see Henry was proud as all get out of Kiz. When

folks accused him of being partial to her, though, he denied it. Said she had more coming to her, being an orphan. Shim guessed Kiz was one reason Henry's family always made more cotton than any other tenant on the place. Of course all of Henry's boys were hard workers too, and a couple of them weren't even as old as Shim.

"How come you don't buy some land of your own to work?" Shim asked. "Like Foots and Caline."

Foots Booker owned eighty acres joining the Govan place on the southwest. His wife Caline was a sister to Henry's wife Aggie. You'd think a man like Henry would want his own land, too.

Henry slapped at a brown lizard that went running along the fence rail, missed, and then shook his head. "You're barking up the wrong snag now, boy. I had me some land once—a hundred and sixty of as good acres as ever laid outdoors."

Shim looked at him in surprise. Henry had been the Captain's straw boss, hostler and general handy man ever since Shim remembered. He tried to imagine Henry anywhere but right here, and couldn't.

"Owning land," Henry went on, "ain't nothing but trouble. My crops would be parching up for moisture, and I was ruined if it didn't come a good rain. Rain would come and before the ground got good and wet I'd be scared it wasn't going to quit till I got too much. Time it stopped and cleared off, I'd be worrying all over again scared it had quit for the season and everything would burn up. Now and then I'd sure enough have that crop failure I kept worrying about, and then there'd be debts to pester me, taxes to get up. Mules would get sick and haul off and die. And the tenants—Lord help! Tenants always grumbling about something, throwing away my stuff, fighting, getting sick, running off right at pickingtime.

Boy, don't never come here talking to me about owning no land. I wants my pleasure in the daytime and my rest at night. I sold them hundred and sixty acres and thanks the Lord for the day I done it. I moved here with the Captain and lets him do the worrying. I gets everything I wants, and never has a bellyache that a dose of baking soda won't cure."

Puzzling over Henry's words, Shim brought his eyes around to the right and jumped quickly down off the stump. Dave was over there, cleaning off a ditch bank with a bush ax, and might decide to make him help if he caught sight of him. Shim was doing what the Captain had told him to do, but Dave was bigger than he was, and the Captain wasn't here. The safest thing to do was not let Dave see him.

He looked curiously toward the wire contraption under the cottonwood tree where Henry had left it. With the white oak cut and ready to carry back with them when they went, and with Henry satisfied the work in the field was going on just right, he was bound to be about ready to tell Shim what they were going to do with that odd-looking thing.

Sure enough, Henry turned from the fence, saw where Shim was looking, and yawned. "If you're going with me, boy, you better rest your feets. We're fixing to take a long, fast walk." He walked over to an old rotting log, sat down and shifted on the log to get his shoulders resting against a hickory sapling. His chin lowered to his chest, and his eyes closed.

Shim looked at Henry's big strong arms and legs and wondered if it was because no matter what was afoot Henry could always sleep a little snatch that he stayed so strong and supple, and his one hundred and eighty pounds could outlift and outrun men weighing a heap more. Shim had learned long ago that impatience got him nowhere with Henry.

Settling down on the other end of the log, he began watching a flock of jay birds chirping and diving at a fox squirrel in a mulberry tree. All he could see of it was a flash of red when the sun caught its tail just right. Mulberries weren't ripe yet, and it was just traveling through the tree to get to some pin oaks beyond.

It was cool here in the woods, the sun no more than a couple of hours high. Waiting for Henry to catch a nap of sleep was no trouble. Time didn't mean anything because there was always more of it than anybody could use. Shim felt slack run in his own muscles, like he could near about drop off to sleep himself, and he slid down onto the leaf mold to have the log for a shoulder rest. From somewhere came a sound like a teakettle just before it boils. Bees. He saw them in a flowering haw tree a little piece down the road. They sounded too busy to belong here in the woods—busy like folks were in town.

Town. The only thing he liked about town was the shows and the good music you could hear. He was just a chap when, visiting with Miss Cherry over in Mooresville in the next county, Aunt Em had taken them to a concert. He'd been carried completely away with the dancing and singing. He'd never seen folks have so much fun and make such pretty music as those folks up on the stage did. The words and tunes of the songs had stuck in his head, and when he got home he'd sung them over and over for Fanchie. Miss Cherry bragged on his singing until he told her he was going to be a singer and dancer on the stage when he grew up. Then she'd changed. He remembered her serious face and her exact words: "Those folks weren't having fun. They were working. Why, you might have to sing or dance sometime when you didn't feel like it."

He could see from the way she said it that about the worst

thing in the world would be to work when you didn't feel like it. So he gave up the idea, but music was still the next best thing to the woods. And whenever the Captain took him to Memphis or Jackson they always saw a show. The singing and dancing and music still made him wild to be up there on the stage having a good time with them, but he'd remember what Miss Cherry said. And except for the shows, towns didn't suit him at all. Too many folks, too many tall buildings, some of them stacked up four or five stories, and the hard walks made his feet ache.

The rough bark of the log was pricking him uncomfortably through his thin shirt, and he sat up. Henry opened his eyes, straightened his shoulders and glanced at the sun. "I was up near about all night last night making that trap." He looked toward the wire box under the cottonwood.

Shim's heart began to thump. A trap? For what? But he waited.

"Otters," Henry said, "makes the finest pets in the world. And I'm fixing to catch us one."

Shim's mouth dropped open and he jumped to his feet. The only thing in the world he wanted right now was a pet otter. "How?" he said. "When?"

Henry yawned loudly and slowly scratched his back against the sapling behind him. "Over here on Muleshoe Lake. I found a slide, and that's where I sets my trap."

Shim had seen otter slides—smooth places in the mud where otters, for some reason unknown to him, dragged their bellies while going from the water out into the woods and back. They always used the same place, so you'd be bound to catch one there first and last. But he'd never in his life heard of petting one.

"You going to pull their teeth so they won't eat you up?" he said.

"Catch a young one," Henry said. "Ain't no kind of young thing mean, if you treats him right." He stood up. "I don't know if it'd be best to go the long way round through the big woods and have easy walking, or cut straight through here to the lake. That little trail that runs from there on is pretty bad, and it will be tough walking that-a-way."

Shim shouldered his ax. "Let's take the short way. I can go anywhere you can."

Henry picked up his trap. They crossed the road and went into the woods, Henry in the lead, Shim following and trying to take steps as long as Henry's. The woods were still and quiet except for the songs of birds.

Suddenly Dave's crazy talk at the breakfast table started worrying Shim's mind again, and before he knew it he said right short, "Henry, what do sawmill folks do to woods?"

The rhythm of Henry's steps broke and he almost staggered, like the words had been a hard lick in his back; then he lined out again and after a few seconds said, "You been hearing talk, boy?"

"Some sawmill folks in town talking about building a sawmill there. Uncle Ben, and Dave too, want the Captain to sell them our big trees, but he won't do it."

"Course he won't," Henry said. He was walking so fast Shim had trouble keeping up with him. A little farther on he stopped short, swung around and looked at Shim like he was mad as a hornet about something. "Has any of the folks around here sold them sawmill mens their woods?"

"The Captain talked like some of them are going to," Shim said uneasily. "What do they do to woods, Henry?"

"What you reckon they does, when they come slam-banging in with their saws and axes and big wagons and cuts down all the big trees and hauls them out to the sawmill?" Henry's lips were poked out, and his voice was rough as a file. "They spoils the woods, that's what they does, plumb ruins them. Drives out all the game, and with the big trees gone the sun gets to the ground, and bushes and briers and vines grows up so thick you can't get through without a bush ax or a cane knife. Hunting is over with, and folks like me and you is done for. Might as well pack us little satchels and put us feets in the road."

Shim's heart seemed to be pumping all the blood of his body into his head till it felt like it was about to float off. "We'll kill them, Henry. You and I can hide behind trees and shoot them fast as they start in. They'll never touch one of our trees."

Henry gave his face a quick rub. "Listen at you—" his voice was easy and natural again—"young as you is, and talking about killing folks. Ain't you just told me the Captain ain't going let them on his land? The Captain ain't near about fixing to have no strays from way off somewheres prowling around in his woods. Besides, how they going get all that big sawmill machinery way out so far from the railroad? Folks always scheming schemes. These men'll go back to that way off where they come from, and nobody'll hear tell of them again."

He shifted the wire trap to his other shoulder. "Are you and me fixing to get us an otter, or stand here mouthing foolishment all day?"

They started off again. The swimming and floating feeling that had been in Shim's head slowly passed down through his body till it was gone, and he felt clear and solid again.

Of course they couldn't get all the big boilers and stuff it would take for a sawmill over those miles of rough road from the depot to Mulberry. Nobody but Henry had been smart enough to think of that.

Their feet were so silent on the leaf mold that a big bullfrog on the bank of the lake didn't let out his grunt and jump into the water until Gimlet ran down and began to lap thirstily. The dark surface of the water, rimmed with big cypress trees and smaller tupelo gums, was smooth as glass, except across near the opposite bank where ripples caught Shim's eye. A string of wood ducks was swimming silently along the edge of some elbow bushes.

Beside each hen, dull brown with light streaks in her feathers, swam a drake, brown and green, his topknot long and curled at the tips. Last year he and Henry had lucked up together on the prettiest sight anybody could ever see—a mother wood duck taking her young down to the water. From a nest high in a cypress tree she pushed them out, one at a time, with her foot, and as each duckling fell through the air she swooped down under it, caught it on her back and lowered it safely to the water.

"The prettiest, fastest ducks in the world, and the sweetest eating. More of them raising here every year. Shooting's going be first class this fall." Henry had seen them too.

They were in the overgrown trail along the lake bank now, and the going was slow and steamy hot. Tree limbs and vines overlapped above their heads, and the trail was strewn with dead brush and sticks left when the high water went down this spring. Through the undergrowth on their left the lake was never more than a few feet away, but on their right the brush was so thick a coon would have trouble getting through it to reach the big open woods beyond. Shim wiped his sweating face on his shirt sleeve. If he hadn't been in such a hurry to get to the otter slide, they'd have been walking through those cool woods now, in dense shade, with no bushes and vines catching at their feet.

A limb that Henry had pushed far out of the way before releasing flew back and hit Shim a stinging rap across the face. He grunted. Embarrassment at his carelessness in not having kept his face protected hurt worse than the pain.

Henry looked back over his shoulder. "Sure is a good thing I kept a hold of that limb long as I did or it would have knocked you down."

Shim, his shame eased by Henry's joking him, grinned sheepishly.

Sweat stung the welt on his face. The walking didn't get any easier. The heat bore down worse. He about had the thumps when Henry at last stopped and beckoned him to close up the short distance between them. "Don't make no fuss," he whispered. "We're right at the slide. It's just t'other side of that log."

The log, a few feet ahead of them, was a fallen tupelo gum, one end in the water, the rest on land. Shim wiped away sweat trickling into his eyes. Beyond the log the ground looked free from undergrowth, a cool place to sit down and get his breath while Henry set the trap. Gimlet was sitting down hassling and panting; Henry was taking time to look over his trap for possible damage from the trip. Shim, eager to reach the cool-looking little open space ahead, moved quietly to the log and jumped up on it, heading for the other side.

Before his back could straighten, he knew he'd played the devil. Overbalanced forward, he heard breath escaping with a loud hiss and saw widespread jaws reaching up for his legs. The biggest alligator he'd ever seen was right under him, and he was too far forward to draw himself back. He jumped as high and as far as he could, drawing up his feet to clear those gaping jaws and reaching ahead with his eyes for a sapling small enough to climb fast.

The open space where he'd aimed to sit down and rest extended back only a few yards from the water and was no more than fifteen feet across. A bitter-pecan sapling straight ahead was the nearest thing for safety. His feet—thank the good Lord he still had them both!—hit the spongy buckshot ground running.

"Run, boy, run." Henry's voice, hoarse with fear, added a notch to what Shim had thought was already top speed. He heard the crash of a tree limb being wrung off and knew Henry was trying to get hold of something to fight with. The only weapon between them was the ax still in Shim's hand.

"Climb a tree, quick," Henry called again.

He strained his legs for more speed—which they didn't have—and heard Gimlet bark his fighting challenge. He risked a look over his shoulder and dug his heels in to bring himself to a stop. The alligator had swerved and was lunging about after Gimlet, who was doing some nimble bouncing to avoid both the thick bushes on the one side and the lake on the other.

Henry, standing on the log, had a tree limb drawn back, waiting for a chance to strike. Gimlet and the alligator were circling, the alligator making short lunges, Gimlet dancing aside.

"Go—go on. Run, I tell you, run!" Henry was bellowing now.

But Shim was looking at the distance between the bushes, which would tangle a dog's or a man's feet, and the lake. It was little more than the length of the thrashing alligator.

Either tail or jaws were everywhere, and Gimlet, jumping around to avoid them, was taking too many chances for such close quarters. Shim's hand tightened on his ax.

Henry jumped off the log and brought the tree limb he held down across the alligator's back. Quick as powder the big tail whipped around and had him leaping back for safety. The long ugly jaws were bent now on dog meat, and Shim saw that Gimlet was being maneuvered toward a network of vines and short oak bushes. He gripped his ax with both hands and took a step forward. A chunk of wood big as a watermelon, thrown by Henry, landed against the alligator's widespread jaws. But the chunk was doted and broke into harmless pieces. It couldn't have hurt the alligator, but it must have changed his mind. He turned and started lumbering slowly toward the water.

Before Shim's racing mind could believe it, Gimlet sensed that the alligator had given up the fight and, making unhesitating use of this first real chance for attack, dashed in, mouth wide. His teeth scraped harmlessly on the armored hide, the powerful tail flipped, and Gimlet was rolling helplessly on the ground. Before he stopped turning, the widespread jaws were reaching for him.

Shim, moving with all the strength and speed he had, felt helplessly slow, with the short-legged alligator only inches from its goal and his own longer legs with yards to cover. So close to the alligator that a cold chill started up his back, he swung the ax with all his strength. The blunt side landed with a keen whack behind the knotty eyes. The jaws closed harmlessly and lay flat and still on the ground.

He had killed it. Gimlet was limping to safety. Anger took the place of fear, and, fighting mad, Shim brought the ax down again on the hated, motionless head. Sudden as a flash of powder, the nose snapped up, and Shim's frantically backpedaling legs felt the wind from a vicious swing of the deadly tail that barely missed. He'd only stunned it, and that second lick had brought it to. Henry grabbed his shoulder, jerked the ax from his hand and sent him stumbling toward the bushes.

By the time Shim got his footing good, the big varmint was dead. Henry's ax blows were hard enough to do more than stun. Shim's trembling knees wouldn't hold him any longer, and he sat down on the ground. Henry went over and sat down on a chunk. Everything was quiet except hearts thumping against ribs, and Gimlet's noisy hassling for breath.

Henry raked a sleeve across his sweating face. "If you ever tells anybody I mistook a gator trail for an otter slide, I'll beat you to death, boy."

Shim worked his dry jaws a couple of times to limber them up. He'd clean forgotten the otter they were going to catch.

Henry was looking at him hard. "How you feel?"

"I'm about half sick," Shim said. "How do you feel?"

"Weak, but willing." Henry stood up. "You set there and get well, whilst I cuts some steaks off of this old gator's tail. Then we'll go by and get our white-oak pieces and go home."

Shim rested his arms on his knees and head on his arms. Henry set to work to get the piece of tail for steaks, and the steady sound of his voice while he worked was familiar and soothing to Shim.

"Old ax, you is the best weapon there is when trouble gets started, because you don't never snap like a gun sometimes do."

Henry talking to his tools while he worked was about the most restful sound in the world—a flat, monotonous talk, not like talk between folks; more like a strange kind of music. It had a meaning that wasn't always in the words and that you couldn't put into words yourself, but that made you feel there was an understanding between him and his tools better than any there ever was between folks.

He heard the blade strike into the tail, and now Henry was talking to the alligator. "Maybe you learned that boy a lesson—not to go headlong through the woods, jumping over logs before he sees what's on t'other side. Lord, Lord, Lord, that boy come close as nineteen is to twenty, getting hurt bad."

Shim's heart was slowing down, and he shifted his head on his arms to hear Henry's words better. A slight change in their tone told him that Henry had caught the movement, knew he was listening, and the talk from now on would be meant for his ears.

"Course," Henry said, "I never taught that boy nothing about being careful. I never showed him, no longer ago than last fall, that big rattlesnake coiled up against the side of a log and chopped all up into pieces by the sharp hoofs of a deer. A deer got sense enough to look before stepping over a log."

Shim's legs felt strong enough to hold him now, and he stood up. His stomach was mighty hollow-feeling, and seeing Henry hacking away on that tail didn't help it any. "You needn't figure on me eating any of that varmint," he said. "But I sure would like a glass of cool buttermilk."

Henry straightened. "Me too. My stomach's about growed to my backbone, and no wonder. Looka yonder at the sun. Miss Cherry'll get after me for making you late for your dinner."

He picked up the piece of tail, shouldered the ax and headed for the log. The wire trap lay where he'd dropped it. He picked it up and flung it far out into the still water of the lake. "Nobody but an old fool would have set up all night making a contraption like that. Don't know how come me to get to studying about otters noway. Probably sink their teethes into our hands clean to the bone if we had of caught one."

"The little ones won't bite," Shim said, and, giggling, ducked back out of reach of the alligator tail Henry shoved at his face.

"You little devil, if you ever tell it . . . Besides, if you had of clumb a sapling like I told you to, instead of turning back to help out a meddlesome little feist bouncing around about like a bee after an elephant, we wouldn't have had all that trouble."

"You wouldn't have got to kill that big varmint, either, if Gimlet hadn't got in it," Shim came back at him.

"Who?" Henry said. "What do I care about killing that old gator?"

"You wouldn't have missed killing that alligator with an ax for a hundred dollars, and you know it," Shim said.

Henry snorted, but a half grin on his face, and his eyes batting right fast three or four times, were a dead giveaway to Shim that he was right.

"Let's go back through the big woods," Shim said. "Tell you the truth, my legs don't feel too steady yet."

"It'll be cooler, too," Henry said. "Danged if this ain't the hottest May day I ever did see."

chapter four

SHIM was under the wagon shed bolting the handles onto a new plow stock when, out of the supposedly clear June sky, a summer shower of rain seemed to turn loose all hold above and begin falling. He glanced quickly at the sky, for this was Saturday and he'd planned to dress up and go to town tonight. But if it rained . . . He saw a rainbow in the east and knew there was nice weather ahead until tomorrow at least, and this little shower while the sun shone was only the devil beating his wife.

He heard Dave's voice at the lot gate. He was talking to a weather-beaten man Shim had never seen before who sat on a horse in the road. The usual greetings were being exchanged between them: "How is your health, your family's health, and how are crops?" Then the stranger handed Dave an envelope over the gate and rode off.

The rain had stopped, and on his way to the wagon shed Dave opened the envelope, took out a sheet of tablet paper and ran his eyes carefully over it. He sat down on the sill.

SHIM 57

"A dance tonight in the hills," he said. "Sugarfoot Simone's house. Note's from Tildy, his youngest girl."

All Shim had ever heard of Sugarfoot Simone was that he lived in the Rocky Ford neighborhood, the roughest place in the county, where outsiders like Dave were pretty apt not to be welcome. Shim was flattered to be taken into Dave's confidence, but he couldn't help a glance across the orchard toward the house. Miss Cherry wouldn't put up with this for a minute if she knew it. She was mighty particular about the folks they mixed with.

"Never force yourself on folks that don't see things the way you do," she said. "Let them alone and they'll let you alone. It's not that you're better than they are. They're just different, and trying to mix means trouble."

From what Shim had heard of the Rocky Ford folks, he bet anything this girl's folks didn't know she'd asked an outsider to come. And he bet Dave wouldn't be talking about going, either, if the Captain and Miss Cherry and Fanchie weren't all gone off for the night.

Shim laid his wrench down and took a seat on the plow stock. "How come that girl writing you?"

"Because she's been knowing me a long time and wants me to come." Dave had a faraway look on his face as if he'd already left for Rocky Ford.

Shim watched a mockingbird in the top of a peach tree pause long enough in his song to pitch straight up into the air several feet and drop back down to the limb he'd left, sending a shower of sparkling raindrops to the ground.

"I thought those were all square dances in the hills," he said. "You don't know how to square dance."

"There you go," Dave said, "prying around asking questions. I'm going, and I told you because I figured it was the safest way. If you should wake up in the night and find me gone, you're so all-fired curious you might get up and get a horse and start trailing me. You'd likely get turned around in those hills and still be out of pocket when the folks get home tomorrow. Then the fat would be in the fire."

Shim's heart began to pound. Dave had given him an idea. Where there was a dance, there'd be bound to be music—maybe more instruments than at a round dance. And surely a bass fiddle. Mulling over in his mind the best way to break to Dave the news of the decision he'd just made, he saw a calf come nosing around the corner of the wagon shed. The shadows of its legs looked extra long. Moving and small, they called his attention to what the shadow of the big, stationary barn hadn't—that the sun was getting low in the west, wasn't more than an hour high.

"It must be a long ride over there," Shim said.

"A couple of hours maybe." Dave glanced at the sun. "Go down in the woods lot and run me up a horse while I put in feed for him."

Shim stood up. "Put in feed for two. I'm going."

Dave looked surprised, and Shim braced himself for an argument. Instead, Dave stood up, a quick grin on his face. "It's probably the only sure way to keep your mouth shut, at that. You will be as deep in the mud as I am in the mire if you ever tell it. Go on after the horses."

Shim headed for the back gate, tickled pink. A square dance—no telling what new sights he'd see, how many instruments he'd hear played.

He didn't pester Dave with a single question while they bathed and dressed. He was going to see for himself how folks did over there. Dave, busy with his own dressing, didn't pay him any attention until, all ready but his coat,

Shim picked up his pistol and stuck it in his back pocket. He'd been caught without his pistol once this summer and like to got grabbed by an alligator. No telling what varmints they might meet on the road, and, more than that, he'd heard folks over there were quick to start trouble.

"You'd better leave that old pepperbox at home," Dave said. "Somebody's liable to take it away from you over there."

Shim looked at the bulge Dave's pistol made in his pocket. Dave's coat would hide it, and so would Shim's hide his. Of course you didn't go out in society with your pistol showing, but you didn't go without it, either. "I don't see you starting out half dressed," he said.

Dave, squinting at himself in the mirror and fiddling with his necktie, didn't answer. Shim settled his pepperbox more securely into his pistol pocket and reached for his coat. They drank some buttermilk and ate some cold biscuits and preserves instead of waiting for Kiz to cook, but even at that it was dusk-dark by the time they got started.

They'd been going up and down hills for what seemed to Shim a long time, and he was beginning to get drowsy in the saddle when he saw what looked like a stretch of sand cutting across the brown road ahead in the starlight. "Rocky Ford," Dave said, and their horses' feet crunched on pebbles and sloshed in dark rippling water.

Shim perked up. "I'm glad of that. I'd about decided we were on the wrong road."

They were on the other side when a man's voice hailing them from off to the right brought them up short. "You fellows come here and help me."

They saw him, standing a few yards down the creek between a clump of willows and a sand bar.

"What's wrong?" Dave hollered back.

No answer came.

"He talked like his teeth are too long," Shim said.

"Hush, he'll hear you." Dave reined his horse off the road toward the willows, and Shim followed.

The man, tall and rawbony, was pulling on a rope that ran out into the creek and around a cow's horns. The water didn't look to be more than three or four inches deep, but the cow's legs and lower part of her body were out of sight.

"You all are the slowest mortals I ever did see," the man stopped hauling long enough to pant. "Help me with this rope. That danged old cow has got stuck in quicksand."

Dave jumped down and hurried toward him. Shim, ruffled by the man's ill-mannered way of talking, took his time about tying the horses to a little willow.

"Where you all from?" The man on the rope looked them over suspiciously.

Dave pointed west.

"Swamp angels," the man grunted. "Way up here." He got a better hold on the rope. "Well, never mind that. Catch a hold there and pull hard. Can't you see she's sinking all the time?"

He was the one wasting time asking questions and making slighting remarks, and Shim wouldn't have laid a finger on his danged old rope if he hadn't felt sorry for the cow. He'd heard quicksand would bog a shadow, and it would take a heap of pulling to drag her out. Dave, not paying any mind at all to the man's grouchiness, had his heels dug into the sand and was pulling with all he had. Shim grabbed a hold and pulled too. The cow moved a few inches, and the man hollered, "Hold on there. You're getting too rampant. Trying to break her danged neck?"

Dave, polite as a basket of chips, said, "The way we do, when they get mired up in a bayou or swamp mud——"

"Pull," the man ordered, "while she's trying to help herself."

The cow was grunting and thrashing around. They all laid back on the rope. She got her feet onto hard sand, and a moment later came wading out of the water, her sides heaving. The man dropped the rope, the cow started off up the road, and Dave and Shim turned to their horses. The man didn't open his mouth to thank them—just stood there looking at them.

They were mounted when he said grudgingly, "You didn't tell me how your folks are getting along."

"Fine, thank you," Dave said.

"How's crops down that-a-way?"

"As good as I ever saw them," Dave answered politely.

"Well," the man said, "if everything is so durned fine down there in the bottoms, why didn't you all stay there?"

Shim wished he was big enough to throw the old buzzard into the quicksand they'd just pulled his cow out of, but Dave reined back toward the road without a word.

On either side of them now, blackjack oaks and scrub pines grew thickly. Riding at a walk, because the road here was going up a long incline, Shim stole a look at Dave, but nothing in the set of his shoulders or his face showed that he was sore at all. Somewhere close by in the stunted growth a horned owl blew his call—"Whooooooooooooo-whoo-whoo"—a mean, lonesome, low-down sound that sent a chill up Shim's back.

"The varmints up here sound about as friendly as the folks," he said.

Dave turned his head to look at Shim. "So that's what's eating you. I knew you were all swelled up about something.

That old man didn't mean any harm. He was just brought up different to what we were."

"A shoat's got more manners than he had," Shim said.

"Just different manners from ours," Dave said, like he knew all about them. "It takes time to catch onto them. Yonder's Sugarfoot's house."

Shim leaned forward eagerly in his saddle. On their right the trees had stopped suddenly, and he had a clear view of a square-looking, lighted house, standing maybe a hundred yards back from the road on a little dogwood flat. There was a cluster of dark outhouses behind it, probably chicken house, tool house and smokehouse.

A road forked off from the one they were on and they followed it, a rail fence and a field to their left, the house ahead and to their right. Horses and wagons were hitched at the front gate, and Shim could see folks moving around on the long gallery and in the yard.

At the corner of the yard fence Dave pulled up. "My horse fights strange horses," he said, and reined in among some dogwood trees to the right. "We'll hitch here."

It was the first Shim knew about Dave's horse being a fighter and it sounded fishy, but if Dave wanted to hitch here away from the others, it was all right with him. Beyond the yard fence, made of poles with the ends flattened and nailed to posts, light shone from the window of a front room, and he could see a lamp was burning in the room behind it. Another one or two rooms, outlined in the starlight, were dark and seemed to be the balance of an ell that ran back on this side.

They walked around to the front gate, an extra heavy one made of oak palings. Going up the walk, they passed several men, but none of them spoke nor, as far as Shim could tell, even looked at him and Dave. At the same time he had a funny feeling that sharp eyes watched their every move, and it made his legs feel stiff.

From inside the house a voice let out a yell that jerked his shoulder muscles taut; music began to play, and the voice went on, calling out strange words in a singsong baritone. To cover his start of surprise, Shim said, "That fellow talks like his mouth leaks air."

"Hush," Dave said in a low voice.

"Well, can you understand him?" Shim said crossly.

Dave's voice close to his ear said, "Forget your smart-aleck stuff here, if you know what's good for you."

They were climbing the steps, and Shim turned his attention to the house. Made of hewn logs chinked with clay and whitewashed, it was two rooms wide, with no hall between. From each room a door and a window opened onto the long front gallery, but only the room on the right was lighted. The other one, hot as the night was, had both door and window shut tight. All the dances he'd ever been to, the whole house was lighted up. If the musicians, and all those feet he could hear scraping the floor, were in that one room, it must be jammed full of folks. It was. He and Dave got just inside the door and had to stop or be run over.

The room was bigger than it looked from the outside. It had to be to hold all the folks in it. Down its middle a line of men and boys stood opposite a line of women and girls, all of them swinging and pulling at one another in time to the music. The men were all in shirt sleeves and were all sort of gaunt-looking, with weather-tanned faces; the women and girls, dressed in bright colors, had faces almost as tanned as the men's. They took up plenty of space, stamping their feet and cutting figures, but there was still room for folks standing along the walls or sitting double on turned-down, shuck-bottom chairs.

Shim located the musicians—to his right, in the corner between the front window and a rock fireplace at the end of the room. He started inching down toward them when, from somewhere, a little slim girl in a yellow dress, grinning as silly as a duck eating briers, swooped down on Dave, grabbed his arm and started to pull him out onto the floor. Dave grinned, just as silly as she was, then said, "Just a minute, Tildy. This is my little brother."

Tildy threw him a glance and a giggle, and she and Dave joined the dancers. Shim looked after them. "Little brother." He didn't lack more than a couple of inches being as tall as Dave, even if he did still wear short pants and wasn't filled out good yet. He'd just stand here and laugh at Dave getting his feet tangled up in square dancing he didn't know B from bull's foot about.

> "All join hands and mind the laces,
> Tighten your back bands and let out the traces."

Shim caught the words and a glimpse of the caller at the far end of the line. He was stamping and kicking up his heels lively as a cricket, if he did look about a hundred years old, his face dry and wrinkled as a dishrag gourd, and his voice the biggest thing about him.

Shim's eyes came back to Dave. He was swinging Tildy around, cutting the same figures the rest of them were, without a bobble, like he'd been square dancing all his life. Shim decided to figure that out later, because right now he wanted to close the small space between himself and the musicians so nobody could cut them from his view. As close to them as he could get, he leaned against the wall and watched their every move.

There was a fiddle, a guitar, a mandolin and a bass fiddle. The bass fiddler, jerking his bow like he was having the time of his life, threw back his head and sang:

> "Baby, with the bread board,
> Working up the dough . . ."

and something about a dog that wouldn't bite that Shim didn't quite catch. But the words didn't matter; it was the rollicking beat of the music that carried him plumb away. He was lost to everything else when, with a long scrape of the bow across the bass-fiddle strings, it stopped. The dancers, out of breath, their faces flushed, backed up against the walls, fanning themselves and talking.

With the middle of the room cleared, Shim saw it was the low ceiling that made things look crowded and brightly lighted. The bright tin reflectors behind the coal-oil lamps high on the walls had nowhere to reflect their light except down and out. A man wearing overalls was passing a hat, and each man he came to dropped money in. It came Shim's turn and he dropped in a couple of dimes.

The musicians beside him were beginning to tune up their instruments, and again he gave them his undivided attention. The mandolin player, leaning close to the guitar player, jerked his head toward Shim and said, "We done charmed a swamp angel."

"That's all right," the bass fiddler said, "he favored the hat with change."

Shim stood a little straighter against the wall, and a wave

of embarrassment swept over him. These folks' way of never seeming to look at him had caused him to forget his manners and let himself be caught staring at the musicians all this time. If he could take off his coat he'd be less conspicuous; he and Dave wore the only coats in sight. But if he did that, the handle of his pistol would show, and that wouldn't do. These men here must all wear theirs in their shirt bosoms.

A grating voice right beside him surprised him. "You folks from the swamps are getting rich as cream selling your woods to the sawmill crowd, I hear."

A dish-faced young man was backed up against the wall alongside him, and although his small, deep-set eyes were looking straight ahead, Shim knew it was he who had spoken. The flat words hung between them, and Shim felt heat creeping up his neck and into his face. This stranger was saying that the money Shim had taken out of his pocket to put in the hat was "sawmill money."

"You heard wrong, sir," he said politely but firmly. "The Govans don't sell their trees."

The pale, deep-set eyes turned to look at him. They had a glitter in them, but if the man said anything, Shim didn't hear it. Another voice, a woman's, was speaking to him. She was about his height, but three times his width, and she was standing in front of him. The fiddler was bawling out "Get your partners for a sandy quadrille," and Shim hadn't caught what the woman said. "Ma'am?" he said politely.

"Be my partner for this dance," she said, still without raising her eyes from about the second button of his shirt.

"Thank you, ma'am," Shim said, "but I've never done this sort of dance."

The invitation was the last thing he'd expected, and he both wanted to and didn't want to. He didn't want to stand here beside this dish-faced young man. The woman settled it. "That don't matter," she said, reaching for his hand. "We'll show you what to do."

His head took a whirl or two and he was lined up facing her. The action was starting; the singsong baritone called out something that sounded like "Ladies, go see dough," and dancers were pulling or pushing Shim this way and that. His feet were as tangled as a fly's in molasses. But the friendly snatching and nodding and pushing kept up, and all of a sudden it began to come natural. It was easy as swimming downstream in swift water; all he had to do was work his hands and feet and he stayed afloat on the music. He was having more fun than he'd ever had round dancing.

He hadn't much more than got limbered up good, though, when he noticed gaps coming in the line where dancers had dropped out here and there. He hadn't noticed them doing that in any of the figures they'd cut before. When the couple right next to him faded out, he watched to see where they went. The man went out the front door, and the woman went and stood with other women, frowning, against the back wall.

The ones left in the lines kept on cutting figures in response to the changing calls, but they were slow about giving Shim his cue when the music changed and didn't seem to have their minds on what they were doing. He tried to swing the wrong girl and was jerked around, a little late, by his own partner.

The music stopped, and loud rough talk from the yard could be heard plainly inside the room. That explained the dwindling dancers. The men had dropped out to join whatever rookus was going on outside. There was trouble inside too. Shim heard sounds of scuffling over by the fireplace and a loud voice saying, "I'm going out there." He caught a glimpse of four or five men crowded around a big man with a face red as a beet, holding him back, trying to quiet him down.

Shim eased over to his former place against the wall near the musicians. The dish-faced man was gone. Feeling uncomfortably small and on ground that was getting a little shaky, Shim looked around for Dave. He caught sight of his dark shoulders across the room, but they were blotted from sight by the big, red-faced man surging away from the fireplace, bringing with him the crowd holding on trying to stop him.

"Ain't enough of you lightweights in the county to stop me," the big man yelled, and with that he slung one arm straight out from his body. It sent three men, who were holding to it, tumbling across the floor like turtles raked off a log with a stick.

"I'm the best man that ever wore shoe leather," he bellowed. He straightened the other arm, and rocked so far back on his heels he almost went over backward. The men holding the second arm had let go in time and it had met no resistance. He got his balance, though, and began walking slow and heavy toward the front door, his head turning from side to side like a big bear. "I am plumb and teetotally poison," he said, "and I'll break their sorry necks fast as I get my hands on them."

Darting down from the other end of the room, a little, narrow-shouldered woman with black hair and black, flashing eyes headed for the door too. She beat the big man to it and stood facing him. He walked straight on like he didn't even see her, until one more step would have brought him smack up against her.

Before he took that step she spoke. "Sugarfoot Simone, get back there and behave yourself, or I'll beat your eyes out with my fists. You know that stump water of yours always drives them crazy. If I catch you passing out any more of it tonight, I'll wrap the jug around your neck till it chokes you to death."

It looked like a rabbit standing up to a hound, but to Shim's surprise the big man turned around, meek as Moses, and started back toward the fireplace.

Into the quiet of the room came a grating yell from outside. "Turn them dudes from the swamp out here, Sugarfoot." The big man didn't even turn, but Shim's eyes flew to where he'd last seen Dave. That voice from outside sounded mighty like it belonged to the dish-faced man, and it sure wasn't friendly. He saw Dave, and that Tildy had him by the arm pulling him toward a door in the back of the room. The doorway was completely blocked by four or five stony-faced women, not moving, not looking at anything, just listening to the loud talk going on outside. While Tildy took one of them by the shoulder and pulled her aside, Dave turned his head and shot a glance back at Shim. His eyes, narrow and extra bright, told Shim there was danger and to follow him quick.

Shim, trying to walk like he wasn't in any hurry, made his way across the room toward the door Dave and Tildy had disappeared through. When he got there the women had closed ranks again. He knew better than to pull one of them out of the way like Tildy had. He hesitated politely before the two directly blocking the door, but they didn't even see him, they were straining so hard to catch the angry words outside. "Rally round," a voice out there yelled. "Let's go in and get them."

Scared witless, Shim sent his eyes flashing around for another way out, and saw a door in the end of the room, opposite the fireplace. With the muscles of his back drawing painfully, and feeling tall and clumsy like he was on tom-walkers, he made a beeline for it. Wherever it led, he would be out of this room.

He opened it, pulled it quietly to behind him and, his heart pounding, waited for his eyes to accustom themselves to the total darkness. Even before they did, he knew he was in the wrong place. Holding his breath, he heard sounds of breathing all around him. A child whined, and a woman's voice cooed sleepily.

The bulk of a bed on either side of him took shape; the floor beyond was covered with pallets, all of them mounded with sleeping forms. He was in the dark, closed room he'd noticed to his left when he came up the steps, and it was filled with sleeping folks—old women and babies who had come along in the wagons with the others to the dance. He'd swapped the devil for the witch. He couldn't go back, and he sure mustn't be caught in here.

He stretched his eyes wide to let in all the light he could get, and saw a dim square of starlight to his right. A window at the back of the room was open. He started toward it, weaving cautiously among the pallets, setting each foot down carefully and silently. He was only three or four steps from the window now and not a board had creaked. With escape so close, his feet got in too big a hurry and one of them struck a quilt. Fighting panic, he eased it up to untangle it, only to feel thick folds wrap around his ankle. Between him and the window a head and shoulders reared up suddenly from the floor. A woman, propped on an elbow, was staring right at him.

He kicked his foot free, cleared her pallet and another beside it in one long leap, swung his feet over the low sill and dropped. His feet hit something spongy, throwing him off

SHIM

balance, and a blood-curdling howl almost deafened him. He had landed on a sleeping hound. Running and stumbling, he was past the first of three rooms of the ell that separated him from his horse before he regained his balance and could make time with less noise.

He rounded the end room, and there ahead of him somebody was standing. Changing his course to pass well out of reach of whoever it was, he saw the dark shape suddenly separate and become two somebodies—Dave and Tildy. He and Dave hit the fence at the same time, grabbed the top pole and swung themselves over.

Dave's horse was the closest. Shim got his horse's reins untied, threw them over its head and was swinging into the saddle when he heard Dave grunt and his foot thump the ground hard. Shim's own horse was acting up, jumping sideways and kicking. He saw Dave stoop and come up from the ground with the stirrup in his hand, saw him catch the saddle horn, jump, and land belly down in the saddle; but he didn't see him right himself, for Shim's own horse whirled and took off like hell after a yearling. Shim gave him his head.

When he hit the main road, his horse lined out in a gallop that broke into a run, and Shim knew he was running away. He pulled up hard on the reins, and his hands flew back and hit his chest. The reins were broken. With nothing to hold to he felt like he was floating in the air. He grabbed the horn, but the horse, with no pressure on the bit, was going like the wind.

Running hoofbeats overtook him, and Dave yelled from beside him, "Hold that crazy horse so I can handle mine." Dave's horse was running just to keep up; Shim had to stop his, or both of them might hit a rough place and stumble and fall. They were going down a dangerous incline and weren't used to these hills. He had to get the shank of that curb bit.

Gripping his saddle horn tighter with one hand, Shim leaned cautiously over the horse's neck until the fingers of his free hand found the head stall. Straining every muscle in him to stay in the saddle and still keep his fingers inching forward, he heard hoofs grind against rocks, knocking water high as his head. They were crossing Rocky Ford at full tilt, and Dave's horse had drenched him.

Going up the incline beyond the ford, Shim's fingers finally got what they were after—the shank of the bit. He got a firm grip and began to pull back. His horse slowed to a crowhop, then to a slow trot, and, still holding to the bit and to the saddle horn with the other hand, Shim swung his leg over and dropped to the ground. The second he left the saddle, his horse put on its own brakes, and Shim had to run only three or four steps before his horse stopped, skittish, but docile.

Dave, who'd whooshed past him up the road several yards before being able to rein his horse up, came riding back. "What you doing letting your horse get the best of you?" he said angrily.

Shim pointed to the loose reins dangling across his saddle, but said nothing. He was busy unstrapping his girths. The broken reins had kept him from controlling his horse, but something else had made him run away to start with. Shoving the saddle back, he ran his hands under the blanket and hit something that stuck like pins.

"The low-down yaps," he said. "Trying to get me killed."

Dave, squatting on the ground, struck a match and lighted a pile of pine needles and sticks he'd raked together with his hands. Shim tossed a prickly mass onto the fire. "Cockleburs. Somebody put a fistful of them under my saddle blanket."

Dave stood up and in the light from the small fire examined his stirrup leather. It had been cut nearly in two, ready to break when he put his weight on it back there. Shim looked down at his own reins. Cut, too, better than halfway through. He felt like telling Dave what he thought of the kind of company he kept, but right now all he wanted was to get out of these hills. "If we just had some lace leather," he said.

"Yeah," Dave said. "If a frog had wings . . ."

Shim dug into his pocket and came up with a generous length of set-hook line. Cutting off a piece with his pocket knife, he handed it to Dave and with the rest began piecing together his reins. They worked silently and hurriedly in the firelight, and in a few minutes were on their way again, riding at a walk and in silence. They, as well as their horses, were pretty well winded. They'd ridden up and down a couple of hills and were passing a dark cabin when Dave spoke.

"Say, that was my set-hook line we cut up back there. What was it doing in your pocket? Someday I'm going to knock a knot on your head big as a goose egg for taking my stuff."

"You left it hanging in the saddle room for the rats to eat. I stuck it in my pocket to save it. It's a good thing I did. You'd have got mighty tired riding home with one stirrup."

Dave grunted and then said with a grin, "Were you much scared back there?"

"Not so much," Shim lied. "I just never wanted to leave a place so bad in my life."

"Was it you half-killed that hound just before you busted around the corner of the house on Tildy and me?"

Shim giggled. Most scary things were the funniest ones of all—afterward; and tonight was beginning to be funny already. "When those women blocked the door again after you and Tildy went out, I had to find another one. . . ."

Time he finished telling Dave about his blundering into the room full of folks on pallets, and diving out the window onto the sleeping hound, Dave was laughing so hard Shim figured now was a good time to get something settled that was bothering him. In a roundabout way, though, without admitting that he might be to blame for the trouble starting.

"Those folks in the habit of running you off this way every time you go over there?" he asked.

"What makes you think I've been there before?" Dave said.

"That square dancing came mighty natural to you."

"Swimming came mighty natural to you once," Dave said.

Shim's mind flashed to the day Miss Cherry took him to the bayou to teach him to swim. Dave knew Shim had been slipping off and swimming with Henry's boys for a couple of years, but he'd watched Shim pretend to be learning and never said a word.

Shim came back to the question bothering him. "You haven't told me yet if this is the way you always leave from there."

"Well, no," Dave said. "They're never overly friendly—except Tildy. You have to watch every word you say, and step mighty light around them, but I always made out all right till tonight."

"You reckon I could have been the cause of it?" Shim blurted the words out without meaning to, and when Dave looked at him in surprise, he let the cat all the way out of the sack.

"Some dish-faced fellow standing against the wall beside me said we swamp folks are getting rich selling our woods. It made me hot, and I told him right quick that the Govans didn't sell their woods to sawmill folks. I said it polite and all, but there was a kind of mean look in his eye. Just then some woman grabbed me to dance, but it wasn't long till that rookus broke loose outside. I recognized that dish-faced fellow's voice, and I'm pretty sure he was the one doing the biggest of the yelling for you and me."

Dave shrugged. "Could have been that. Could have been anything. You never know what riles folks that are different from you. 'Most every time I go over there, trouble of some kind gets started. They get full of old Sugarfoot's pop-skull, and then they've got to have meanness of some kind for exercise. Tonight, it just happened to be us. There's no harm done."

Dave wasn't blaming him for maybe causing the trouble; more than that, he wasn't taking this chance to lecture Shim for being so hardheaded about selling the woods. Shim's chest felt light. Maybe Dave was beginning to see that he and the Captain were right about the woods. He felt a new, grown-up feeling of companionship with Dave, and sat straighter in his saddle.

Now and then on one side of the road or the other the woods opened and they'd ride past a field and the bulk of a dark cabin; then woods hemmed them in again. He and Dave and their horses might have been the only things alive in the world. The steady movement of the horse under him, the monotony of clear, starlit sky and timber line, the stillness of the night—all ran together in rest and contentment.

The last hill was a mile or more behind them and the welcome smell of swampland was heavy in the air when nearness to home roused Shim. He slid over and rested one thigh in the saddle. "That cut in your stirrup leather won't be seen. The fender hides it."

"I know," Dave said, straightening slack shoulder muscles. "I was just thinking about that. I've got a pair of new reins at home you can have."

Shim nodded. He and Dave were in this together—to keep the Captain from noticing anything out of the way and start asking questions. He felt good, like he and Dave would never be at loggerheads about things again.

chapter five

TENTS, light brown and A-shaped, stood among the big oaks between the lake and a green wall of cane. Women walked around like they were hunting something to do—not work, for they were dressed in their Sunday best. From the log where he sat, Shim watched Foots Booker and his wife Caline stack cooking tools beside a pile of wood they'd gathered. Soon the fire would be built and the cooking start. Shim, with Henry, Foots and Caline, had been here since daybreak. He'd watched the tents go up and the wagons and folks come rolling in. He always came in the first wagon, not to miss a minute of this August camping trip they all came on every year.

Another wagon bumped noisily out of the trail and stopped. It was Cousin Jeff Ferguson's boys and girls and their two girl visitors from Yazoo. The two boys jumped out and stood beside the front wheel; the girls, one at a time, put a foot on the wheel, gave a hand to each boy and were lowered to the ground.

Other young folks ran around among the tents and down to the boat landing, chattering like a flock of geese, trying to get a game of some kind started. Now and then a girl would let out a squeal, and Shim would smile to himself. At home the old folks would never put up with such an unladylike forgetting of manners by the girls, but out here in camp everybody was plumb carefree and happy.

Two more tents were going up, and in a shady spot between a couple of big red-oak trees Henry was unloading long planks from a wagon. Four posts, sharpened at one end, would be driven into the ground and tied together with crosspieces to hold the planks and make a table.

Here and there among the cypress trees along the lake's edge people stood like statues, holding out fishing poles, the red-and-white-painted corks of their lines floating in the water. Out on the lake Dave was paddling a boatload of girls around. Somewhere out of sight the Captain was off in a boat, aiming to harpoon a few buffalo fish.

A span of slick horses pulling a topless buggy came from under the low-hanging tree limbs of the trail, and Shim's eyes brightened. It was Judge Short's rig, and his boy, Mack, was the one town boy Shim's age that liked the country. But Judge and Mrs. Short were alone. Shim's moment of disappointment passed. It would have been fun to have someone here his own age, but he was used to being the youngest in the crowd. He was always welcome to join in the games with the young folks of courting age if he wanted to, and he could hold his own with the men in hunting and fishing.

Walking along in front of the tents came the four-piece band from Jackson. Each man had his instrument in one hand, a cane-bottom chair in the other. They selected a place where the hard, dry buckshot earth was clear of leaf mold or brush, sat down and began tuning up. A mandolin, trombone, cornet and bass fiddle, and they were hired for the whole week. Shim drew a long breath and slid his hips along the log to where he could rest his shoulders against a little ash sapling while he listened. Life was perfect. A whole week of this lay ahead—folks, music and good food, here in the woods beside Beaver Lake. At home the crops were laid by, needing nothing but time and sunshine to ripen the sorghum for grinding, the corn for pulling and the cotton for picking.

Another wagon, heavily loaded by the way the thimbles clucked on the axles, came out of the trail and pulled up beside a big, freshly dug hole in the ground. The driver, jumping down and lowering the back endgate, began unloading big crokersacks full of ice. It would keep—what was left of it after the long drive in the hot sun from the railroad depot—for days down in that hole. Wick, Henry and Foots, opening up cases of soft drinks and beer, stacked the bottles on the ice and stretched a tentfly over the hole to keep the heat out.

The musicians were playing a song that was new to Shim, and catchy. When the bass fiddler bawled out the words to the chorus Shim listened closely, and it suited him to a T. It was about a place called the Congo, where there seemed to be plenty of woods, game and warm weather the year round.

Some of the young, courting-age blades—Sank, Rance, Cholly and Irvin—had made themselves brooms by tying a handful of brush together, and were sweeping a level space of the crusted ground free of leaf mold. If there was much dancing and stamping on that ground, there'd soon be a layer of dust to be swept off. Three or four of the older women were watching them. "If you intend to try dancing there,"

Miss Cherry said, "those little sprouts will have to be uprooted." Cholly found a hatchet beside the table lumber and went to work on the root of a knee-high sprout.

Shim heard a sound like a happy sigh from the women and a grunt from the men. He saw why. J. Ney Ward was riding out of the woods on a slick black horse. A little way behind him, on another pretty horse, came his servant; and behind him, two hounds trotted out of the bushes—J. Ney's bear dogs. J. Ney always had the best of everything—clothes, riding stock and dogs—and he never missed a chance to show them off. He always carried a roll of bills big enough to choke a mule, and pulled it out every chance he got.

J. Ney Ward was a bachelor—older than Uncle Ben and Wick and their crowd, but not nearly so old as the Captain. He had plenty of kinfolks, even a couple of married sisters, but he lived by himself in a big old house, and a tenant woman on his plantation cooked for him. He usually dropped in on these camping trips for a day or two, and the men were never easy when he was around. He was the kind that just didn't fit. He was too full of himself to begin with. And more than that, he was bad about saying things that didn't set well with other men. Shim had heard them say J. Ney had always been that way, but since he'd killed his best friend over a poker game a couple of years ago he'd got a heap worse. Was so fractious and quick-tempered he was dangerous as dynamite. But the ladies seemed to like his strutting, dandified air, and mostly he stayed around with them.

Dismounted, hat in hand, J. Ney bowed admiringly to the ladies, then turned to the men. "You all are the sorriest lay-out I ever saw. You ought to be out getting some bear meat, instead of scratching around camp doing nothing."

Nobody had anything to reply to that.

Betty Lou Holliday drifted over close to Shim. As girls went, Betty Lou was better than most. Her hair was the red-gold color of black-gum leaves after frost, and in the sunshine her brown eyes seemed that same warm color. She wasn't as silly and put-on as most girls. She leaned over and whispered to Shim in a funny, half-choked voice. "What do you think is keeping him?"

He knew who she meant. Uncle Ben had seemed to be studying about Betty Lou pretty much lately. But he didn't know why Uncle Ben was so late about coming in. So he just shrugged and went on listening to Judge Short talking to Miss Cherry in his loud, speechmaking voice. "Cherry, folks are queer. When it comes to vacations, Yankees go north and rebels go south. City folks go uptown, and country folks, like us, take to the woods."

J. Ney said, "Ah, Miss Betty Lou, pretty as ever. You know what I'm going to do? This fall I'm going to get you a big bear hide and have it mounted for a rug."

Betty Lou sort of fluttered her long lashes. "Why don't you get it now?"

"They're not much good now," J. Ney said. "But come to think of it, I'll just get you one this week. Those dogs of mine are the best that ever breathed fresh air."

Betty Lou fluttered her lashes again. Shim looked at her right hard, puzzled. One minute whispering that frantic way in his ear about Uncle Ben, and the next making calf eyes at J. Ney.

It was almost sundown. Uncle Ben hadn't shown up yet. The long rough table was set as neatly for supper as if it was in somebody's dining room. A big platter of fish was in the middle, and more fish—buffalo, perch and bass—were browning in the pot of boiling grease over the fire. The women sat around the table on cane-bottom chairs, the men on empty soft-drink cases and spring seats from the wagons. Shim sat on a block of wood. Over to one side, on a log, Henry was cleaning lamps and lanterns that would have to be lighted before another hour passed.

They were at the pie, cake and coffee stage of the meal when Uncle Ben rode into camp. He hitched his horse to a swinging limb, exchanged cheerful greetings with everybody and, bending over Shim, laid a shiny four-bit piece on the table. "A present for you," he said, and pulled up an empty box to sit on.

Betty Lou, in a voice that sounded like a knife on whetrock, said, "What on earth delayed you?"

Before Ben could answer, J. Ney said, "Guess he's been after some more of those foreigners' gold."

"Foreigners" meant the sawmill men, and mention of them drew Shim's cheeks in like a green persimmon. There'd been no more talk of the sawmill at home. He'd overheard Dave tell the Captain a few weeks ago that the folks weren't selling their woods very fast, but this sounded like Uncle Ben was still working on them. Frowning, he put the four-bit piece in his pocket and went down to the lake bank. He didn't want any more to eat, and he'd better get the boat while the getting was good, before somebody beat him to it. The money wasn't a present. It was payment to Shim for slipping out and hiding a good boat so Uncle Ben could take Betty Lou riding after supper. He'd hidden out boats for Uncle Ben on too many camping trips not to know without question what the money was for.

The best boat at the landing was chained to the exposed root of a tupelo-gum tree. He untied the chain, stepped in and paddled silently up the lake. He turned in at a little pocket with bushes growing thickly on both banks, his paddle noiseless in the shallow water. A few yards and he was in a thicket of elbow bushes growing in the water. He worked his way through them to the bank, landed and pulled the boat well up between two bitter-pecan trees.

He followed the bank of the little pocket for several yards before turning through a patch of mutton cane considerably higher than his head. Shadows were getting thick, but he could still easily tell a stick from a snake; and hitting camp this way, nobody would be apt to backtrack him. There were going to be more courting couples wanting boats than there were boats.

He was near the pit where the ice and drinks were kept when he heard a voice coming from beside a big red-oak tree. It sounded like somebody was mad, and he stopped to listen. It was Uncle Ben, and he was talking mighty serious. "I only brought the men out to your place and had absolutely nothing to do with the price they paid you for that three and a half sections of woods."

J. Ney Ward's voice answered. "Other people are getting a lot better price than I did. How do you explain that?"

"You sold them your woods. I'm not responsible for the price you agreed on."

Suddenly Shim remembered that when J. Ney made that remark at the table about "foreigners' gold," Uncle Ben, sitting beside him, had made a quick, curious move—nothing you'd really notice, just sort of a quiver. He should have known then that trouble could come up mighty easily. Setting his feet noiselessly as an animal's in the leaf mold, he headed for camp in a hurry.

He found the Captain at the table, playing a friendly game of poker with five other men. Shim leaned over his shoulder. "Uncle Ben and J. Ney are arguing back there by the ice pit."

Low as he spoke, all six men heard him and, at the same instant, dropped their cards on the table and were up and in motion. Shim stood perfectly still and listened, until he knew by the quietness of things that they had got there in time to stop the trouble. Then he went on to the row of women's tents to find Betty Lou and tell her where he'd hidden the boat. He didn't feel like seeing Uncle Ben right now. To tell the truth he was about half sore at him for getting mixed up with those sawmill folks.

The hour was getting late. Out on the lake courting-age boys and girls made merry with songs and boat riding, but the older women were asleep and their tents dark. Only a few of the older men were still up, over at the table, playing cards or talking.

Shim, Henry and Foots sat on chunks beside the campfire. Shim guessed Betty Lou and Uncle Ben had found the boat all right. He'd seen them with a lighted lantern going through the woods toward the pocket where he'd hidden it. Betty Lou hadn't batted her eyes that silly way at J. Ney Ward since Uncle Ben got here. Henry threw a fresh stick on the fire, and Shim shoved his chunk back a little from the heat. "You going to keep a fire all night?" he asked.

"I never lets a fire go out at night when I'm camping," Henry said, and, brushing his hands together to knock off the trash, he went on in a lowered voice. "This-here Mr. J. Ney is stamping around, raring so for a bear hunt it's going to take one to calm him down."

"No hunt nor nothing else never is calmed him down since I been knowing him," Foots said.

Ignoring the interruption, Henry went on. "What I figures is that just to humor him the men will plan a hunt tomorrow, likely for the next morning. If they does, I wants you all to help me get out of camp with a good horse tomorrow night."

"For what?" Shim said.

"The Captain's dogs and mine too needs a good hunt much as Mr. J. Ney Ward's does, don't they?" Henry said.

"Mr. J. Ney will be mighty mad." Foots cackled. "He's aiming for his dogs to get all the credit."

"I'll guarantee you'll get a horse," Shim said, "and maybe I'll go with you."

"When you're fixing to slip out and do something, one is company and two is a crowd," Henry said. "I'll go by myself."

Shim yawned, and Foots looked at him. "You're so sleepy your face looks long as a ax handle."

Henry looked at him too and said, "I fixed you a bed that will sleep fine as frog hair. Go to it, before you falls off that chunk and hurts yourself."

In the right-hand corner of the dark tent Shim felt around quietly with his feet and found his bed—a blanket spread on top of a pile of fresh-cut, springy switch canes. This was a luxury he hadn't expected and didn't know whether he wanted. Maybe he'd rather sleep on the bare ground as he usually did on camping trips. This seemed sissy, like townfolks, and not the way to stay strong and tough.

In the back of the tent someone snored softly. He knew that snore. Judge Short was sleeping back there with the Captain. There was no sound of breathing from the corner opposite Shim; some courting fellow would be coming in later on to sleep there. Shim lay down, pushed his hat off to one side and fell asleep.

Sure enough, like Henry had guessed, the men agreed the next day to the hunt J. Ney Ward kept bantering them for; and that night, when the camp grew quiet again, Henry was on his way through the dark woods to the Govan plantation. His dogs and the Captain's weren't going to miss the fun in the morning if he could help it.

Before daylight Shim awoke to find himself being pulled, feet first, from the tent. Outside, in the rays of the campfire that shone among the trees, he sat up. Henry said in a low voice, "If it wasn't for me, you'd be sleeping till doomsday."

"Who?" Shim said. "I've been watching all night for you to get back with the dogs."

He went down to the lake in the darkness and washed his face in the cool water. Henry's two hounds and the Captain's four nosed around him excitedly every step he took. When he joined the rest of the hunters at the table the hounds stopped politely a few feet away, but one of them let out an impatient howl. The men, talking in low tones so they wouldn't disturb the folks who were still asleep and not going out, glanced up. They saw the hounds at the edge of the lantern light, and J. Ney stood up.

His face was fiery red, and he looked like he was trying to smile but couldn't get the corners of his mouth up. "Whoever went to the trouble of going after his dogs for this race wasted his time," he said. "There's no need for you all to go, say nothing of those extra hounds. I'll do the killing this morning."

Everybody knew that anything that was said would only rile him further, so they kept quiet, while J. Ney untied his horse from a swinging limb and climbed into the saddle. Dave got up too and got onto his big black hunting mule that loved a hunt as well as any man did. Dave and J. Ney were mounted, because they were going to do the driving.

They disappeared around the right end of the canebrake, the eight hounds following, moaning and whining for action, and the men left behind began to gulp their coffee. Ben stood up, cup in hand, to finish his. "I know right where that bear will try to cross Wrong Prong Bayou," he said, "and that's where I'll get him. Shim will go with me and take the stand by the broken-top ash."

Henry laid a shotgun and six buckshot shells on the table by Shim. Cholly, shouldering his own shooting iron, looked at Ben. "You and Shim will hold the east then. The rest of us will cover the stands to the north and the Indian mound to the south. J. Ney and Dave will likely get him up in that thicket by Round Lake and cut him off from the west."

Ben nodded.

"Let's go," Rance said. "Some of us have got a right smart of foot traveling to do."

Sank, Wick, Rance, Cholly and Henry went off into the darkness. Ben's stand, and Shim's, were closer and they had plenty of time, but they shouldered their weapons and circled the canebrake to the left.

Daylight caught in the treetops and held a few minutes before sliding leisurely downward to the leaf-covered ground. Shim, still groggy from heavy sleep, stumbled over a decaying stick, and Ben said, "How are you coming along?"

"About like a frog walks, slow by jerks," Shim said.

A little farther on Ben stopped and looked around. "Well," he said with a grin, "they say the best of friends have to part some time." He pointed northwest. "You go across there, and just beyond that hickory ridge you'll see a broken-top ash. Anywhere within a hundred yards of that is good. I'll go over here to the Bayou."

Shim struck out for his stand. He had no more than found it when he heard the dogs, to the west, open up. The tracks they'd picked up were cold, though; the slow, long-drawn-out, occasional sounds from their throats trailed off into sadness.

The sun climbing in the eastern sky turned the cool dampness of the woods into steamy heat and stirred swarms of mosquitoes into activity. They bit Shim's face and hands and shoulders, where he sat on the ground resting his back against the broken-top ash tree, and their constant buzzing seemed nearly as loud as the now steady barking of the dogs. They had jumped the varmint where Cholly had guessed they would—in the tall buckvines beyond Round Lake. J. Ney and Dave would be in the open woods now, big-eyed from watching so hard for something moving and every now and then turning loose a whoop long as a plowline to encourage the dogs and also to keep the wolves notified that men were present so they wouldn't take it into their heads to run afoul of the dogs.

Shim parted his jaws a little to take the pressure off his eardrums and to hear better. The steady barking was a little closer but doing a mighty heap of zigzagging and crosscutting. That meant the bear had got hold of too much to eat last night and didn't aim to do much running if he could help it. Shim wondered what bears ate beside roasting ears and acorns. He'd heard they liked pigs and shoats and had even been known to kill a cow by breaking her neck with their fists, but he didn't know how true it was.

The dogs seemed to be lining out and bearing pretty much in his direction. He began to shake his legs and work his feet to make sure they would be limber for action and not stiff from sitting. He tried to figure out which dogs were ahead, but their voices now were one prolonged ring and he couldn't tell. He was getting excited fast. His mouth was dry, and he could hear the blood rushing by his ears.

The dogs were so close that he was getting on his feet when they suddenly turned north. Maybe heading for Persimmon Tree stand, where Henry, Sank, Rance, Wick or Cholly, whichever one was there, would get a shot—and, if he missed, get his shirttail cut off when he got back to camp. If he hit, J. Ney Ward wouldn't get a hide to give to Betty Lou. Shim would like mighty well to get the bear himself, of course, but it didn't really matter who got him, just so it wasn't J. Ney. J. Ney had sold his woods to the sawmill men, and besides, he'd been trying to flirt with Uncle Ben's girl.

The dogs had hit the tupelo brake now—about twenty acres of water full of old treetops, logs, elbow bushes and all sorts of mess except where the water was deep. At the north end they swung over east, then back south. That bear was trying to shake the dogs off his trail by going down one side of the brake and up the other. He could wade in many places where they would be slowed down by having to swim. At the south end they turned back again, and Shim figured Uncle Ben was running himself into a case of the thumps up and down Wrong Prong Bayou bank, trying to be at the right place when the bear lined out again, and praying he would line out before J. Ney or Dave caught up with him. Shim knew Uncle Ben wanted to kill the bear, just like they all did, but more than that, Shim knew that for J. Ney Ward to get that bear and give the hide to Betty Lou just wouldn't do. Not with bad blood already boiling between Uncle Ben and J. Ney.

The dogs were on their fourth round of the brake when

most of the pack of a sudden went silent. Only three—and they were the Captain's hounds, Rowdy, Rope and Music— were holding the trail. The others, Shim figured, had got tired of being tricked and were cutting across to the other side, aiming to break it up—meet the bear so he'd either have to fight or give up the water and take to his heels on solid ground.

J. Ney's two hounds opened up again. The others quickly joined their voices in, and a couple of minutes later the whole pack was in full cry and coming. Shim checked his gun breech again and strained his eyes among the big tree trunks, his heart beating his ribs like a hammer. He glimpsed movement about a hundred yards away. Luck was against him; he was in the wrong place. Jerking his eyes to a bigger opening among the trees a little to the left, he saw the black hunk of fury flash by, heading southeast like hell beating tanbark.

Well out of shooting range, the bear made it to a thicket that looked, from where Shim stood, as solid as the side of a hill, and to his astonishment the bear disappeared into it. Running his best, he saw the dogs vanish at the same place. The thicket was a place where the trees for some reason had been blown down or died, letting the sun through to the ground so that switch cane and every sort of brier and bush had grown up there thick as hair on a dog's back, and all of it was woven tightly together by tough, entangling vines.

Reaching the spot where the bear and dogs had vanished, Shim found the opening and stooped to look down it. It was a tunnel, ranging from knee to waist high, going straight through the thicket, and at the far end of it he saw the bear, bayed. His back against an old clay root, his red tongue was bright in his half-open jaws, and his deadly paws were raised and ready for the dogs barking and snarling just out of his reach. Shim's heart pounded with eagerness, but nobody with a lick of sense would crawl down that twenty-five or thirty yards of tunnel, with no chance to stand up and fight if things went wrong. He'd have to find another way to get to the bear.

Shim was running again. The thicket proved to be small. Circling it, he reached the other side, where his ears told him he was close to the raving dogs and growling bear. But he was slowed by briers, the biggest and tallest blackberry briers he'd ever seen. Using his feet and gun barrel to break trail, he worked his way into the brier-laced top of the old down tree against whose clay-covered roots the bear was backed up. From this side, the broken and dirt-caked roots pointing toward the hot clear sky concealed the sight he had seen through the tunnel. Working his way through the branches, onto the trunk and past a couple of limbs, he was stopped short by briers laced and lapped across before him so thick he couldn't have cut his way through them with anything smaller than a bush ax. He was so close that the barking of the dogs almost deafened him, but he still couldn't see them over the roots.

He backtracked a couple of steps to a limb big as his thigh that ran up at a pretty sharp angle from the trunk. It was exactly the thing he needed. Climbing with a shooting iron in one hand was hard work, but he managed to make it up to a protruding knot big enough to hitch one leg over, and stopped there to catch his breath. He could see the top half of the bear from here, but a shot was impossible with the dogs out there in line with the hot lead. He'd have to climb a few feet higher and get the lower part of the bear's back in his sights before a shot would be safe.

A movement beyond the thicket caught his eyes. It was J. Ney, already dismounted, tying his horse to a swinging limb and coming at a run to the mouth of the tunnel. He dropped out of sight, and Shim grinned, knowing how J. Ney was feeling, looking at that sight and not being able to get to it. Shim gripped the dry hard bark with arms and knees to hoist himself higher, but his tightening muscles froze where they were and the grin left his face, for through an opening in the overhead brush of the thicket he saw movement. He didn't want to believe his eyes, but there it was. J. Ney, on elbows and knees, was crawling down that tunnel and was about to beat him to the bear.

Gripping the limb in frantic haste, Shim inched himself up, one eye trying to keep track of J. Ney's progress. Suddenly, through another thin place in the brush, he saw the face, red from heat and excitement. Neck craned up, eyes hard and unfriendly were staring straight into Shim's. Resentful at the glint in those eyes, Shim pulled himself up another long notch. Still he wasn't high enough, and the dogs, knowing help was close, got too daring. One of the Captain's, Rowdy, the big spotted one, got too close. Shim saw him scooped up in a black hairy arm that could break a mule's back, given a quick squeeze against that black chest and dropped, limber and dead. Another black hairy arm swung out and this time caught one of J. Ney's dogs with a blow that sent him winding among the bushes.

J. Ney was out of sight in the tunnel, but in another minute he might be crawling right up among the dogs where he could shoot without hitting any of them. Frantic at the thought of missing his chance at the bear, Shim lifted a foot high and set it on a knot that stuck out a couple of inches; with a hard surge he pushed himself up to a crook in the limb he had been aiming to reach. He was raising his gun when he heard the sound of cracking wood and knew he'd been careless in his hurry and gone too high. He was falling.

With swishes ending with a *whoom* the limb crashed through briers to the ground. Scratched and torn, Shim landed on his feet. Not much over the length of a fence rail away he saw the bear lunge forward, slapping dogs every which way, and charge through them straight at J. Ney in the tunnel. J. Ney's face was white as cotton, his eyes wide with horror, and Shim cringed for him. His first thought was to shoot, but his arms were so caught in briers he couldn't possibly move them to raise his gun.

He saw the bear's big paw hit J. Ney's head, pushing the white face into the ground; another paw hit his back. Then the bear was gone, and all the dogs, in full cry at its heels, were charging down the tunnel over the length of J. Ney's flattened body. Neither bear nor dogs had paid any more attention to J. Ney than if he'd been a chunk in their path. All that bear wanted was distance. Shim's mixed feelings—embarrassment and fright at falling, and disappointment at losing his chance at the bear—turned to relief that J. Ney hadn't been killed. He was bound to be bruised up, though, and the thing now was to get to him to see if he was hurt badly. With clothes and flesh tearing in the dense briers, Shim worked himself up onto the old tree trunk to backtrack out of there.

Suddenly, to his surprise, he heard J. Ney yelling like a wild man. "I'll break your neck, you little devil. Running a four-hundred-pound bear over me that way. You low-down trash, I'll cut your tongue out."

All Shim's confused feelings of the past few minutes turned into anger. The words were meant for him. J. Ney was accusing him of falling into a brier patch for the sole purpose of scaring the bear so he'd run over J. Ney. The man must be teetotally crazy to be saying things like that.

Shim was almost out of the tree limbs and briers when he

heard J. Ney yelling again, this time at his horse. He sounded like he was fixing to overtake that bear and tackle him with his naked hands. He couldn't be much hurt if he'd made it back through the tunnel to his horse that quickly, and Shim began listening to the dogs. They were making a turn now near the north end of the tupelo brake, and he'd better try to get back on his own stand fast as possible. If the bear swung east when it left the brake, he might get another chance.

He wiped away blood trickling down into his eyes from the brier scratches on his face and started to retrace his steps when he heard J. Ney's voice again, still raving and much closer. He heard, too, the sound of a horse coming fast around the thicket toward him. J. Ney couldn't be after the bear, not headed this way. Shim's brain took a spin. J. Ney was hunting him. It was crazy, but it was true. And nobody was close enough to help. He whirled and made tracks for a clump of bitter-pecan bushes.

Hidden among them, he found an old decaying stump he could use for a breastwork, if necessary. Bleeding and stinging from dozens of scratches, much of his shirt and pants gone, he waited, his heart thumping. J. Ney had stopped yelling, but it wasn't long before Shim heard the hoofs of a horse, slowed to a walk, stirring the leaf mold as they hit the spongy buckshot ground. With one hand he cautiously parted the leaves before his eyes. He saw J. Ney, sitting straight and forward in his saddle, his clothes spotted with leaf mold, his face dirty, and blood trickling down the side of his neck. Turning his head from side to side, he was sweeping with his eyes everything in range. Shim had once tried to look a dead panther in the eyes and had failed. He felt the same fear now. If ever he saw a man looking for mischief, this was one.

SHIM 95

Silently Shim let go the parted leaves and waited, all his senses listening.

He'd never heard of a grown man jumping on a boy, but everything had to have its first time. Maybe J. Ney, proud and fractious as he was, would kill Shim rather than risk folks finding out he'd blundered around and let that bear run over him. Maybe he meant it about cutting Shim's tongue out. If he did, it wouldn't be long, because Shim's tracks coming across the open woods were right there plain to see and, if J. Ney wasn't too blind crazy to follow them, would lead him straight to this clump of bushes.

Shim cocked the right-hand barrel of his gun and felt a chill run down his back like a possum had walked over his grave. No matter how bad—nor how good, nor how strong—a man was, hot lead stopped him. He'd seen men killed, and he knew men who had killed. Now it looked like he was going to be forced to stop a man. Afterward would he be like the Captain's cousin, Joe—afraid to sleep in a room by himself ever since he'd killed a man? Or would it make Shim like Dr. Zuey, who'd killed a lot of men and couldn't talk about anything else but the good shots he'd made and how he'd beat men to the draw?

Something he'd heard the Captain say came to him. "First make up your mind there's no other way out, but don't waste any too much time making it up, or the other fellow may beat you to it." It steadied him. The hoofbeats were so close that he could hear the squeak of saddle leather. If J. Ney turned into these bushes, Shim would know he had to do it—pull the trigger, or be killed himself by a crazy man.

Far away over on Wrong Prong a shotgun roared, and Shim felt a moment's connection with friends and safety. It was bound to be Ben, and, since there was no second shot, Ben's aim had been right. He'd got the bear and the race was over. But Shim's trouble wasn't. Beyond the bushes everything was silent. Not a hoofbeat, not a sound, since the shot. J. Ney was still there, but not moving. Shim held his breath, his mouth dry from straining to hear.

The horse moved; hoofs hit the ground—not into the bushes toward him but going away. Silently he parted the leaves. J. Ney was lined out straight for camp. Carefully Shim lowered the hammer of his shotgun into place and sat down on a stump to wait until his trembling legs would get strong enough to use.

Inside the tent, Shim pulled off his torn clothes and stood before Henry, who sat in a cane-bottom chair, working the cork out of a bottle of liniment with his teeth. Foots came in carrying two buckets of lake water and emptied them into a tin tub. Henry motioned for Shim to get into it. "What ails you, boy? You ain't said a mumbling word since you got back here, raggedy as a keg of kraut and all scratched up like you is been tangled up with a pa'cel of wildcats."

Shim stepped into the tub and winced as Foots began rubbing soap on him.

"Look like somebody been frailing him with a thorn bush," Foots said.

"I already told you I fell in a brier patch," Shim said. He was trying to overhear the talk going on outside, the joking and laughing that always went on after a hunt, over the blunders and mistakes each hunter had made. But this time the remarks kept pointing at J. Ney. Shim wondered how much they knew about what had taken place and soon found out they didn't know much.

"I've seen a heap of things in the world," he heard Wick say, laughing, "but I still can't figure how a dog got up high enough to put his toenail marks on a tall man's neck."

Rance said, "J. Ney is trying to forget something or other, the way he's over there by himself, laying to that beer like a sick kitten to a hot brick."

J. Ney must be standing over by the pit, but their voices were meant to reach him and banter him into telling them what had happened. Shim wished uneasily that they'd stop it. If they knew what Shim knew, they'd quit.

"Well, I would have been there in time to see what went on, but I got in the wrong company. . . ." That was Cholly, and for a few minutes he held their attention. "I'd left my stand and was cutting across the woods when the dogs bayed. I ran up on Dave and got up behind him on his mule. We went rip-snorting through the woods so fast Dave didn't watch where he was going, and he let that dang mule run under a low limb. Dave grabbed the limb and saved himself, but I got wiped off backwards and hit the ground like a sack of meal. Time we got our breath and caught the mule, the bear was running again, ka-hellity split, and it was too late."

The band started playing, mixing music with the men's laughter, and Shim couldn't hear any more. Somebody pitched his voice high enough to be heard and said, "What I want to know is why J. Ney on his horse didn't cut that bear off when he swung back east."

They were razzing J. Ney again, and Shim frowned. He was glad of one thing, though. He noticed Uncle Ben had sense enough to be keeping his mouth out of it. J. Ney might take it from the rest of them.

"Something terrible must have happened by the looks of one man and one boy, and you can't get a word out of either one of them." That was Wick's voice, and Shim's faint hope that nobody'd noticed the shape he was in when he got back to camp vanished.

Henry, rubbing a handful of fiery liniment on Shim's scratches while he squirmed and flinched, mumbled, "I hopes they don't keep on out there until they outspeaks theyselves and gets Mr. J. Ney stirred up hot as a skillet." He put the cork back in the liniment bottle and said, "Hurry up and get your clothes on, boy. We got to go hunt up old Rowdy. He ain't come in yet."

"He isn't coming in," Shim said.

"How come Rowdy ain't coming in?" Henry said quickly.

"He got hugged," Shim said. "One of J. Ney's dogs isn't coming in either."

Henry groaned. "Lord have mercy on me when the Captain finds out about Rowdy. What happened?"

It was Henry's first direct question, and Shim didn't answer. He had already said more than he'd aimed to. He got his clothes on and went outside for fresh air. Miss Cherry, standing near the lake watching Dave and two or three more fooling around out on the water—diving off their boat and just about turning it over every time they did—must have been keeping one eye on the tent too, because the minute Shim stepped outside she beckoned him with a nod of her head.

Shim joined her and said quickly, "There's nothing wrong."

She brushed at his tousled hair with her fingers. The band was still playing, but his mind wasn't following the music like it usually did. Miss Cherry was waiting for him to talk. Speaking low, he said, "I climbed a dead limb so I could see better, and it broke off with me, landed me in a brier patch."

She looked more closely at the scratches on his arms and

hands and said quietly, "It's a good idea to wait until a safer time to tell what you saw from that limb."

Shim cut his eyes up at her gratefully. She could always read him and knew things without being told. She smiled and headed for the pit. "Come on and let's see if a cold soda water won't brace us both up a little."

"I'll tell you when we get back home," Shim said, and she nodded.

He took the thick round bottles of red soda water out of the pit, hit the protruding wire loop of one of them with the ball of his hand, driving the stopper down inside and out of the neck, and handed it to her. Opening the other one, he began to drink. The coolness felt fine to his dry throat. By the time he finished it a crowd of women was around them, chattering about starting a Flinch game. Miss Cherry laughed and said that playing Flinch in the morning seemed all out of kilter, but maybe that was why camping was such fun, because you did things just whenever the notion struck you. She brushed Shim's hair back out of his eyes and said softly, "Take care of yourself" before going with the others toward the long table.

It struck Shim that except for the women and their chattering the camp had become unusually quiet and deserted. Outside of a few couples out on the lake there wasn't a man in sight. He threw down the empty bottle and walked along the first row of tents. Hearing talking beyond the bushes, he kept going. He found Henry, Foots and J. Ney's servant, Dabs, kneeling around a little cleared-off spot on the ground, shooting craps.

Foots rolled the dice and crapped out. Without looking up he said, "This boy that come back to camp looking like a steamboat runned over him comed up here and Jonahed me out of my luck."

Henry picked up the dice. "You couldn't hit with a stick." He threw down a silver piece. "Four bits I rambles, and kiss your money good-by when you fades me."

Foots covered the bet. Henry rolled the dice and caught four for a point. "Little Joe, pick the cotton," he said, rubbing the dice together in his hands.

"Two bits says you won't see it again," Dabs joreed.

"Put your money where you mouth is," Henry came back with a grin.

"Any man that will catch a four for his point is low-down as a snake's belly," Foots said.

Henry kept on rubbing the dice in his hands. "Me and dice gets along smooth as owl grease," he said.

Shim heard other voices nearer the lake. Looking through the trees, he saw just about all the men from camp. They were gathered at a hickory tree where they'd skinned the bear. The hide hung over a swinging limb. To Shim's surprise, J. Ney was there with the others. He'd been keeping strictly to himself since the hunt, but there he was, walking around right jerky, waving his arms now and then and talking sort of thick-tongued. That beer he'd been drinking was most likely taking a hold on him.

Henry, still rolling the dice, let out a cackle. He'd made his point with a pair of twos. "I'm going to break both you all so flat the seat of your pants will be dragging your tracks out when you leaves here."

Shim's interest in the crap game wiped out by the sight of the bearhide, he strolled over to the crowd of men and stopped beside Judge Short. Uncle Ben, settling the bear's vicious-looking head more securely on a fork of the limb, ran his hands over the small ears and said, "I wish the hair was better than it is, so I could have it mounted. But I will say the job of skinning is first-class in every way."

He stepped back, looking at it proudly, and before his voice stopped, Shim knew J. Ney was going to pick up what he'd said—knew it like he'd seen it worked out on paper. Ben's careless brag gave J. Ney the opening he wanted.

"You ought to be able to skin a dead bear," J. Ney's thick voice grated. "Good as you are at skinning your neighbors out of their timber."

He and Uncle Ben were about fifteen feet apart. Uncle Ben's eyes flashed, and his hand reached for and closed on the handle of an ax stuck in a tree root beside him. J. Ney's hand came from his pocket and there was bright steel in it. In a flash Shim knew J. Ney had planned it; had seen the ax handy, known that his insulting words would make Ben, unarmed, reach for it, and that when he did, J. Ney could shoot him and claim self-defense.

Uncle Ben saw the gun, let go the ax handle and jumped behind a small black-gum tree. His shoulders stuck out beyond the trunk on both sides, but it was the best he could do before J. Ney's pistol spoke. The bullet tore the outer bark, making a white spot on the tree where it went in. Uncle Ben wasn't touched.

Before J. Ney could shoot again the Captain was in it. Almost like he'd been expecting something like this, and knowing Uncle Ben wasn't armed, the Captain was close enough to J. Ney to land a long straight. The blow caught him at the bur of the ear and flattened him. Before his pistol could go into action from the ground, the Captain had dived and wrung it out of a hand that wasn't much strong right then. Uncle Ben, raging like a wild bull to get to J. Ney, was helpless in the firm grips of Wick, Rance and the Judge; Cholly and Ed Fergusson were helping J. Ney up from the ground and brushing the trash off his clothes. Trouble was over, for the present. It had happened the way trouble always seemed to—over nothing, if you didn't know what was back of it.

Shim turned and walked away. The bitter taste that had been in his mouth since his own encounter with J. Ney seemed to be spurting through his body with every beat of his heart. By keeping quiet, Shim had got out of his trouble pretty well by himself. But J. Ney wasn't satisfied till he'd started something with Uncle Ben. The Captain had had to get in it because Ben was kinfolks, and now they were all in it. Shim didn't feel like running into Miss Cherry right now, nor into anybody else. Skirting camp, he went down to the lake, shoved out in the first boat he came to and paddled off. He wanted to be by himself.

He wasn't scared. He had plenty of confidence in his folks' ability to protect themselves and him; and since this morning, when things got to their worst and his folks hadn't been close enough to help, he had a new confidence in himself. It was something worse than fear that was tearing him up inside; it was a boiling hate because J. Ney had stuck something in their craws they couldn't get rid of.

It was to keep this very thing from happening—this strain that could flare into serious trouble at any time and involve Shim's folks—that had made Shim decide never to tell the insults J. Ney had shouted at him. Calling him "trash," which insulted his folks too, might have led to trouble if Shim had told it. He hadn't told it, and never would have, because he wanted more than anything for folks to be friendly and peaceable. But J. Ney hadn't stopped till he'd got trouble started. The damage was done now. Even after both sides cooled off this wouldn't ever be quite forgotten. From now on there'd always be a strain whenever his mother's and Ben's folks—the Caulfields—or a Govan met J. Ney Ward or any of his kinfolks.

Suddenly some words of the Captain's came back to him. "Easy money is bad for everybody." That was what was at the back of the whole thing—the sawmill. Ben's taking the sawmill men to see J. Ney, and J. Ney's selling them his woods, had started it all. Already, before the mill was even here, it had near about caused a killing. And a killing didn't often stop at just one. Any little thing a person did, like climbing a tree limb to get a shot at a bear, might wind up in bad trouble, when folks were already stirred up and greedy inside.

Bad as he hated it, there was nothing he could do about it; and when the muscles of his face no longer felt tight, and his chest moved easy to his breathing, he paddled slowly back to the landing.

Before he nosed the boat onto land, he saw the unusual activity in camp and felt his heart sink like a rock in clear water. It could mean only one thing: they were breaking camp. Everybody was moving around, busy; not hurrying, but working: loading mattresses and blankets into wagons, bringing valises out of tents, undoing guy ropes, taking tents down. He stepped slowly out and tied the boat to a cypress knee.

The Captain came down the bank, heading for a tupelo tree where his harpoon and trammel set stood propped.

"What's the matter?" Shim asked from a tight throat. "What's the reason for tearing up camp?"

The Captain looked him over, looked at the boat and then back at him. "Get your stuff together. We're going out."

"Why?" Shim asked.

The Captain glanced back up toward camp. "Well, son, a little trouble can go a long ways, sometimes. Neither J. Ney nor Ben will volunteer to leave, and they can't stay here together. We can't send one off without sending the other, because the first one to go would wait for the other one up the road somewhere and trouble would break out again. So, we'll all go, and keep them apart till they have time to cool down." He looked at Shim and smiled. "I know it's tough, but it's the best way."

Shim walked over and shouldered the Captain's trammel net. He didn't have any gear of his own that Henry wouldn't take care of. "J. Ney will be after you, too. You hit him," he said.

The Captain said quietly, "I hope after he thinks it over he'll see it was for the best."

Shim cut a quick eye around to see that nobody was within earshot. "He was crawling through a tunnel in a thicket to get to the bayed bear. I'd got to the tunnel ahead of him but was scared to go down it, so I had run around to the opposite side."

"Did you shoot?" the Captain said quickly.

Shim shook his head. "I couldn't get to the bear for the briers, so I climbed an old dead limb sticking up from a log. It broke, and I fell in the briers. It scared the bear and he tore out, straight into the tunnel and at J. Ney. Ran right over him like he didn't even see him, and the dogs did the same thing. Must have tromped him up right smart."

"Uh-huh," the Captain said. "So that's what was in the wind."

"He got sore at me, and I hid in a thicket till he left." Shim was unexpectedly having trouble keeping his voice from trembling.

"I see," the Captain said gently. "I'm proud of you for keeping quiet about it."

Two or three folks were coming toward the lake. The Captain picked up his harpoon and laid a hand on Shim's shoulder. "We'll finish this later. It's time to go now."

Shim went to the Captain's wagon and laid the net in the bed. Dave was there, straightening blankets and mattresses. Dave looked at him right hard and grinned. "What you looking so long-faced about? I've got an idea you and that brier patch started all this fuss."

Shim wasn't feeling like foolishness. "Maybe I did," he flared. "Now you get smart and stop it." He was sore. He hadn't started it and he knew who had. Dave and Uncle Ben and all the crazy folks who wanted the sawmill to come were the ones who'd started it. But nobody but the Captain and Henry would ever see it that way.

He hesitated. Ordinarily he'd wait and leave in the last wagon out, with Henry and Foots and Caline, making the time in the woods last a little while longer. But for some reason, today he felt like staying close to his folks. He'd go find Miss Cherry and bring out the valises for her and Fanchie. Maybe he was glad to go home. It would be good to see Gimlet.

chapter six

SHIM LAY, HALF DOZING, IN A HAMMOCK SWUNG UNDER the black-gum tree in the front yard. From the kitchen the tart smell of boiling muscadines came to him, wrinkling his nose and making the insides of his cheeks draw. Henry had brought Miss Cherry a water bucket full of muscadines, and she and Fanchie were making jelly. It was a good smell, but today it made his stomach feel funny. That's how he happened to be lying down in the middle of the morning to start with. When he stood on his feet he felt right lap-legged, and when the sun hit his skin it burned like fire.

Lying there, his eyes closed, his ears still ringing with the quinine he'd finished taking yesterday, he wondered if the round of calomel Miss Cherry had made him take was entirely to blame for the way his stomach felt. This was the worst bout of chills and fever he ever remembered, and it might be those cucumber pickles he'd eaten yesterday had something to do with it. He'd known better than to eat them when the calomel was still in his system, because that might mean getting salivated and having his teeth drop out; but by yesterday he'd figured it was safe, and he'd had such a craving for those pickles, he'd waded in and eaten half a jar before he stopped.

He wished there was something he could do to make him forget the sore, gutted feeling inside him, but every time he got in the sun his head began to ache and swim and the quinine-ringing in his ears grew louder. He sat up suddenly, roused by the dogs charging full cry to the gate.

"Wake up, it's daytime," Mack Short's voice called.

Three boys on horses were at the gate—Mack Short and the Calhoun twins, Dick and A. C. Waving a welcoming hand and calling back the dogs, Shim walked to meet them. They all sat stiff and proper in their saddles, not fitting down in them like country folks did, and they were all giggling and talking. He never could figure out how town boys found so much to talk and giggle about all the time, but today they were just what he needed.

"Get down and come in," he said.

"Get ready to protect us from that flock of dogs so we can," Dick said.

"I'd just as soon face a pack of wolves," A. C. said.

Shim didn't say anything, because he didn't see anything to say. The dogs were already sauntering quietly back toward the shade of the high front gallery.

The three boys swung down from their saddles, cautiously, like they were trying to protect their clothes from getting wrinkled or dirty or something. Town boys were always thinking about their clothes. Dick, wrapping his reins around the top of a fence picket, said, "Danged if you don't live so far back in the woods you must have to break day with an ax every morning."

"What do you tell time by out here if the clocks stop?" A. C. asked with a wide grin.

Shim was always tickled over the way A. C. sort of repeated everything Dick said. Dick set the screw, and A. C. turned it. Used to their friendly ragging him about living so far back in the woods, he just grinned with them.

"We rode out to take you back to town with us," Mack said.

Mack was Shim's favorite of all the town boys. He liked the country and sort of fit in better than the others. At his words, Shim felt a sudden craving to go to town. He'd been lying around all the week getting over the chills and fever, and a change sounded like just what he needed. He led them along the walk toward the house.

"Yeh, comb the hayseeds out of your hair," Dick said. "It's time we took you to town and showed you a little life."

"Lying up in a hammock this time of day," A. C. added.

Sometimes A. C.'s habit of driving home everything Dick said got a little old, and Shim, glancing at him, saw a chance to change the subject. "Who knocked those knots on your head?" he asked, eying a couple of bruises on A. C.'s cheek.

The smiles on his visitors' faces turned into dry grins.

"Orland got a hold of him," Dick said, like he'd just as soon the subject hadn't come up. Come to think of it, Shim had seen all three of these boys at one time or another bearing the marks of Orland's fists, and he began wondering about it. Orland Moulton, about their age, but fat and overgrown and with the manners of a shoat, seemed to make a habit of beating up everyone anywhere near his size.

They climbed the wide steps and sat down in chairs on the gallery. Shim, backed deep in a rocker, said thoughtfully, "It seems like you all town sissies could make arrangements to whip Orland Moulton some way or other."

"He always picks somebody he can handle," Dick said, and A. C. added, "He's all muscle and no brains."

"Clumsy," Shim said, as if talking to himself.

A. C. jerked a thumb toward Shim and grinned at the others. "Smart Aleck here thinks he could take care of Orland."

"There are ways of getting around difference in size," Shim said slowly. Henry had taught him that.

"Used to be," Dick said, "before Mulberry had a marshal. Now they've got a law about hitting somebody with a blunt instrument, and if you hit with anything but your fist, old Eagle Eye Moulton hauls you in."

Shim slid forward to the edge of his chair. "You mean it's against the law to wrap a scantling around a fellow's head to get him off you when he's jumped on you and is beating you up?" He looked at Mack.

Mack shrugged. "Unless you want to pay a fine to keep from going to jail," he said. "Mulberry is changing. Folks like the Moultons been selling their woods to the sawmill folks, and with a stack of dollars in their pockets, they get highfalutin ideas about what they call 'improving' the town. What they mean, Papa says, is that they want to run it. They stirred folks up about all the outsiders that will be coming in here with the sawmill, and made them think they had to have somebody besides the Sheriff to keep law and order. Next thing anybody knew old Eagle Eye Moulton was walking around, feeling important and messing everybody up. Orland was bad enough to begin with, but now his uncle is town marshal he's worse than ever."

That was the most words Shim had ever heard Mack put out at one time, and he understood why anybody would be upset. Why, how could there be a law against a person defending himself any way he had to? The earliest lessons Henry had ever taught him were ways to defend himself against attacks from animals and, later when he started to school, from bigger boys. "If a big boy jumps on you," Henry had told him, "try to kill him and maybe you'll whip him." Shim frowned. What Mack had just said sounded all backwards.

Dick's voice broke into his thoughts. "Shim's studying about how he's going to handle Orland." The others giggled.

"Me?" Shim said, surprised. "Orland never has bothered me, and I'm sure not going to bother him."

A blast blown on a conch shell from the back gallery, and right along with it a noisy braying from the lot, jerked all of them but Shim straight in their chairs. Shim grinned. "Dave's hunting mule. He always does that when he hears the conch shell. It means dinner will be ready in about thirty minutes."

Around the dinner table greetings were exchanged, questions asked and answered about all the boys' folks. Mack told Miss Cherry they'd come to take Shim back with them. She didn't much like the idea, bad as he had been feeling all week. But he told her he felt fine, and, after he ate a hearty dinner to prove it, she finally said he could go. When they left the table she went to the kitchen to gather up butter and preserves and a bucket of muscadines for Mrs. Calhoun, and some wild crab-apple jelly she'd been wanting to send to Mack Short's mother to try.

With all her bustling around she didn't forget to hide Shim's pepperbox. When he slipped back to his room to get it, just before they were ready to leave, it was gone from the drawer where he kept it. Both Miss Cherry and the Captain had laid the law down about his not carrying his gun when he went to town. Of course he didn't have any use for it there, but he felt half naked without it. Besides, they could have had fun with it on their ride in, shooting at snakes or at anything that made a good target.

When he came out on the gallery where they were waiting for him, Miss Cherry caught his eye. She knew what he'd gone back for. He grinned a little sheepishly. She handed him a tightly covered tin bucket. "You'll have to carry these muscadines, Shim. Henry has the other things in a meal sack tied to your saddle." He saw his horse at the gate with the others.

Miss Cherry turned to the boys. "Tell your mammas I'll have some wild grapes to send them before long, and you all come back again and stay some with Shim." She laid a hand on Shim's arm, her dark eyes warm and laughing, but serious underneath. "Behave yourself, son, and don't get into any meanness."

In chorus the boys assured her they wouldn't, and with polite good-bys and thanks for the fine dinner they headed for the gate. They were mounted and turning their horses' heads toward town when Fanchie came tearing down the path. "Shim, oh, Shim," she called. Shim reined up.

"Go by the drugstore and tell Bunk to give you a bottle of rose water for my hands. They're just ruined with those old muscadines. Tell him I've got plenty of glycerine to mix with it. I just want the rose water—a good big bottle."

"All right," Shim grumbled. Fanchie and Miss Cherry went to town a dozen times to his once, but if he'd ever got off without Fanchie thinking up some foolishness for him to bother with, he couldn't remember when it was.

"Don't you dare forget it," Fanchie called.

Shim grunted again, and pressed his heel to his horse's side a little harder than necessary to start him.

The road to town was shady most of the way; the dinner

he'd eaten turned into strength and energy fast, and by the time they got there the joreeing and talk of boys his own age had taken up the slack in muscles and spirits left there by a week of sickness. Mrs. Calhoun acted mighty well pleased to get the muscadines and preserves and stuff, and asked a hundred questions about all his folks.

By the time supper was over and first dark came, he was thinking town wasn't bad at all. Mack was spending the night with the Calhoun boys too, and when the four of them left the house and headed down the plank walk towards the Square, around which the business section of town was built, Shim was feeling right excited and a little reckless.

The different smells of town were thick all along the street —a soft smell like chicken and dressing, the richer smell of fried ham, the dusty smells that come from crowded places, and now and then a whiff of what they called table scraps in town but at home was put in the slop bucket and the hogs ate it up. At home tonight the only smells would be from the earth—woods, and crops that grew, all cooling off in the damp night air. Here it was still hot. A strong, sharp smell of ammonia reminded him that the livery stable was just a little piece down the street they were crossing.

At the corner of the Square they stopped in a patch of light from a swinging lamp in a general store. They glanced up the streets both ways, looking and listening for some more of the boys their age. Different smells wrinkled Shim's nose —paint and oil from hardware and plow stocks, dye from dry goods, dust from the road. Lamps, inside the stores that surrounded the Square, shone out through open doors and laid checkerboard patches of light across the plank walks, the spaces between them black-dark. The light from the poolroom halfway up the block to their left shone clear across the walk and out to the hitching rack, where three saddle horses were tied. They could hear the clicking of balls occasionally, but none of their crowd would be there because no minors were allowed inside.

A low whistle came from the west gate of the iron fence surrounding the courthouse yard, and Mack, with a low "come on," led the way into the darkness of the road. The dense mass of mulberry trees around the dark and deserted-looking two-story brick courthouse in the middle of the Square was the last place Shim had expected a sound of life to come from, but he followed the other boys toward it. The round dome on the top of the courthouse caught a little starlight, and Shim raised his eyes higher. Faintly he made out the small statue of a woman holding a pair of scales. The Captain had told him once that the statue meant something about weighing the evidence so that each man could get his just dues.

They walked between a horse and buggy and a saddle horse, hitched to the fence, and it still looked black-dark to Shim in there under the trees. He decided it must be the lights from the stores around the Square that kept his eyes from adjusting to the darkness and kept him from recognizing Scott Gibbs at the gate until he spoke.

"I was just going after you fellows," Scott said in a low, excited voice. Scott was a year or so older than they were, and the main thing Shim remembered about him was how he wore his pants, low and slouchy, sort of swaggerified.

Scott dropped his voice to a whisper. "Listen, the Moultons are gone off for the night—Orland's folks. Let's go over here and do our planning."

They followed him to a long bench under the mulberry trees and sat down in a huddle; Scott in the middle, the boys on either side, leaning forward to hear what he said. Shim leaned forward too, politely, but he couldn't catch on to what all the excitement was about. Town boys sure got stirred up about funny things. What did anybody care whether the Moultons were gone off or not?

His toes began working to the rhythm of a good two-step somebody was beating out on a piano. The sound came from down the street that led off from the southwest corner of the Square. Now that was something worth looking into. He nudged Dick with an elbow. "Let's go down where that music is and dance, if there are any girls there."

Dick looked around at him like he thought he was crazy. "Girls, my foot," he said. "Didn't you just hear what Scott said? We've got business to attend to."

"We can get all the honey we want," Scott said.

Shim thought of the crock of honey in the smokehouse at home and the long row of beehives in his back yard. "I didn't know you all wanted honey," he said, puzzled. "Miss Cherry would give you a tubful of it."

Nobody paid that any attention.

"We'll have to have a tin bucket and some gunpowder if we're going to rob a beehive," Mack said.

Shim might not know what they were so worked up about, but he knew one thing. "You're fixing to get stung to death if you start robbing bees," he said flatly.

"They won't sting because we'll kill them all," Scott said.

The talk, that up to now had just been puzzling and without any point, suddenly didn't suit Shim at all. "I never killed a bee in my life unless he stung me," he said.

"These are Orland's bees," Mack whispered in his ear. "It's our chance to get back at him for some of his meanness."

Orland's meanness didn't seem to Shim to have anything to do with killing a lot of bees that hadn't done anybody any harm. If all they wanted was to rob Orland's hives, he could tell them how to do that without hurting a bee.

"All you need is some mosquito-bar netting to go over your head, and a pair of gauntlet gloves," he began, but Scott was standing up, and none of them was listening to Shim.

"Mack and I know where we can get some gunpowder," Scott whispered. "A.C., you go home and get a bucket and a kitchen knife or spoon to dip the honey out with. We'll meet at the Moultons'."

Shim opened his mouth to repeat what he'd said about the mosquito bar, but before he could speak, Scott had grabbed Mack's arm and the two of them disappeared in the darkness. A. C. was gone in another direction. Shim and Dick were alone.

Shim began following the piano music more closely, to get out of his mind what Scott had hatched up. He didn't like it, but the others seemed to, and he didn't exactly see any polite way to get out of going when he was their visitor. After a few minutes he said restlessly, "Let's go down there and dance while we wait."

"And let folks see us?" Dick whispered. "With something like this on foot, we don't want to be seen tonight. Let folks think we're in bed asleep. And watch out for Eagle Eye. He may come from behind a tree or around a dark corner any time."

"What if he does?" Shim asked.

"Because he'd figure there was something on foot," Dick said impatiently. "Tomorrow when he hears about this he'd remember seeing us here tonight, and might say we were acting suspicious. You don't know how to act in town, sure enough, do you? Well, just act like I do. Sit here and wait until we figure the others have had time to gather up the stuff they went after and get to the Moultons' house, and then we'll ease out and down there to meet them."

Shim felt more and more like he was getting into something that he'd wish he hadn't. He was being told to look out for the law, to act like he was scared of old Eagle Eye Moulton, a little old town marshal who couldn't even arrest anybody out in the woods or on a plantation. He reached up to a low limb, broke him off a short, leafy piece and began using it as a fan to keep off the mosquitoes that were working on his ankles.

A man came out of a store next to the poolroom, tied a bundle on the back of his saddle, climbed on his horse and rode off into the darkness. One by one the lights were blown out in the stores around the Square, and their owners went home. A welcome breeze riffled the leaves of the mulberry trees for a minute, and they gave off a faint, musty scent. Shim shifted his hips around on the hard bench. He'd like to get down on the soft grass, but he had on his best clothes, and the courthouse yard, which so many folks used, wasn't clean like the woods.

Dick stood up. The last rigs and horses were gone from along the courtyard fence and from the hitching rack in front of the poolroom. Everything was dark except the drugstore. "Let's go," he whispered, and led the way out of the courthouse yard and down the middle of the dusty street.

Shim's heart began to pound, and he felt suddenly wicked and strange. He had never in his life thought of even going on any man's property uninvited, to say nothing of going to do any damage. Now he was fixing to do both.

The Moulton house was tall and dark. Big square columns that held up the gallery roof gleamed in the starlight. A low whistle came from the yard, and Dick and Shim crossed the sidewalk and went through the gate. Three figures came from the deeper dark under the shade trees, and they all lined out single file around the corner of the house, between flower beds. Shim thought about tracks, but with so many, maybe it wasn't likely anybody could tell one from the other.

At the back they found a path leading through a grove of trees. When the barn and chicken house loomed up ahead, they turned left a few yards to a fence where a row of beehives stood. Scott knelt before one of the hives and the other boys stood close around him. Shim, a little piece back, lay down on the ground to watch. He could see better from there because they were above him, and he was also safe from being seen.

Scott took a piece of paper from his pocket, unfolded it and from it poured gunpowder in a pile before the two little A-shaped entrances to the hive. Taking his knife blade, he pushed the powder through the openings. He struck a match on the handle of the knife and stuck it to the powder. There was an instant flash, and he and A. C. began pulling the top off the hive. With a big kitchen spoon A.C. began lifting out nice hunks of comb.

There wasn't a bee humming. They were all dead. The bucket was full, and A.C. handed it to Dick. Scott set the lid of the hive carefully back on, bumping it with the heel of his hand to push the nails back in place. Everything looked as if nothing had been bothered, but in daylight the telltale powder burns would show on the front of the hive.

Walking on tiptoes and at a much faster clip than they had come in, they went back around the house, Dick in the lead. At the gate they hesitated, listening to make sure nobody was on the dark street. Hearing no sound of footsteps, they headed down the walk away from town. They all seemed to know where they were going except Shim, and he soon found out. They went into some woods. With his feet on familiar-feeling ground—exposed tree roots, dead limbs and leaf mold—the uneasiness he felt at all this scheming around and killing bees weighed a shade lighter on him.

They stopped on the bank of Platinum Bayou. While Shim stood looking at the reflection of stars in the water, the rest of them gathered up some dry sticks and built a fire for light. They began lifting out chunks of dripping honeycomb with their hands, holding them to the light to see there were no dead bees on them. The bucket came to Shim last, and he took out a small piece, just to be sociable.

"What's the matter with you?" Scott asked from a dripping mouth. "You got a dainty appetite like a canary bird?"

"I'm just not much hungry," Shim said, and went down to the water and washed his sticky hands. When he turned back, they had all found seats on tree roots or chunks and were eating like hungry wolves.

"You all better slow down, if you don't want to be sick as mules," he said, sitting down on a chunk by the fire and laying a stick on it to keep a little light.

"We haven't been down with chills. It won't hurt us," Mack said, leaning over so a fresh chunk of comb he was lifting from the bucket wouldn't drip on his clothes when he popped it into his mouth.

A. C. got his breath from eating so fast and said with a grin, "Maybe if we had as much of everything as Shim's got down on the plantation, we wouldn't be hungry either."

"Maybe it's something else bothering Shim," Scott said. "Maybe he just don't like our way of doing things."

Scott had pretty near hit the truth. Shim couldn't see any fun in sitting around hogging down honey when you weren't hungry. He was getting sleepy and tired. If anything was on foot, like a coon hunt or a dance or anything that *was* anything, he never even thought about getting sleepy, but his eyelids were mighty heavy now. Remembering his manners, he straightened his back and said politely, "You all are figuring me out wrong. I was just studying about a coon hunt I want to take you all on this fall so I can pay you back for all this."

Scott spit out a big wad of dry honeycomb and leaned back against the tree trunk behind him. "Shucks," he said, "what's an old coon hunt? Nobody cares if you kill an old coon. But tomorrow when Orland finds his bees have been killed, he'll be going around swelled up mad enough to bust, and he can't do a thing about it because he can't find out who did it. Besides that, old man Dillon will come across where we've had this fire tonight, and he'll carry on like somebody crazy because somebody has been fooling around in his woods. And he won't know who, either. Folks act so ticky about their old woods and their old bees. You all don't know what fun is out there in the country."

None of the boys but Scott was looking at Shim. In the light from the fire, Mack's round face was one big frown, and Dick and A. C. were licking the honey off their fingers like it took all their attention but not like it still tasted good. Shim got a sudden notion that the way Scott had just put it made them see tonight's work in a way that took the edge off their appetites. Scott, though, didn't notice that slack had run into their enthusiasm.

"Wait till that sawmill gets here," he said, chuckling. "They're aiming to build a little town of their own, right on the edge of Mulberry. Those outsiders will be so green we can play jokes on them all day and all night, till they won't know which way to turn."

Dick got up and went down to the water's edge to wash his hands. He came back and sat down on the chunk he'd been using for a seat. "Cousin Ab," he said, "says sawmill folks are the roughest and toughest folks he's ever seen. He says that up near Memphis at that sawmill where he's been working there's something going on every night—crap games, poker games—and as sure as the weekend comes there's a shooting scrape."

"Shooting scrape over what?" Mack said.

Shim was glad Mack asked it, because he wondered too, but he wouldn't ask a question about the sawmill folks for anything.

"I asked Cousin Ab that," Dick said in a puzzled voice, "and he just said the men work too hard and get too much money for it."

"I don't see anything to that to make them fight," Mack said.

Shim didn't exactly see anything either, but it sounded like what the Captain had said about too much money ruining folks. If just he and Mack were together, maybe they might try to puzzle it out, but not with Scott here.

Scott had the floor again. "I may get me a job at that sawmill when it comes," he bragged.

Dick let out a whoop. "I can just see your folks letting you work for wages, like you were trash."

"Is your Cousin Ab 'trash'?" Scott said.

"He's a civil engineer," Dick said. "That's different, and you know it. It's like a—well, like a——"

"Like a doctor or a lawyer," A. C. said, coming to his brother's rescue. "It isn't working for a salary."

Shim's stomach was feeling funny. Maybe there'd been a dead bee on that little piece of honey he ate. Henry always said he "must have et a fly," when his stomach hurt. Scott's talk about liking to make folks mad had started Shim's stomach to churning, and this talk about sawmill folks was worse still. Warm as the night was, he felt chilly, and threw a little chunk on the fire.

The flames caught and brightened things up, and just then he heard a stick snap somewhere pretty close by in the dark. "Hush," he said, and cocked his head to listen. The other boys were gone. Quick as rabbits, they'd dived in among bushes beyond the firelight. He caught up with them in a cluster of small red oaks, just as an angry voice called, "You all needn't to run, because I'll get you."

They stopped still, huddled close together, sheltered by the darkness of the trees. The small, angry man who stamped into the firelight was carrying a shotgun. Running made too much noise while they were within reach of that gun.

"Old man Dillon," Mack whispered in Shim's ear.

The old man looked, and listened, and muttered to himself. He was mad as a hornet, but he didn't know which way they'd gone. Laying down his gun, he broke off a branch from a tree and began raking dry leaves back away from the fire. They could catch what he was saying now. "Everything dry as doodle dust, and folks got no better sense than to build a fire. Burn a man out of house and home. Get my pasture and barn sure."

A swipe of his branch hit the tin bucket. He picked it up, held it in the firelight and grunted like he was pleased. Then he saw something else that helped his feelings. "Ah-hah . . ." He reached down and came up with the big spoon. "I'll just find out whose house these things came from and . . . " He dropped both bucket and spoon and began snorting and raving. He rubbed his hands on some leaves, smelled of them and cussed. "Honey, by gosh. The low-down, thieving, no-account hellions have robbed somebody's bees sure as shooting. If I get my hands on the low-down . . ."

Shim fought a tightening knot in his chest. He wasn't used to taking talk of this kind, and he was getting sore fast. If the Captain heard anybody talk about him that way—— His thoughts broke off short. The Captain better not hear about any of tonight's doings. Shim was in the wrong, and so he had to take that rough talk. But he sure didn't like it. The other boys seemed to be tickled by it, especially Scott. He was doubled up laughing. A choked giggle got away from him, and that was too bad.

Old man Dillon, with a quick swipe of his sticky hands on his pants, grabbed up his shotgun. "There you are. I'll make you smart alecks sorry of this," he yelled, and dived straight in their direction. They lit out, dodging around stumps and trees in the darkness, really running this time. They knew the old man couldn't catch them, but they also knew good and well that he mustn't.

They were back at the Calhoun house and ready for bed when A. C. said, "We've got to get another spoon before Mama misses the one we took."

"I've been studying about that spoon," Shim said. "You don't reckon there's any mark on it that would help old man Dillon find where it came from, do you?"

"An old kitchen spoon?" A. C. said. "Everybody's got one like it. Say . . . come to think of it, maybe you better be studying about that tin bucket. It came from your house. It's the one you brought the muscadines in. I grabbed it off the table on the back gallery when I came home after the spoon. Is there anything different about a country bucket?"

Shim shrugged, and hoped his face didn't show what an unpleasant piece of news this was. "Mama doesn't want the bucket back," he said quickly. "It's just an old tin bucket." He added more slowly, "I'd give a lot if I had it right now, though."

"Shucks," Mack said with a yawn. "You all quit gabbing and go to sleep. Nobody can tell one tin bucket from another, nor kitchen spoons either."

"I reckon not," they agreed, and were asleep.

chapter seven

THE TOWN CLOCK WAS STRIKING ELEVEN NEXT MORNING when Shim hitched his horse to the courthouse fence. He would have been gone long ago, but he'd waited around at the Calhoun house, hoping the other boys would get over their sick spells and come uptown with him. He hadn't any more than dropped off to sleep last night when Mack, in bed beside him, had started tossing and groaning, and before daylight all three of them had been as sick as he'd figured they would be after eating all that honey.

They were still pale as sheets, with no interest in anything he mentioned and with just one idea in their heads—to keep Mrs. Calhoun from guessing what had made them sick. A few minutes ago Shim had decided to do Fanchie's errand for her and go on home. He had paid his respects to Mrs. Calhoun, saddled his horse and told the boys good-by.

He crossed the street. The drugstore smell met him on the sidewalk before he got to the open door. It was a smell to put anybody to guessing—many kinds of drugs, scented soaps, sweets from the soda fountain; the mixture was always a wonder to his nose. He stepped inside, and a little catch of surprise ran from his legs to his chest. Beside the door, sitting on a small stool with his back against the wall, was Orland Moulton, his eyes on the floor and looking like a thundercloud.

Shim's face didn't change, and his voice was clear and steady. "Howdy," he said politely.

Orland glanced up, mumbled "Howdy" and dropped his eyes back to the floor.

Shim was suddenly painfully conscious of his feet. Maybe Orland had found tracks when he got back this morning and was sitting here to look over the feet of everybody who came in the drugstore.

"Come in," Bunk called from halfway down the store, where he was straightening some bottles on a shelf. "What can I do for you?"

Fighting a slow, unwilling guilt that was smoldering in his chest, Shim went back to where Bunk was and leaned across the showcase. "A bottle of rose water for Fanchie, and charge it to the Captain, please."

Bunk took a gallon glass jug from the base shelf and went behind the prescription partition. Shim, waiting, saw, uneasily, from the corner of his eye, that Orland's head was still down. Was he matching the shape of Shim's feet with tracks he had found in the Moulton yard? His feet felt so heavy and big that they ached, but he wouldn't risk a direct glance to see. He looked around at bottles, read labels, studied the showcases of toilet articles and writing paper and wished Bunk would hurry. Why couldn't it have been Scott who'd stumbled upon Orland this morning instead of him? Scott would enjoy it, and Shim wasn't enjoying it.

Somebody came in the front door and fell into a low conversation with Orland. Somebody else in the room made the air a little easier to breathe and Shim's heart slowed down. A sharp hammering on the marble top of the soda fountain with a piece of money gave him an excuse to look down that way. The man who had come in was J. Ney Ward.

"We'll have a drink if we can get somebody to wait on us," J. Ney said, tapping impatiently. His eye fell on Shim, and he said, "Come have a drink, boy."

"No, thank you, sir," Shim said with stiff politeness.

J. Ney was mighty friendly this morning. He and Orland ought to get along fine together; neither of them could get along with anybody else. Shim sure didn't aim to get thick with either of them.

Bunk came out and handed him a thick, short-necked bottle wrapped in paper. "What else?"

"Nothing, thank you," Shim said, wondering why anybody working in a place with all kinds of drugs had to have as many pimples on his face as Bunk.

"Much obliged and come back," Bunk said cheerfully. "And tell Miss Fanchie I said come to town and do her own shopping. I haven't seen her in a month of Sundays."

On his way out, Shim heard J. Ney say importantly to Bunk, who was fixing a couple of tall glasses of soda water, "I was just telling Orland, I've about decided to rent my land out and move to town this fall. No need for a man to bury himself in the country when the sawmill folks will pay him more money than he can spend, for just a few of his trees."

Shim suddenly couldn't wait to get home, and hear no more talk of sawmills. He was almost to his horse when he heard Orland call his name. He turned, pushing the bottle of rose water into his pistol pocket to have his hands free.

SHIM

"Wait right where you are," Orland said. "I'm going to give you a whipping."

Shim waited for him to say something about the bees, but he didn't. His face puffed up and red, and his little eyes full of meanness, he kept coming, and, still walking, threw his right. Shim stepped far enough out of the way to get only a bruise on his forearm and a sting over his ear. The left came around, Shim ducked under, closed in and drove right and left to Orland's ribs. They didn't do much good. This town boy was tough as whitleather, and came in, arms spread for a clinch. Shim's elbow held him off, and he and Orland were both swinging fists.

Shim's sight was failing him. There seemed always to be a fist before his face. His head was suddenly swimming and he felt himself hit the ground. He got back on his feet, holding his arms high and his head low, but was still being hit so fast he couldn't count the licks, and his legs were weak as water. He was about to be whipped and he didn't aim to be. With all the force he had he shoved out his open hand. It caught Orland's face and sent him back a step. That gave Shim time. He jerked the bottle of rose water out of his pocket and brought it down on Orland's head. Liquid and shattered glass went every which way. Orland turned and with hands over his eyes staggered blindly for the drugstore.

Shim was in the saddle, reaching forward to jerk the reins loose from the fence, when a firm hand caught his leg. Eagle Eye had hold of him. "Wait a minute, Govan. I saw you hit that boy with a blunt instrument."

This was Shim's first brush with the law, and the disgrace of jail flitted across his mind. He was scared and mad, but he wasn't running-scared, nor blind-mad. "That was just a bottle," he said.

"Hitting somebody with a blunt instrument is a violation of the law," Eagle Eye said.

Shim thought fast. His head cleared a little. Orland didn't know about the bees. If he did, he'd have said so. He was just sore at everybody and when Shim happened along had decided to take it out on him. Maybe J. Ney had even put him up to it. The thought of J. Ney stiffened Shim's shoulders. Nobody knew anything about the bees. All he'd done—that anybody knew about—was keep Orland from beating him up, and if that was against the law, the law was just plain crazy.

He remembered Wick Beckham's brother, Harvey, was the Captain's lawyer. Harvey would never let old Eagle Eye put him in jail.

"If I've violated the law, sir," he said from a dry mouth, "go and see Lawyer Beckham."

Eagle Eye hesitated, frowning, then took hold of the rein. "You're the one in trouble, but I'll take you over there." Walking beside the horse's head, he led him across the Square to a little two-room wooden building on the northeast corner.

Shim dismounted, tied his horse at the hitching rack and glanced up over the whitewashed door to read the sign: SHORT AND BECKHAM, ATTORNEYS-AT-LAW. Times he'd been here with the Captain, he'd never thought he'd be going in on business of his own. He stopped politely at the steps, for Eagle Eye to go in ahead of him, but Eagle Eye motioned him to go in first. It made him feel mighty funny to go through a door ahead of a grown person.

Harvey Beckham, alone in the office, leaned quickly over his desk and began tinkering with some papers, frowning like they were interrupting deep study about something. He looked up, like he'd just now seen them.

SHIM

"Howdy, Marshal," he said. "And how are you, Shim? How's everything down your way? Miss Cherry and Miss Fanchie, and Dave and the Captain. Haven't seen your Pa in a coon's age."

"They're fine, thank you," Shim mumbled.

Harvey glanced at Eagle Eye, then back at Shim. "What brings you to town?" he said.

"He's been fighting," Eagle Eye said. "Hit another boy with a blunt instrument in violation of the law."

"Orland jumped on me. I just got him off me was all," Shim said.

Harvey looked at Shim's left cheek that was swelling, and smiled. "Boys will get a little rough sometimes in their games and play." He shoved back in his chair and said offhandedly, "Well, Marshal, the fist is a blunt instrument, I believe, but not much harmful, generally speaking."

Eagle Eye shifted his chew of tobacco. "This wasn't his fist. It was a bottle of Cologny water, judging by the smell of things it splattered on. The glass may have injured Orland. 'Personal injury' charge it may be against this boy before he's through."

"Well, now, Marshal, I don't believe a little bottle of perfume could have much hurt a big, strong boy like your nephew Orland." Harvey, leaning back in his chair, had his elbows on the arms and kept bringing the widespread fingertips of his two hands slowly together and apart as he went on. "You've got to keep in mind, Marshal, that here in town we all live off each other, but when it comes down to brass tacks, it's these heavy-spending farmers who really keep us going. If we're going to make it unpleasant for them to come to town, they'll go somewhere else to spend their money. If they want to they can buy in Jackson, or Memphis, ship it to the depot, and they've got plenty wagons and teams to haul it home from there."

Eagle Eye's chest was swelled out, and his deep-set eyes were snapping. "I'm getting sick and tired of trying to do my duty in this town and having all you smooth-talking jackleg lawyers running my business for me. If you fool with me, I'll have this boy in jail...."

Harvey raised one eyebrow and looked at Eagle Eye right hard before he spoke, extra soft and low. "Put Cap Govan's boy in jail? Now, Marshal, you know as well as I do there'd be more Govans and Caulfields in here to tear this town up than ten town marshals could handle."

Eagle Eye cleared his throat and spit his wad of tobacco into a stained spittoon at the end of the desk. "I know as well as you do that I got an uphill row to hoe before these hot-headed folks around here will ever knuckle under to the law. And you jackleg lawyers back them up. All I was fixing to say, if you had let me finish, was that I'd put this boy in jail unless you make bond for him."

Harvey picked up a pencil and, shielding the writing with his other hand, dashed off a few lines. Folding it neatly, he handed it to Shim, saying, "Excuse me, Marshal. Shim, I wish you'd deliver that note to Wick in the next day or so."

He turned back to Eagle Eye. "Of course I'll make bond for the boy, if it's necessary." He stood up suddenly, his face serious, looking out the side window, and like he had just thought of something mighty important. He took Eagle Eye by the arm and said, "Say, step in the back room with me a minute. I want to see you privately."

The door closed, and Shim was alone in the little office. He started to put the note in his pocket, but noticed something written on the back. *Read,* it said. He opened it and read. *Straddle your horse and get the hell out of town quick.* Shim was out the door and on his horse in a flash.

When he rode into the barn lot he was glad to see by the sun that it was well past dinnertime. He wasn't ready to face any of his folks yet and had killed enough time on the road to make him late. Nobody was in sight. The hogs were lying in the shade down by the pond; the chickens were dusting themselves under the shade trees. The Captain's horse was gone, and Miss Cherry and Fanchie would be lying down. Hot and hungry, he unsaddled his horse and headed for the kitchen.

He was crossing the yard when he saw Henry come out of the kitchen and head for the back gate at a swift walk. His heavy lips were poked out, and his nostrils flared wide like a mad horse's. He didn't so much as glance at Shim, passed him up like a pay car passes a tramp. Shim frowned with surprise. Trouble was in the air. Henry was worked up like he'd never seen him before.

In the kitchen Kiz was rattling pots and skillets around in the dishpan. She didn't speak either. He sat down at the kitchen table before he noticed that she was slinging tears and wiping them away with her apron.

"What's up?" he asked uneasily.

Kiz gave a snort and tossed her head. "Henry—old biggety Henry. The Captain done spoiled him till he thinks he runs this whole place, but he sure don't run me. I'm grown now."

Shim couldn't believe it was Kiz talking this way. Kiz was a fool about Henry. Suddenly he remembered hearing Miss Cherry tell the Captain a while back that Kiz had moved over to stay with Foots Booker and Caline, and that she was afraid Kiz and Henry had had a falling out over something. Of course Caline was Kiz's aunt, just like Henry's Aggie was, but Kiz never had stayed with them before that Shim could remember. Miss Cherry had said she hoped it would blow over soon whatever it was, because Kiz had a heap farther to walk to the house from Foots's place and was late getting to work some mornings. She didn't act like herself either.

Shim hadn't paid any attention much to what Miss Cherry said at the time, but, remembering it now, he looked at Kiz curiously. She looked back at him right hard. "Your face is red as a turkey-gobbler's snout," she said. "How come?"

Kiz was acting enough like herself not to miss anything out of the way about him.

"I'm hungry," he said.

"Hold your horses, boy." She opened the warming oven. "I'll have you some victuals in a minute."

While her back was turned he ran fingers gingerly through his hair. He was pleased to find the knots on his head were getting smaller; the swelling in his left cheek was going down some, too. Kiz set meat and potatoes on the table and turned away to catch up her apron and wipe away a sudden fresh rush of tears. Shim pretended not to notice. He took a long drink from the big glass of buttermilk she had set beside his plate. Whatever the trouble was between her and Henry, she wouldn't tell him until she'd cooled down, and anyhow he had troubles of his own to worry over. A few days later, when it was too late, he was to look back and wonder if he had pressed Kiz to talk there in the kitchen that day things might have turned out different. But he didn't.

When suppertime came he couldn't put off facing his folks any longer. He no sooner sat down at the table than Fanchie lit into him about her rose water. Miss Cherry asked a whole parcel of questions about the Calhouns and what they had to eat for supper last night, and Dave wanted to know what he'd run against that bruised his cheek that way. He made out pretty well, though. He answered Miss Cherry as fully as his memory would permit; told Fanchie straight out that he forgot her rose water, and Dave to tend to his own business.

After supper they sat out on the front gallery to catch the little cooling breeze that usually sprang up right after dark. Miss Cherry and Fanchie were rocking and fanning themselves; Dave, sitting on the top step, was mulling something over in his mind; the Captain was in his big rocker, smoking his pipe; and Shim, in a straight chair tilted back against the wall, was worrying. Night bugs sang, and a distant thump came now and then from down at the barn when a fractious mule let fly with a hoof against the stable wall.

Gimlet, at Shim's feet, gave a warning growl low in his throat, and a second later they all heard the buggy. It came down the lane and pulled up at the gate. In the light summer darkness Shim recognized Harvey Beckham's buggy and span of bays, and, shifting uneasily, dropped the front legs of his chair to the floor.

Harvey hallooed and the Captain answered him. Dogs, pouring out from under the house, blocked the walk, and Harvey, stepping high as a blind goat, seemed like he was going to walk right into them before the Captain could call them back. Shim's heart pounded so hard against his ribs he was afraid Miss Cherry would hear it. Maybe the business about the bees had been traced to him; maybe that glass had put Orland's eyes out.

Harvey came up the steps, saying he was on his way to see Wick and just dropped by. He shook hands with the grownups and asked how they all were. No matter what news he was bringing he'd go through all this politeness first, and Shim didn't relax. Harvey stepped over to him and slapped his shoulder so hard it almost knocked him out of his chair. With a big laugh that hurt Shim's ears he said, "The country boy put the town bully in his place."

Shim stood up. "Have this chair, Mr. Harvey, or would you like to have me get you a rocker?"

Harvey sat down, still laughing, but shut his laugh off right suddenly and looked at first one then the other of the puzzled faces. He wound up looking at Shim. Shim tried to laugh, but didn't make much of an out at it. "You didn't think I was coming home and tell it, did you?" he said.

Before Miss Cherry and Fanchie had got their mouths open to ask the questions Shim knew were coming, the Captain said quickly, "If you ladies will excuse yourselves, I've got a little matter I want to talk over with Harvey."

Miss Cherry got up and went into the house; Fanchie followed her, slowly, looking back over her shoulder just dying of curiosity.

When they were out of earshot Shim turned to Harvey. One of the questions pressing his mind he could afford to ask. "Was he cut?" he said.

"Not a scratch," Harvey said.

Shim turned to the Captain and described the morning from the time he got to the drugstore till he left town. He finished, and Harvey said quickly, "That's the first whipping that bully Orland Moulton ever got, to my knowledge, and now the boys are calling him 'Rosewater Orland' and making him like it."

The Captain didn't smile. "Did Eagle Eye put you under arrest, Shim?"

"No, sir, I don't reckon he did," Shim said, glancing at Harvey.

"Of course not," Harvey said quickly. "Don't get your dander up, Captain. Eagle Eye got all right as soon as I talked to him privately. He's mighty sensitive about that overgrown nephew of his, and then too, he's getting politics on his mind. He wants to stand in good with all these folks who have been selling their timber and got it in their heads they're going to make the town over. Forget about the whole thing. Everybody in town but the Moultons has been hoping somebody would give Orland a good currying."

The Captain turned to Shim. "If you violated the law, you'll have to pay the fine. However, the law does say a man has a right to defend himself. It's time you boys went to bed."

Shim and Dave said good night and went inside. On the gallery the two men sat in silence. A tree toad shrilled in the hot night, and the sound of water spilling from the artesian well at the side of the yard sounded cool and refreshing.

"Sorry I blurted it right out in front of the boy," Harvey said. "I figured he'd told you and you all might be worried."

"I am worried," the Captain said, "but not about Shim. I'm worried about Eagle Eye Moulton threatening to arrest my boy for defending himself. It's a straw showing the way the wind is blowing. When too much money flows, everybody gets greedy and goes to grabbing for it anywhere they can find it. These folks selling their timber are going to find the money in their pockets won't cure the trouble that comes with it."

The Captain's voice was harsh, and Harvey said quietly, "I'm afraid you're right, Captain. But there's mighty little we can do about it. Times aren't going to stand still. Folks around here are going to see more money than they ever dreamed of seeing. The ramshack wooden buildings of Mulberry will be replaced with brick. There'll be brick sidewalks and maybe even roads. These farmers will be renting out their plantations and moving into that town, or a bigger one, buying their wives and daughters diamonds and carrying them to New Orleans every year and maybe to Europe. I'm no fortuneteller, but I firmly believe we're in for some big changes."

Harvey broke off with a short laugh and got to his feet. "You've got me stirred up. Why don't you ride over to Wick's with me? It's a mighty fine night and too hot to sleep awhile yet."

The Captain stood up. "I'll do that," he said slowly. There was a strange look on his face that Shim, if he had been here and could have seen it in the darkness, would have read. Because he, like the Captain, would have caught the undertone of excitement in Harvey's voice, even while he called himself not liking the changes that were coming.

Shim heard them ride off and felt suddenly comfortable and sleepy. To his relief, Dave hadn't asked a single question since they came inside to go to bed, but now, from the other bed, he said suddenly, "What you reckon Orland jumped on you about?"

A shiver went through Shim, even though he was pretty sure all danger of suspicion about the bees was past. The fact was, Orland did have a reason to jump him this morning, even if he didn't know it. Shim was sick and ashamed of the part he'd played in killing those bees, and nobody would ever find out about it from him. He didn't answer.

"Quit possuming and answer me." Dave said. "How come Orland to jump on you?"

"I don't know why the fool jumped on me," Shim said hotly. "Just wanted to beat up a country boy, I reckon." He flopped over onto his stomach and felt around with his feet for a cool place on the hot sheet.

"The son of a gun," Dave said. "I'll go in there tomorrow and pull his teeth for him."

Shim sat bolt upright. "Let him alone," he said angrily. "I don't need you fighting my battles." And he flopped back down on his stomach.

He'd never go to town again the longest day of his life. Tomorrow he'd go fishing and wipe out the memory of the whole thing. He wriggled to the edge of the bed and hung an arm down to pick up any coolness that might come through the window. A wet tongue began licking his hand. Gimlet, looking for coolness too, was on the floor under the bed. Shim scratched the soft head and thought about how nice and cool the nights would be when coon-hunting time came.

chapter eight

NOTHING MOVED ON THE TURNROW SHIM WAS FOLLOWing except him. The narrow field road that separated one cut of land from another was hard and firm to his feet in the middle, but the edges were deep in soft gray dust, where the plows, turning from one furrow to start back down the next, had torn it up during plowing season. He was walking slowly, like anybody ought to in such hot sun.

Tired of waiting for Henry to show up, he was going to find him. Henry had been hard to catch up with ever since the day a couple of weeks ago when Shim got back from town and found him leaving the kitchen looking mad as a hornet. He'd quit coming around the house and, when Shim did see him, acted like his mind was way off somewhere. Yesterday evening at the lot, though, he had hinted to Shim that he had some plans on foot for the two of them for tonight. Now, with the day half gone, he hadn't laid eyes on Henry yet, and he wasn't going to wait any longer to find out about it. Whatever it was, he didn't aim to miss it.

These hot days between the laying-by of crops and the coming of gathering time were long days of rest and enjoyment. The tenants slept a heap, and the fields were silent and deserted. The only noisy thing was the chickens. One was cackling now out in the cotton somewhere. This time of year when you heard one cackle it didn't always mean an egg; but, with the crops grown so high and vegetation so rank everywhere, just that the chickens were scary, afraid some varmint or other was hiding unseen, ready to grab them.

This time of year was like when you throw a ball or bottle straight up in the air to shoot at, and the moment comes when it stops there, stands still, before starting down. That was the instant a keen eye could hit it with a pistol. It seemed to Shim that vegetation, crops did the same thing. They grew tall and big, and then came these late-August days when they suddenly reached their full growth and stopped, waiting and silent, as if gathering their strength to break into harvest. For folks, these days of rest were a deep drawing of breath for the coming race to get the crops in while the weather was pretty—ahead of the fall rains.

Henry's four-room house faced the turnrow, and Shim saw him lying on the floor of his front gallery, asleep. Part of the hard smooth dirt of the yard was already shadowed from the afternoon sun. Shim went noiselessly through the front gate and up the path bordered on both sides by carefully tended flower beds. A big palma-Christi plant in the fence corner was the only other growing thing in the yard. Not a spear of grass or weed was allowed to grow on the baked smoothness of the clean-swept yard.

Shim sat down quietly on the top step and watched a swarm of butterflies, all with different markings, mixing with the bees in the flowers along the path. Wide bands of heat waves quivered on the hot still air. In the early spring, buffalo gnats danced in dense formations like that, only they were black. These bands seemed to be made up of what looked like millions of tiny silver rings, dancing like bubbles. Not silver either, he thought, rings of light—not just sunlight, but sky-light, earth-light, tree-light, all mixed up.

Henry rolled over on his side and opened his eyes. "Get up from there, boy, and sit in a chair," he said.

"You didn't come by like you said," Shim replied, and stayed where he was.

Two quail zoomed up from the turnrow in front of the house, flew out over the sorghum patch a ways and almost stopped still in the air before cupping their tails and wings and easing down out of sight below the tall stalks of sorghum.

Henry sat up and hung his feet over the gallery's edge. "I didn't come because I think maybe you ought not to go," he said.

"You're up to some sort of skulduggery," Shim said, and turned his head and looked at him.

"It's this-a-way," Henry said. "If anything was to come up, the Captain wouldn't like it about you being there."

Inside the house Aggie yawned loudly and mumbled something about keeping up so much fuss out there. Henry stood up, yawned and started for the gate. "Let's go get us a watermelon." Shim yawned too, and followed him out of the gate and down the turnrow.

As soon as they passed the corner of Henry's yard fence, cotton stalks rose on their left, high as Henry's head; and on their right, late corn, so tall it would have hidden a man on horseback, was such a rich green it looked blue in the shimmering heat. They walked a good little piece before they came to a break in the cotton stalks where two long rows were being used for a watermelon patch. They each pulled a fair-sized melon and took it to the shade of the little cotton pen beside the turnrow.

Shim took out his knife, and Henry said, "Wait a minute. That little short blade ain't no account." With the knuckles of his fist he beat a shallow groove the length of the striped rind and, lifting the melon up a few inches, bumped it firmly against the hard ground. It burst open with the sweet red heart whole and in perfect shape.

Shim, his mouth watering, gouged out a good section of the red meat from one end next to the rind and used it like a wet sponge to wash his hands in the juice. Henry did the same. Then each lifted out the heart and started to eat. The warm, sugary goodness ran down over Shim's chin. Miss Cherry always wanted her watermelon tied up in a clean flour sack and lowered into the well to cool before she ate it, but, to Shim, cooling took away the biggest half of the sweet flavor.

Henry downed an oversize mouthful, wiped the dribbling juice from his mouth and chin with the back of his big hand and brought the palm slowly back across to finish the job. "It's this-a-way," he said. "I got some prowling to do in that canebrake between Frying Pan Bayou and Bear Track Slough. My aim was that me and you would put out the word that we is taking the dogs out for exercise tonight, and that will give me a chance to tend to some private business I got down there. But after figuring things out I see that there'll more than likely some trouble come up." He bit off another piece of watermelon and dropped his voice to a more serious tone. "It just won't do for you to get mixed up in it."

Shim's eyes didn't lose the brightness that had come into them at Henry's first words. He'd outtalked Henry before, and he could do it this time. He sure didn't want to miss going with him tonight. Over in that canebrake, not far from the lick-log where the deer went for salt, there was a shack he'd like to get a close look at. It was built mostly out of big slabs of bark, shed by some of the big old cypress trees. Shim had always itched to make some use of that bark. He'd seen slabs of it four or five feet wide and eight or ten feet long that had broken off the tree and fallen whole to the ground. If the ground and the roots hadn't been there to prevent, he wondered if it wouldn't slide off whole and round the way a snake sheds its hide, like pulling off a sock. But he'd never seen the bark used for anything, until he'd caught sight of that shack a few months ago on his way back from hunting. He'd wondered about it, and not more than a week or so later he'd seen the man who built it.

It was one day right after dinner. Shim and the Captain came out on the front gallery just as a strange man came in the side gate and started across the back yard, heading for the field. Shim stared, and the Captain stiffened. That was a thing folks didn't do. Even your neighbors and your kinfolks respected you enough not to go about over your plantation without first coming to the house and politely explaining their business. The Captain hailed the stranger.

He turned, snatched off the cap he had on and came to the gallery edge, moving as fast and easy as a mink, for all he was tall and water-jointed and hump-shouldered. He wasn't old, but he wasn't exactly young, either; and the one time he looked up at the Captain, Shim got a glimpse of the strangest eyes he had ever seen—big and bulging, and with a shine to them like they'd glow in the dark.

When the Captain asked him who he was and what he was

doing here, he said, humble and polite as could be, that his name was Jeems Yarn, that he was a sawmill worker and had thrown himself up a little shack over in the woods to live in, bothering nobody, till the sawmill opened up in Mulberry and he could get work. As to what he was doing here on the Captain's place—he was just walking about.

The Captain told him he didn't allow strays on his land and asked him not to come on it again. Jeems Yarn apologized, said he didn't mean any harm and would stay off the place.

Shim knew you couldn't allow strays on your plantation; you had to protect your fields just like you did your house, because the fields were your living. Strays didn't care what they did—leave a gate open, or even tear down a panel of the fence, and the cattle and hogs and other animals would get in the fields and destroy the crops. Strays didn't work, and had to eat, so naturally they'd steal food and anything that was loose, like plow tools and gear, even mules and hogs, and take them and sell to somebody else. Besides that, they were natural troublemakers—stirred up the tenants, got fights started and maybe somebody hurt or killed. As well as Shim knew this, Jeems Yarn's eyes were so big and shiny and sad-looking, and he'd built himself such a neat little shack with that cypress bark, that Shim had felt half sorry for him for just a second that day as he'd watched him go out the front gate and off down the road. He hadn't seen Jeems Yarn nor, to tell the truth, thought about him or his shack since then, until now.

"Reckon we might get a good look at that old shack made out of cypress bark over there?" Shim said. "I'd like mighty well to."

"I aim to," Henry said in a hard voice. "I aim to tear that shack teetotally down, and when that Jeems Yarn gets back there tonight I'll stamp his eyes out."

"What you mad at him about?" Shim said. "I didn't know he ever was on this place but the one time the Captain told him to stay off, and he was so humble and polite I felt sort of sorry for him, even if he is a stray."

Henry gave a snort and blew a mouthful of brown seeds from his mouth. "You sound like you ain't got no more sense than that crazy ignorant Kiz—talk about feeling sorry for a owl-eyed varmint like that."

"What's Kiz got to do with him?" Shim said, puzzled.

"God himself only knows," Henry said. "Caline figures Jeems done put a spell on Kiz some way or other. She took to slipping out meeting him of a night. I put a stop to that, and Kiz and me had a big round about it. That's when she left to go stay with Foots and Caline. Now Foots has done caught up with her doing the same thing over there, slipping out and meeting that varmint in the woods. Last night Caline slept in the bed with Kiz, to make sure she didn't slip out. Way up in the night a low keen whistle came from back of the house, and Caline say Kiz laid there beside her and shook like a leaf, but never tried to get up because Caline took a good hold of her arm. Caline say she didn't quit shaking for the longest, but she never would say nothing. I'm fixing to get rid of that Jeems before Kiz drives her ducks to the worst market in the world. I tell you that long, disconnected, water-j'inted stray ain't right. His eyes ain't right, and he ain't right."

Shim remembered the day he got back from town and found Kiz in the kitchen crying. "Why don't you tell the Captain?" he said, frowning.

"What I'm going to tell him?" Henry said. He was mighty

worked up. "He ain't been on the Captain's land since he was told to stay off, as anybody knows of. The Captain can't do nothing about his tolling Kiz out, if she's crazy enough to follow whenever that Jeems crooks his ugly finger."

Henry threw away what was left of his watermelon heart and pulled off some cotton leaves to wipe his hands. "I tell you what I'll do. I done promised you I'd take you with me tonight. So we'll go and I'll see can I get something on him that the Captain can do something about. The varmint's bound to be getting something to eat, and that means he's prowling of a night, stealing folks's corn, plow tools or anything that ain't nailed down. Maybe he's making liquor. We'll take the dogs out tonight like I said and let them get some exercise on a smart coon's trail, and when we get to Frying Pan you can make a fire and wait, whilst I goes over there and sees what that varmint's got in his rat den. Something he stole maybe, or if he's making liquor I can smell the mash mighty good on still, damp air."

"Suppose he's there and jumps on you?" Shim said.

"Well, now," Henry said slowly, "I would just enjoy that in the full. I'd a heap rather wring him in two with my own hands than have to bother the Captain or the Sheriff either. But there won't be no such luck. He'll be sneaking around over in the woods back of Foots's house, blowing his whistle for that poor conjured Kiz to come out to him."

Henry was so wrapped up in what he was saying that Shim heard it first—someone picking a guitar and singing. Pewatt Hodges came in sight down the turnrow. Pewatt and his wife, Parafina, had the best corn over in the new ground that ever had been made on the plantation, and he was feeling good. His guitar hung by a string around his neck, and he was moaning a song.

"Oh them chickens up that tree
And there's nobody here but me. . . . "

"Where you going with all that fuss?" Henry called.

"Hunting me a watermelon," Pewatt said with a wide grin.

Shim knew as well as they all did that Pewatt hadn't been going anywhere—just drifting around in the good sunshine with his guitar. He stooped over to thump a melon to see if it was ripe.

At that instant the keen report of a rifleshot ripped the hot, motionless air. All three of them were on their feet, standing straight and tense, looking across the cotton in the direction the sound had come from—the strip of woods in front of Foots Booker's house. A man's squall over there tore the silence wide open, and Henry started running. "Come on," he said. Pewatt shifted his guitar behind his back to protect it from thumping cotton boles and limbs and disappeared at top speed behind Henry into the tall cotton.

Shim stood for a moment, wondering what he should do. He could hear either yelling or mighty loud, confused talking going on now at Foots's house. There was trouble there. The Captain and Dave were both in town, and Shim felt an unwelcome weight of responsibility press him suddenly. There was another shot, and now loud squalling was going on over there continually.

He struck a swift trot back down the turnrow. A third shot rang out—all from the same gun—before he got to Henry's house. The gate that opened out on the road from Henry's side yard stood open, and down the road he saw the reason why. Aggie, in spite of her size, was carrying her weight at a speed Shim himself couldn't beat. He lit out following her. A shrill whistle from up the road behind him made him look around. He stopped. The Captain was sitting on his horse where this road joined the one from town. Relief swept over Shim. The Captain, on his way home, had heard the rookus and would see about it. He was reining down the road toward Shim at a swift single-foot. Even with him, he pulled up.

"Do you know who's fighting?" he said.

"No, sir," Shim said. "I just started down there."

"Go back to the house and stay with your mama and Fanchie. Dave's still in town." The Captain slacked on the rein and his horse lit out again down the road toward Foots's house.

Shim sat on the back steps, anxiously listening and wondering. Miss Cherry, standing on the gallery behind him, said uneasily, "I wish your father would come on back." Fanchie, beside her, said nothing, but he could feel her impatience in the way she kept twisting and fidgeting around. Trouble excited Fanchie the same way a frolic or party did, made her eyes bright and her cheeks pink, and she couldn't be still. Shim frowned. If the Captain hadn't shown up just when he did, Shim would be down there where the trouble was, right now, instead of here waiting at the house with the women.

"Hush," he said, and held up a hand.

"Yeheeeeeehoooooooooo."

The news, whatever it was, was beginning to travel. Powerful lungs were sending the word across fields and woods to wherever there were ears to hear. Three times the squall was repeated, and then he heard answers coming back from far distances and from every direction: from the woods where somebody who happened to be hunting or making rails or cutting wood heard the news, acknowledged it, and passed it on; from the back of the place to the north and east and west; from the next plantation to the south, beyond Foots's house. Everywhere folks were hearing and spreading the news. Close as Shim listened he knew he wouldn't catch a word. He'd heard messages passed this way all his life, heard them close at hand, known what they were, and still had never been able to distinguish one word from another. He knew only one thing: the news was bad.

The Captain rode in through the back gate and up to the gallery. He looked placid as lake water on a still day, all but his eyes. They were too bright and quick. Even Fanchie didn't open her mouth to ask a question. The Captain dropped more quickly than usual from his saddle, and stood straight and motionless among the flock of dogs gathered around him.

He looked up at Miss Cherry. "It's bad. That infernal Jeems Yarn. He's run amuck. King Sommers is dead. Old Caline got shot through the hand. Jeems got away." He hesitated long enough for Shim to know he hadn't told it all. "He carried Kiz with him," the Captain said.

Miss Cherry let out a small "Oh" and put her hand to her mouth. Fanchie started to cry. The Captain frowned, and swept his eyes over the field and road. His horse was cropping big mouthfuls of Bermuda grass, and the craunching sound of it being wrung off by the strong teeth was unnaturally loud in the stillness.

The Captain pulled up on the reins. "I'm going to the barn. We've got to look up some chains and good locks for the barn and the gates. Henry and his crowd are bound to catch him before night, but if they shouldn't, we've got to make sure he doesn't steal a horse or a mule to get away on after dark."

SHIM 149

"What did he carry Kiz with him for? Why did she go with him? Where did they go?" Fanchie was twisting her hands together.

The Captain sat down on the steps, a thing Shim had never seen him do before. Shim guessed the Captain knew Fanchie would never get quiet till she knew it all.

"As I get it," the Captain said slowly, "Jeems has been after Kiz to marry him. She's been slipping out meeting him at night, and nothing Foots or Henry said could stop her. Jeems knew better than ever to show up at the house, but Kiz would slip out and go to him whenever he whistled. A couple nights ago Jeems told her she'd marry him or nobody, and she told him it would be nobody then. But it scared her, because she told Caline about it. Caline slept in the bed with her last night. When he whistled, Kiz just stayed in the bed, and Foots and Caline were mighty well pleased—thought that was the end of it and that Kiz had come to her senses.

"About an hour ago Jeems showed up, from nowhere, in Foots's front door with a rifle on his arm. Foots was in the front room, in the bed, with chills and fever, and Kiz was there putting cold cloths on his head. King Sommers had dropped by to visit and was sitting on a chair against the wall opposite the door. Jeems up with his rifle and shot King without a word. King fell out of the chair dead, and Jeems started toward Kiz. Foots was too weak to walk hardly, but he jumped up and grabbed the rifle. Jeems knocked him out with his fist and followed Kiz, who had run out the back door. He ran down the back steps and saw Caline come from behind the henhouse with a cutting colter in one hand. She'd been out setting a hen when she heard the shot and grabbed the first weapon she could find. Jeems took a shot at her and would have missed—because he was watching Kiz tearing out down a cotton middle—but Caline threw up a hand and he accidentally hit that. All this time he was calling to Kiz to come back. She kept going, and he hauled off and shot at her.

"At the sound of the shot she stopped, then whirled around and came back toward him. He went to meet her, grabbed her by the hand, and they disappeared together down a little path that leads across the cotton fields to Black Hawk Brake. It's dry as a powder house in there now. You can go anywhere in it."

The Captain stood up. "That's the last anybody saw of them up to the time I left. They haven't had time to get far. Henry had a crowd together and started after them in a mighty short time. It's a mystery to me we haven't already heard a signal saying they've got them."

He headed for the barn. Shim went with him. Neither of them said anything. Shim's chest was full and tight and the hot air seemed too heavy for his lungs to drag enough in to do much good. They got trace chains laid out for the gates and found some locks that weren't too rusty to use. They were listening all the time for a sound from Henry's posse that would tell them what they were doing wasn't necessary. But no whoop nor holler came, no call signal—three shots evenly spaced—to tell them the fugitives were found.

When they got back to the house folks were already gathering. Rance Lavender, Irvin Balfour, Cousin Cliff and his oldest boy, Ab, were standing at the front steps talking to Miss Cherry. Others were coming down the road. In no time, it seemed to Shim, the hitching rail was crowded with hot, tired horses.

As a usual thing, weeks might go by without anybody coming in sight of a plantation except those who lived on it, but let trouble come and folks appeared from everywhere in less time than seemed possible. Two Denmans came up the road, their horses at a fast trot, and hadn't finished hitching them to the fence before Brook Slater and Cholly Sheffield rode up.

Shim looked closely at the shooting irons every man had. Most of the saddles had long-barreled six-shooters hanging on their horns in scabbards, and shotguns and rifles stood against the fence. Everybody asked the same questions. "Have they caught them yet?" "What's the best thing to do now?"

Ben and Wick rode up and right away were raring to form another posse and start out. Plenty of time had passed for Henry and his posse to have caught Jeems. Shim thought so too and was trying to figure some way he could slip and go with them, but the Captain shook his head.

"No. Henry's got a big posse by this time, out there somewhere. With vegetation so thick, if another crowd went out, we're liable to run into one another without knowing it and get a lot of folks hurt for no use."

Men stood around in restless huddles, asking more and more uneasily, as the time passed and no signal came from Henry's crowd, how it was that men who could follow a deer's tracks that were twelve hours old weren't able to handle the fresh tracks of two people no more than a half hour ahead of them.

Shim overheard Ben say impatiently, "That Jeems must be some kind of witch, or they could have caught him in fifteen minutes, it looks like."

Dave rode up with Deputy Sheriff Hoskins and T. Parks Early, their horses blowing like they'd run all the way from town. When they'd heard all the details and got the straight of it, T. Parks Early threw back his head, that looked too big for his body because of the thick white hair that grew long on his neck, and said, "Well, gentlemen, when you're as old as I am you'll believe folks when they say, 'You can't tell who'll win a card game, who a man will vote for, or who a woman will marry.' "

"Kiz wasn't figuring on marrying that stray," Dave said.

"Well," T. Parks said, "she was fiddling around with him. They say all romance leaves an afterglow of misery."

Sometimes it tickled Shim to listen to T. Parks Early's highfalutin talk, always taking the longest way round to say the least thing, but right now it didn't. Whoever the "they" was that T. Parks was forever quoting talked too much and too fancy.

Ben was talking again about starting out another posse, doing something besides stand around waiting. But the Captain was still against it. The sun was down and it would be night before they got good and started. The danger of the posses running into each other and somebody getting shot would be even greater in the dark.

The Captain turned to Shim. "You and Dave see that all the mules and horses are in the lot. Then put those chains and locks we got out on all four gates." He turned to the others. "Looks like we'll all have to sleep with one eye open tonight."

T. Parks Early cleared his throat. "Gentlemen, I agree with Captain Govan. We're just wasting time here. My feeble opinion is that we had better repair to our respective domiciles and protect our families, smokehouses and saddlestock from a madman who has obviously run amuck and will stop at nothing. Only God knows where he will strike next."

Deputy Hoskins started toward his horse. "Let me know if you need me, Govan," he called over his shoulder. The other men moved toward the gate, slowly at first, and then, as if what T. Parks Early had said about the possibility of Jeems showing up at their own places had just sunk in, they peartened their gaits. In a few seconds the last sound of horses' hoofs died away.

Miss Cherry and Fanchie went to the kitchen. Dave and the Captain and Shim sat on the front gallery in the gathering dark, listening, waiting for some sound to come out of the night stillness. But the only sounds that came were the water splashing at the well, the occasional shrilling of an insect and the soft sucking of the Captain's pipe.

Shim got up and walked restlessly back to the kitchen. Fanchie and Miss Cherry seemed to be getting in each other's way. Miss Cherry, usually so quick, never making a waste motion, would pick up a stack of plates and just stand there like she'd forgotten what she meant to do with them. Fanchie went to the cupboard and suddenly started blubbering out loud, pointing to an apron hanging on a nail behind the door. "Kiz left it there just a few hours ago," she sobbed.

Shim got out of there in a hurry and back to the front gallery—to sit, and listen, and wait.

When Miss Cherry called them to come to the dining room, all there was on the table was some fried meat, hot biscuits and the molasses pitcher. Shim wasn't hungry to start with, but he kept right on eating because nothing hit his stomach just right. Nobody said much at the table except Fanchie, and she rattled on enough to run anybody crazy—low-rating all the menfolks in the country for not finding poor little Kiz.

"Looks like anybody with half-sense could have found them before now," she said again.

"You've said that a hundred times," Shim said. It grated on his nerves so bad because it was the same thing that was going over and over in his own head. Henry could follow tracks that nobody else would ever find, and yet, with no head start at all to speak of, a man, with a woman along to slow him down, had got clean away in broad daylight. Somewhere Shim had heard that crazy folks had ten times as much strength as an ordinary person. Maybe they had ten times as much sense, too. Jeems was crazy all right, killing King Sommers without a word, shooting at Caline and at Kiz.

After supper, the sitting and waiting and listening started again on the front gallery. Shim's stomach felt too full. He guessed Miss Cherry and Fanchie weren't much cooks. Before long Miss Cherry sent him and Dave and Fanchie inside to bed.

Shim lay on his bed, but felt like only his hips, heels and shoulders touched it. Nobody for miles around would sleep easy tonight. Every tenant house would be locked up tight, doors and windows fastened. A little breeze stirred the curtain of the open window beside his bed, and with his heart thumping he eased a hand down to the floor for his pepperbox. A wet tongue licked his hand, and, hoping Dave hadn't noticed his movement, he turned over onto his back, feeling sheepish. If anybody had been prowling outside, Gimlet would have let him know it, to say nothing of the dogs out in the yard. His eyes on a thin quarter moon, its points turned up meaning dry weather tomorrow, and his ears straining for any sound of trouble breaking out afresh, or signaling that it was all over, Shim fell asleep.

chapter nine

THE HEAT THAT HAD LASTED ALL NIGHT BEGAN TO BEAR down hard when the sun rose. Green leaves hung motionless in the breezeless air, and no sound of song or talking came across the fields or from the woods.

At daybreak Jim Stegog had come by to bring news from Henry and the posse. They had hunted all night and found no trace of Kiz or Jeems. The strain of listening and waiting, forgotten for a few hours of sleep, clamped down again.

The morning was half gone. Shim was in the hall making feeble strokes with a broom Miss Cherry had given him, telling him to stop standing around like a gosling in the rain and do something. He heard the sound of running feet come in the back gate and Pewatt's voice calling the Captain. Pewatt was one of the posse. Shim dropped the broom and hit the back gallery almost as soon as the Captain did.

Pewatt, his face ashy, and too out of breath to speak, was pointing to a place on his ankle.

"Lie down here on the gallery," the Captain said. "The

biggest thing a snake bite does is scare you to death. Your eyes are big as saucers. Lie down and let your heart rest."

Shim could tell the Captain was as disgusted as he was that this wasn't news of Jeems and Kiz, but just Pewatt scared silly over a snake bite. Shim went inside and brought out the bottle of turpentine, a teaspoon and a lamp. He set them on the floor and lighted the lamp.

"Don't let nobody tell you snakes won't bite under water," Pewatt got breath enough to say, "because this one did. We was wading across Bee Tree Slough with our breeches rolled up when my foot come down on him, and he fastened me with his teeth. I jerked my leg up, and that big old cottonmouth was swinging to it. I dropped my gun and took a hold of him and wrung him in two."

The Captain, standing on the ground beside the steps, leaned over and looked closely at the ankle. "Look here, Pewatt," he said in a relieved voice, and Pewatt rose up on an elbow. "See those little marks in a sort of half circle? That wasn't a cottonmouth. It was nothing but an old water moccasin, not even poisonous. A cottonmouth, or rattler either, leaves just two holes. You'll be all right. It's not even swelling. Get that turpentine hot, Shim. Now, Pewatt, what have you all done all night?"

Pewatt shook his head. "Nothing at all. Them two just naturally took wings and vanished from the earth. Not a track or a sign did they leave. Henry is going to go teetotally crazy if somebody don't get him to quit awhile and get some rest. Him and four or five more stayed in the woods all night. And they ain't heard a fris-fazzling thing, nor seen a thing. The rest of us knocked off and caught a couple hours sleep, two or three of us at a time, and we was all back and at it again by good daylight. We been through the woods, all through the fields. We done looked in every cotton pen and old empty house and every thicket where them two could be hiding. Henry runs right up and sticks his head in, and if he had of runned up on them, Jeems would have done blown it off, long ago, him got that rifle, and God only knows how many bullets."

The Captain glanced at the teaspoon filled with turpentine that Shim was holding over the lamp to heat. "Where did you all lose the trail? Where did they come out of Black Hawk?"

Pewatt, with one eye on the turpentine Shim was heating, said, "Well, sir, that's the strange thing. Twenty or thirty of us circled round that brake two or three times, and we ain't seed no tracks coming out nowhere." He gripped his leg with both hands. The Captain, with the point of his knife blade, was opening each little hole the snake's teeth had left in Pewatt's ankle. Taking the spoon from Shim, he poured the warm turpentine into them. Pewatt gritted his teeth and rolled his eyes, while the turpentine spread over his leg and dripped onto the floor.

The Captain laid the spoon down and straightened. "Just don't get dew poisoning in that and it'll be all right." He looked at Pewatt like he was studying hard about something, and spoke, like he was talking more to himself than to Pewatt. "I don't believe it, but it's just possible Jeems Yarn might have outfoxed Henry in that brake. But Kiz is with Jeems, and there's not a woman alive that could cross it and come out without leaving a pretty easy trail to follow." His voice sharpened. "How far inside the brake did you all lose their tracks?"

Pewatt sat up, his legs dangling over the edge of the gallery, and began rubbing his tired face with his two hands.

"Us never went into the brake, Captain. Dry as it is now, we knowed they'd be across it and somewhere on t'other side before we got good started. First thing we done, not to lose no time, was spread out and circle round it to find where they come out at and pick up from there. Only we never found no tracks."

"Where did you leave the posse, and which way were they heading?" the Captain said.

Pewatt pointed west. "I left them at Bee Tree Slough, but they was heading on north."

An idea struck Shim. Pewatt was a good chance for him to get away from under the keen eye of the Captain and Miss Cherry. Used to being free as air, and nobody ever worrying about him, the way they had kept him hemmed up at the house this morning was making him mighty restless. He slipped back to his room and hid his pepperbox in the bosom of his shirt. On his way back he met the Captain heading down the hall to the front door, frowning, and walking like he was in a mighty big hurry.

Back on the gallery, Shim found Pewatt limping around trying out his leg. When he headed for the back gate Shim walked along beside him. If Miss Cherry happened to look out and see him, she'd figure he was just walking a little piece with Pewatt. By the time they were out the gate and turned into the main turnrow that ran straight down through the field, he felt safe about not being called back.

"I'm going to scout around a little," he said. "Come on and go with me." If Pewatt would go with him, he'd go down and look around that brake, just to be doing something.

Pewatt opened his big mouth and yawned, with a string of grunts that sounded like the tail end of a blast from a conch shell. "I'm fixing to go home and sleep me some," he got out before another yawn started.

The cotton on their right gave way to long rows of sugar cane. They both turned aside into it, cut themselves a stalk and went on down the turnrow, peeling it and chewing the sweet juice from the fiber.

"Where you reckon Henry and them are now?" Shim asked.

"A little north of west," Pewatt said, pointing. "About in them woods between here and Frying Pan. But Henry done lost all the sense he had and is rip-snorting like hell beating tanbark. His eyes is red as foxfire, and he's so short-breatheded he was blowing like a spreading adder when I left them."

They heard children's voices, and at a log cotton pen beside the turnrow came upon Henry's two youngest boys, Toddy and little Henry, knocking peaches off a tree with a long fishing cane. Their tap sticks lay on the ground, and Shim looked them over admiringly. They were brand-new ones Toddy and little Henry had made themselves, smooth hickory sticks between two and three feet long; one of them had a heavy iron tap from a wagon axle on the end of it, and the other had a smaller tap from a buggy axle. Henry had taught Shim to kill rabbits with a tap stick when he was little, and they were just as good for defense. You could knock a panther out with one of them if you hit him just right.

"You all want to go look at Black Hawk Brake with me?" Shim asked.

Toddy and little Henry rolled their eyes and giggled. "You is joking. You is scared like anybody else. You ain't allowed to go no further from the house than what you is now, any more than us is."

Shim sat down on the ground beside a little pile of ripe peaches. He broke one open with his fingers, dropped the clear seed out and with his teeth skinned the meat out from each half, careful not to let his lips touch the stingy fuzz of the peeling.

Pewatt, tall enough to reach the lower limbs, was loading his pockets with fruit.

"You gets to prowling around these brakes and things, you liable to run up on Jeems," Little Henry said, ending with a grunt, as he jumped to catch a plump peach Toddy had just knocked off with his fishing cane.

"Shucks," Shim said, "Jeems is going to be laying low while it's daylight." He finished his sixth peach, and had enough. A vine, clinging to the logs of the side of the cotton pen, caught his eye. He got up and went over and pulled off a couple of brown, wrinkled maypops. Putting one in his pocket, he broke the other open with his fingers and sucked out the sweet, seedy pulp.

"You must ain't et today," Toddy said. "You act like you is hungry as Jeems must is by now."

"I bet that scamp *is* hungry," Pewatt said. "They say a man always gets powerful hungry right after he kills somebody."

"Wherever he is," Shim said, "I don't guess he's had a chance to steal anything to eat, because folks all over this part of the country are watching for him."

"He could be done killed a varmint and cooked it," Little Henry said.

Toddy grunted in disgust. "You ain't got the sense God gave a peckerwood. He'd be a plumb fool to shoot or build a fire either, with the woods full of folks looking for him."

Shim looked at Pewatt. "You going with me?"

"I better stay off this leg awhile," Pewatt said, "and you better go back to the house, where it's safe."

"I'm just going down here a little farther," Shim said.

He went on down the turnrow alone with only Gimlet frisking along behind him. He came to the ditch that led to the left, took off down the bank and followed it almost to the fence. He was now just about straight out in front of Foots Booker's house. Since he'd got this far, he would go on. It wouldn't do for anybody who happened to be around Foots's house to see him, because they'd try to send him back home. He turned into a cotton middle and, dropping to hands and knees, began to crawl. The stalks here weren't tall enough to hide him. When he was a good piece below Foots's house he worked his way across rows to the fence, climbed it, crossed the road, and beyond the fence on the other side he could walk upright in tall cotton.

Over here in Foots's field the rows ran in the wrong direction to follow a middle, and he had to walk across them. Coming to Foots's watermelon row—wide, because it was two rows thrown into one—he was almost across it when he stopped, his eyes on a man's tracks in the dust. They were strange to him. He knew the tracks of everybody around here, and these were none he had even seen before. He followed them a few steps and came to the print of a crokersack in the fine dust, and on the ground beside it the smooth, oblong spot where a watermelon had lain. Not many hours ago either, for the stem where it had been broken off the vine was still green. He counted where three more melons had been pulled right recently, jerked off in a hurry, pulling the vines out of place.

A little farther down the row the crokersack had left its coarse markings again in the dust, and this time beside them was the unmistakable print of a rifle butt. Shim tried to figure it out. In the woods somewhere way back over yonder the other side of the field, thirty or forty men—all of them good trackers and led by Henry, who was the best—were beating around looking for tracks and finding none. Here were tracks, strange ones, that didn't belong here and ought to be looked into.

His mouth was dry, and the sweat was pouring off him. He followed the tracks into the cotton. Slipping his pepperbox out of his bosom, he stuck it outside under his belt, in a handier place. Whoever had made these tracks had made them sometime before daylight, because they had been crossed and recrossed by insects and small animals and in one place were wiped out where quail had dusted themselves.

The cotton stopped, and the tracks led on into a cut of young corn, just in good roasting-ear stage. A dozen or more ears had been pulled from stalks on either side of him. It was a narrow cut of corn, just a few rows, and he came out of it onto the bank of Black Hawk Brake. Vegetation had grown here all summer undisturbed, and he was in waist-high weeds. He stood still, listening, but all he could hear was his own hard breathing and the beating of his own heart.

Into the upper end of this brake, just back of Foots's house no more than a quarter of a mile away, Jeems and Kiz had disappeared yesterday. The brake wasn't more than a hundred yards wide—a mass of undergrowth and old logs and a smattering of trees—but Kiz and Jeems had gone into it and vanished. Nobody had found a sign anywhere showing they had come out of it. These tracks he was following might be Jeems's. He couldn't stop now.

He looked about on the ground and in the weeds. His job of tracking was harder here, but, searching carefully, he found a little scuffed dry earth, then a bruised weed. They led to his right, along the edge of the brake. A few more yards and there was no more sign. He was puzzled. Whoever made those tracks couldn't have left the ground here. His heart gave a hard thump, then seemed to stop for a second before picking up again. There was only one explanation. The man who made those tracks had taken off his shoes in order not to scuff the ground or scar the weeds.

Shim looked down at the brake. Quiet was everywhere. Not a bird sang or moved, not a cricket chirped. The leaves were still as rocks. The sun blazed down out of a sky without a cloud. He felt sweat running down his legs, and he wanted water so bad he felt dry as doodle dust inside. He wanted to turn back, but his curiosity was too strong. For a little ways out into the brake the undergrowth was scattered and scarce. He could go that far and just make sure the tracks went into the brake.

Noiselessly he went down the gradual slope of the three- or four-foot bank to the flat bed. Here the hard ground was almost bare of leaf mold and had deep, dry-weather cracks in it, half an inch wide in places. A bare foot wouldn't leave a mark. He'd gone an uncomfortable ways when he saw sign again: a little pile of leaves had been stirred and some of them crushed as if by a foot. A few steps farther, he stopped. A dead stick lying on the ground had been broken recently, a stick too big to have been broken by the weight of a light animal, and no big animal would have been around here with all those men in the woods last night.

He wasn't going any farther. His legs told him before his mind did. They wouldn't carry him forward another step. Standing perfectly still, he searched everything his eyes could reach without turning his head—the ground, the bushes, the trees. His eyes hesitated on a spot some thirty steps ahead and to the left where a couple of old choctaws lay on the ground, big old down cypresses four or five feet thick that for some reason never rotted.

Just beyond them rose a big drift where old tree laps and small logs, swept along by the high water that filled the brake every winter or early spring, had caught there and held. The drift had been there ever since Shim could remember and, with each year's high water adding to it, was now seven or eight feet high and matted over with bushes, briers and vines.

Suddenly Shim was the worst scared he had even been in his life. Two red eyes were looking at him from that drift. A metallic taste poured from his cheeks and filled his mouth too full to swallow. Every nerve and muscle in him felt like they were drawing up to make him as small as possible. He tried to tell himself he was imagining things, that, thick as that drift was, nothing bigger than a rabbit could get into it, when a sudden memory came to him. The drift wasn't caught against the choctaws like it looked from here, but on a couple of standing trees back a little ways from them. He'd found that out one night last fall when his and Henry's dogs had treed a possum there. There was a narrow space between the choctaws and the drift—plenty of room for a man to be hiding, with the drift at his back and sides and the five-foot-thick choctaws in front of him.

As sure as he was living, red eyes were looking through the brush straight into his. His own eyes began to sting and dance. He wanted more than anything on earth to run, but knew that was the one thing he must not do. His flesh felt like it was crawling about under his clothes, and, in spite of sweat pouring off him, he felt cold. He couldn't stand here another second. Even if whatever he did was wrong, he had to move.

Gimlet, smelling around close by, stopped and cocked his head at Shim, and it gave him an idea. He began to quarrel at the dog. "Sorriest feist I ever saw," he said with a stiff jaw and dry lips. "Lead me way off down here after a varmint you never did smell to begin with." His knees moved. Stiff-legged, he turned his back to the drift and retraced his steps, still quarreling loudly at Gimlet and with the muscles of his back knotting up in dread of the rifle bullet that might hit him any minute.

After what seemed the longest distance he'd ever walked in his life, he was in the corn and hidden. He broke into a run. Distance and action cleared his head. He wished he could see the Captain, but that would lose time getting word to Henry and the posse, who were somewhere in those woods to the northwest. When he hit the main turnrow in the Captain's field he turned north.

He was nearly to the woods at the back of the field when above the noise of his own breathing he caught the sound of other feet than his own hitting the ground. Then he saw them, coming out of the cotton onto the turnrow—Henry, Happy Jackson, Nizer Sparks, Jim Stegog and his grown boy, Briff, and Mason Scully. All of them walked like every step might be their last, heads and shoulders drooping. He'd never seen men look so tired and worn out.

Over hollow cheeks, Henry's eyes were hard on Shim. "Now here you is, out here to make more trouble for me." His voice croaked like a frog's. "Go home before I wear you out."

Turning and falling into step beside him, Shim said with what little breath he had left, "There's somebody in Black Hawk Brake."

"Sho," Henry said. "The Captain just now near about rode his horse to death finding me to send us over there."

Instead of acting glad to get some track of the killer, Henry talked like he was mad about something. The Captain must have lit out after them as soon as he found out from Pewatt that the brake hadn't been searched.

Shim frowned up at Henry. "Where is the rest of the crowd that was with you?"

"I left them back yonder where they ought to be," Henry growled. "There's enough of us here wasting time fooling around with that brake."

"There's somebody in there," Shim said again.

"I reckon you seed him," Henry said.

Shim felt the muscles of his face tighten. "Not exactly," he said. He'd halfway expected nobody would believe him, but one thing was in his favor: he had something to show them once they got over there. "But I felt somebody looking at me. I tracked him from Foots's watermelon row."

"Boy," Henry said, "you used to tell the truth, but now you is talking like you is right wool-gathered."

"If you has found some tracks," Nizer said, "I wants to see them. I been looking for tracks till I'm about blind."

"I don't know whose tracks they are," Shim said, "but I never did see them before, and whoever made them was in that brake when I left."

"You all stop so much talk and get your minds off foolishness," Henry grumbled. "I'm hot as a washpot, and about got the thumps from so much gabbing and walking."

Happy Jackson lifted tired eyes and looked Henry over slowly. "You going to pass out if you don't lay down and rest some."

A funnel-shaped whirlwind of dust and trash, made by some freak draft in the still, hot air, crossed the turnrow ahead of them, went whirling on a straight course across a couple of hundred yards of cotton, then faded and vanished. Gimlet, trotting beside them, made a dash at a dove in the edge of the turnrow, and it struck Shim that Gimlet was going to be in the way. There was a cotton pen just ahead. He picked Gimlet up, dropped him down inside, swung the high door shut on his disappointed yipping and walked on.

"You ought to be fastened up in there with him," Henry growled, "so you'd stop bothering folks that's busy and full of troubles."

Far across the dark-green field a shadow appeared, traveling mighty fast. Shim glanced up to see a white fleecy cloud passing between the sun and the earth and wished that some of the breeze driving that cloud up there would drop down to earth and cool their sweat-soaked clothes. Maybe it would clear Henry's hot and pestered mind so he'd pay what Shim was saying some attention.

"I followed those tracks from the watermelon row, through that strip of corn and into the brake, until I felt two red eyes looking at me from the old drift. I tell you I felt those eyes just as sure as if they were two sticks punching me."

Henry, and the others too, kept slogging along like they didn't even hear him. Henry was going to search Black Hawk Brake, but it was mighty plain he was doing it just to satisfy the Captain and not because he believed Jeems was there.

Nobody spoke again until they had climbed the fence, crossed the road and were in Foots's woods lot. Then Jim Stegog looked up at Briff plodding along beside him and said in a worried tone, "Boy, you is about gived out. You better lay down here somewhere and rest. We'll wake you up when we come back by."

Briff worked up the first grin Shim had seen on any of them and looked down at his father, a head shorter than he was. "It's you old folks needs rest. I'm young, and good from now on."

Everybody knew Jim was a plumb fool about his boy Briff, and Shim wondered if he'd tried to leave Briff behind because he believed maybe Jeems was in the brake.

When they came through Foots's yard gate, Preacher Haymo was sitting on the gallery with Foots and Caline. Foots looked ashy and peaked from his chills and fever, and Caline had her left hand in a sling.

"You all ain't found no sign of them yet?" Foots said.

"Not nothing," Henry answered.

"Lord help!" Caline moaned. "You all mens want some cool water? Some victuals?"

"All I wants," Henry said, "is to get my hands on that varmint."

"Which-a-way is you all headed now?" Caline asked.

"The Captain wants us to look in this brake back here." Henry was keeping right on walking, tired as he was.

They were near about across the yard when Preacher Haymo spoke. "The good Lord will reward you all for the work you is doing."

Shim could tell from their voices that not one of them believed Jeems was fool enough to have stayed that close. They went silently out the back gate. Instead of heading straight for the brake, Henry turned right down a cotton middle. Shim felt a big relief, and a heaviness was gone

SHIM 169

from his feet. Henry was going by the watermelon row to look at the tracks Shim had found there.

They came to the watermelon row and slowed their walk, every eye searching the ground. Henry, in the lead, stopped. "It's him." The words sounded like they were jolted out of him. The others were crowding around, staring at the track.

"It is, so help me, Lord," Nizer said. "I'd know them tracks, big as hamper sacks, in purgatory, if I was to see them there. I can't miss knowing that right track, shaped like his foot's got a kidney in it."

Henry, still staring at the ground, said slowly, "I never would have believed that cush-footed varmint would be fool enough to stay this close, knowing I was after him." He drew a deep breath and threw a quick glance at each of them. "Let's go. And you all hear this: he's mine, if the Lord lets me live to get to him."

"He's in the old drift," Shim said.

Henry looked at him, hard, like he'd forgotten Shim was there. Their eyes held, and Shim saw Henry remember that possum and the space between the choctaws and the drift where a man could hide with all ease.

"Boy, you go home," Henry said, and turned to Happy Jackson. "We got to outflank him. You take Mason and one more and go in above the thicket just north of the drift. You can't get to him from there, but you can kick up some fuss to worry him whilst the rest of us slips in below the drift. And keep low as a toad. Don't forget that scamp can pick a man off at a hundred and fifty yards."

"You all better be the ones to remember that," Happy said. "We'll have the thicket and the drift twixt us and him. You all won't have all that much cover out in front."

The men had changed. Sagging shoulders were straight; eyes dull with tiredness flashed bright and quick; flabby faces had got smooth and hard. They believed now that Jeems was in the drift. It was Jeems's tracks Shim had followed, Jeems's eyes Shim had seen in the drift. Such a bad taste came in Shim's mouth suddenly that he knelt down and burst a small watermelon with his fist. He took one bite of the heart and threw it down. It tasted bitter as quinine. He straightened up and Henry saw him again.

"I done told you to put out home. This ain't no place for you, and I'm tired of worrying with you."

Shim knew better than to try to argue. Henry was right, but, just the same, Shim wasn't going. He'd have to make out like he was, though. He turned slowly, intending to walk off a few steps, when here came Foots carrying a wagon spoke, Preacher Haymo a gun, and Caline a good tap stick.

"I is proud to see you all," Nizer said. "I was just fixing to ask Henry didn't he think we better send for some more men." He pointed to the ground. "Look at all this sign he left here last night."

Three pairs of eyes stared and three voices said, "It's the whole truth."

Foots said, "Well, Caline, this is far as you're going."

"You come here telling me to go back, when you done found that varmint's tracks?" Caline's cheeks puffed out.

Briff Stegog lifted his eyes from a close search of the ground all around and said with a frown, "One thing got me bothered, Miss Caline. There ain't none of Kiz's tracks around here nowhere. Looks like if they was this close, Kiz could have slipped off and come home whilst he was out here stealing these watermelons."

Caline's eyes snapped like a snapping turtle's. "If you're

trying to say Kiz runned off with that baboon because she wanted to, and that she ain't trying to get away from him, you ain't got the sense God gave a monkey wrench, Briff Stegog. She tried to run from him yesterday, till he took and shot at her."

"You go on back home, Caline," Foots said right easy, so as not to rile her up worse. "Where we're going ain't no fit place for a woman."

"That's right," Henry said. "If he's in that old drift, he's going to be mighty hard to get out of there."

"Kiz is there if he is, ain't she?" Caline said, her head lowered and stuck forward. "You just as well save your breath. I'm going. My own flesh and blood laying out there in them woods all this time, mosquitoes eating her up, snakes trying to bite her, nothing to eat but watermelons, and you come here trying to tell me I ain't going? If you all don't want to go with me, just get out of my way, because I'm going out there and joog that Jeems's eyes out, so help me, Jesus, and bring Kiz home."

Big, good-natured Caline had a temper that not a man on the place wanted to tangle with when she got riled up. She was hot under the collar now and stout enough to handle any of them with that tap stick she had in her hand. Foots's eyes dropped to the ground, and he kicked at a small clod.

"What you all standing here waiting on?" Caline said, throwing back her head.

Preacher Haymo cleared his throat. "Brothers, and one sister, we is going into danger. Some of us might not come back. I think we ought to have a little word of prayer."

Knees bent in the watermelon patch. Preacher Haymo cleared his throat again. "Good Lord bless and keep each and every one present here from harm." He stopped. They all stood up, and every face was suddenly long as an ax handle. They knew that in the next few minutes, or hours, somebody would be pretty sure to meet his Maker if Jeems was in that drift. God willing, it would be Jeems, but it might be one or more of them here.

Happy Jackson and Mason Scully led off into the cotton, bearing a little to the left.

"Briff, you go long with them," Jim Stegog said. Briff frowned, but when Henry said, "Yes, Briff, that's right," he went. Right away Jim's face looked smoother and looser, and Shim guessed it was because he'd got Briff headed where there'd be the least danger.

"Come on," Henry said, and led off, bearing to the right, with Jim Stegog close behind him, then Nizer, Foots, Caline and, last of all, Preacher Haymo.

Shim waited until they were across the cotton and out of sight in the corn before he fell in behind them. He reached the far side of the corn patch in time to see them, single file, keeping about two yards between them, ease noiselessly from the weeds on the bank down into the brake, slipping from one small red oak or water oak to another, then to a bush or a down log that would conceal them from the drift.

Henry, in the lead, soon stopped and lay on his belly behind a down log. Jim, Nizer and Foots passed him and went on beyond to drop on their knees behind separate trees. Caline, only a couple of steps into the brake, had stopped behind a big cypress stump that suited her for protection, and Preacher Haymo was behind a down log between her and Henry.

Shim swung a little to his right and behind them before crawling out among the buckvines at the brake's edge. Lying there, flat on his belly, he could watch the drift and see the backs of the posse. They were spread out like the broad base of a triangle, with the drift as its peak. Henry was directly in front of the drift. He was making signs with his hands, warning the others to keep quiet and wait. For all their quietness Jeems was bound to have heard them, but nothing moved at the drift. It looked as motionless and dead as the old choctaws.

Shim's ears rang with the waiting stillness. The hot sun beat down on his back, and sweat stung his eyes. If Jeems started shooting, Shim was in line of possible fire himself. The brake was so still something had to burst loose soon. A redbird whistled somewhere, and Shim jerked his head to the ground, scared, before realizing what it was. When he looked up again his tight muscles had relaxed, and for a flash the brake looked harmless and peaceful as it always had until today. The drift looked innocent and empty of anything more dangerous than a snake or a lizard. He was still sure Jeems had been there, but that was an hour or more ago.

Shim looked at a bitter-pecan tree a few yards away and thought that, if he could climb it, he could see over those choctaws and find out quick whether anybody was there. Once up there, though, he might find himself right in the sight of a rifle that would bring him tumbling out of that tree like a dead coon.

Again he looked over the open space stretching out in front of the posse and wondered if anybody would try to cross it. His throat muscles tightened at the thought of what would happen if any of them did try, because Jeems, if he was in the drift, would sure stop all he could with that rifle. He looked at Caline's broad back, hunched down and still, behind the stump. The others, even Henry, were motionless too—just waiting. Shim couldn't figure out what they were waiting for. It looked like Jeems had them trapped as much as they had him.

Suddenly there was a loud, crashing sound, as if an elephant was loose out there among those bushes and dry limbs beyond the drift. It stopped, Shim heard only the thumping of his own heart for a few thundering beats, then it came again. His heart slowed. It was Happy Jackson and Scully and Briff, trying to kick up enough fuss to the north, behind Jeems, to bumfuzzle him and make him show himself to the men in front of him.

Henry was moving. Shim saw him lay his hat and gun on the ground and pull his knife from his pocket. Everything was dead quiet again, except for a flock of peckerwoods and jay birds squabbling noisily over roasting ears in the cornfield. Henry was motionless again.

The racket started up once more in the thicket beyond the drift—a terrible fuss, like they were beating limbs off trees with big sticks—and, behind the down log, Henry straightened up on his knees. Shim caught his breath and flashed his eyes to the drift. There was no movement there. A sound like grunts of surprise and pain came from the posse, and he saw why. Henry had jumped the log, and, stooping low, his open knife in his hand, he was out in the clear, running with everything he had, straight toward the drift.

Without catching a breath, the grunts from the posse rose to a wail, dropped to rumbling groans, rose again, dropped again; faster and faster, louder and louder the voices sounded, up and down, never stopping. The blood rushed to Shim's head. He'd heard this strange sound from their throats before in times of distress. He caught only a broken word now and then, but, clearer than any words, it was a prayer asking everything pure and strong to send help today and every day to folks who wanted only to live in safety and peace, and pleaded not to die for it. A humming roar, it seemed to Shim to come now from above and below and from all sides, with Henry in its center. Suddenly Shim knew that was a part of its reason—to cover the sound of Henry's running, to rattle Jeems with noise on all sides of him.

Forgetting danger to himself, Shim rose on all fours to see better. Still nothing moved at the drift. Within a few yards of the choctaws, Henry, without slowing his speed, straightened to his full height, took a couple more steps and jumped. In the air he sort of bunched himself, and was coming down bent almost double. A rifle barrel flashed up into sight and landed against the side of his head, smoke squirting from the muzzle. By the time Shim heard the report, Henry, rifle and all were out of sight behind the choctaws. The shot couldn't have touched him; the muzzle had been inches above his head. Henry had him, but was he going to hold him?

The sound in the brake was no longer from throats but from feet. Careless now of noise, the posse ran headlong toward the silent drift, each spurred by the fear he wouldn't get there in time to help Henry and keep that rifle from speaking again.

Shim was up and following them. He saw Caline, the third one to reach the choctaws, lift her long skirts, clear the logs as easy as the men and, landing, throw back her head. A high-pitched shriek lasted the limit of her breath, and ended with a call to the Lord. It told Shim that either Henry or Kiz was dead. Nothing but the death of some of her folks would wring a cry like that from Caline's strong body. A man straightened up beside her. It was Henry.

Shim jumped up on the choctaws and looked down. Watermelon rinds and corn shucks littered the trampled ground.

Jeems lay flat on his back with one sign of Henry's knife in his side; the other sign was under Jeems's chin and reached from ear to ear.

Caline, a high-pitched wailing still coming from her throat, squatted beside another still figure on the ground. It was Kiz. She lay close up against the drift, and the front and side of her dress were dark with blood. Caline's hand was moving light as a leaf over the still, gray face.

"She ain't been long dead. She still limber. Oh, Jesus, Jesus, Jesus." Caline's wild squalling lost the shape of words but went on. A coarse, powerful voice rose above hers. Preacher Haymo was hollering a long, slow call to tell other folks that the hunt was over. He dropped a hand on Caline's shoulder.

"The innocent has to suffer with the wicked, Sister Booker. Only the good Lord knows why."

Henry spoke. His face looked made of wood, and his words fell heavy like big chunks. "It wouldn't have helped none if we had of got here sooner. He killed her yesterday at Foots's house. She turned and come back to him because she was hit."

"You got it right, Henry," Nizer said. "That shot in the back killed her. She most likely went down soon after they got out of sight. Jeems got her this far and began fetching her watermelons and corn to get her strength back so she could go on with him. She ain't been long dead."

"It's unknown what a man will do when he sets his head on a woman," Preacher Haymo said. "He might could have got away by himself, but he wouldn't leave Kiz whilst there was breath in her body."

"If I'd killed him the first time I caught him making up to Kiz . . . " Henry's voice sounded like it was being torn from his throat. "But I fiddled around trying to do it the Captain's way, according to the law. I should have killed him like I would a mad dog." The wooden look on Henry's face began slowly to split up, and it was more terrible to Shim than anything he had ever seen. He whirled, jumped down from the choctaws and began walking fast out of the brake.

"Get on to the house and get things ready," he heard Foots say to Caline, and then he was beyond sound of their voices.

He was through the corn and in the cotton when something about his legs slowed him down. His knees were trembling. There was something packing up inside his head that didn't belong there. He'd seen dead folks before, but it hadn't affected him like this. He kept seeing Henry's cheeks gone hollow, his eyes big and blank as a cow's, Caline looking so wild, all of them looking unnatural and strange. But most of all Henry's face breaking up like it was going to fall apart. Shim's knees gave way, and he sat down. He was glad nobody could see him because every muscle in his own face felt like it was hanging by a string.

He wanted Jeems dead; he'd have killed him himself if he'd had a chance. That was right. But the hate and fear that made it right was gone. And the still body that was Kiz wasn't right. Kiz was never still in all her born days. Always running to get a knife to scale his fish or skin his squirrels, always carrying on foolishness, teasing him; always dancing around the washpot in the yard while the water got hot, because she couldn't be still and wait for anything; always flirting with the young bucks on the place, but not letting any of them make any time with her. Until along comes a sorry stray, and now Kiz was dead.

Loud talking from way across the field brought him to his feet. Folks had heard Preacher Haymo's call and were coming. The Captain would be coming and mustn't see Shim over here in Foots' field near the brake. He straightened his shoulders and shook them. Nobody must see him. He was more ashamed than he'd ever been in his life. At a time for showing strength he'd been sitting here acting weak as a kitten.

He began moving noiselessly but fast through the cotton. If it wasn't for the sawmill talk, Jeems never would have come here to start with. Kiz never would have laid eyes on him. Jeems was just the first. The sawmill would bring more and more meddling strangers to change and spoil these familiar roads and woods and bring trouble.

At the fence he climbed high enough to see there was nobody in the road in either direction, then dropped down, dashed across, over the fence on the other side, and was in the Captain's field. The cotton here, about a ten-acre strip, wasn't tall enough to hide him when standing straight. He struck a run to be across it before anybody came in sight. On the other side he remembered Gimlet and angled off toward the cotton pen to get him.

Keeping Gimlet close by him, he traveled, hidden in tall crops, until he was beyond the house. He'd show up there through the barn lot, and Miss Cherry and Fanchie wouldn't suspect he'd been anywhere. In the barn lot, Gimlet ran to the little ditch that brought water from the artesian well to the pond and began to drink, lapping noisily. Looking at the fresh, clear water made Shim realize he too was dry, hot, and his heart was going so fast he almost had the thumps. This was no condition for him to be in when he met Miss Cherry. He stopped and leaned against a post under the wagon shed to sort of get at himself again.

In the fence corner two mules stood in the shade of a

sweet-gum tree, licking each other's shoulders. He watched them for a minute. They looked so undisturbed and contented he began to wonder why folks didn't have sense enough to keep out of trouble and just enjoy life and all the good things around them.

His heart slowed, and he felt some cooler. Time he got to the well and washed his face and drank about a gallon of cool water, he'd be able to face Miss Cherry. If she hemmed him up with questions about where he'd been, he'd think of some tale to tell her. He straightened his shoulders and started for the orchard gate.

"Come on, Gimlet," he called, "before you founder yourself drinking too much."

chapter ten

THE EIGHT-DAY CLOCK ON THE MANTEL POINTED TO twelve-thirty when Shim got home from school. He laid his books and jacket on a chair, washed his hands in the bowl at the washstand and went to the dining room where the Captain and Miss Cherry were eating dinner.

"Did you tell your teacher you were coming home?" Miss Cherry asked.

"I even asked her permission." Shim grinned, reaching for the bowl of collards and helping himself. "I didn't tell her why, though."

"That wasn't necessary," Miss Cherry said, "but I do think it's only polite to let the teacher know you're leaving, and not just walk off like you do sometimes."

Light feet scraped on the steps and came skipping down the hall.

"Fanchie!" Shim exploded. "I told her she couldn't come, but she must have left right behind me."

The Captain looked at Miss Cherry. "What's she doing home?"

"Afraid she'd miss seeing a new boy, that's what," Shim said. "Hear her? She's going straight upstairs to her room to primp, before she even eats."

"Oh, yes, Dave's bringing that Dobson boy home with him," the Captain said, frowning.

Miss Cherry laid down her fork and said quietly, "Now you all just leave Fanchie alone. Her reason for leaving school is just as important to her as yours is to you, Shim." A little smile came at the corners of her lips. "Your teacher is right young herself, and I expect she'd understand Fanchie's reason for coming home better than she would yours."

Shim grunted. Fanchie might be all keyed up over meeting Dave's new friend, but as far as he himself was concerned he'd like what was on foot a lot better if Jans Dobson wasn't coming. The words *secretary-treasurer* sort of ran around in Shim's mind. He'd never heard them put together that way till Dave had said that's who Jans's father was—secretary-treasurer of the sawmill they were talking about building in Mulberry. They were from California or Oregon or somewhere way out west—rich folks, city folks. This Jans wouldn't know B from bull's foot about the woods.

Dave had met him in school in Mulberry and had been wanting to bring him here to spend a week end ever since. Shim had an idea Miss Cherry had sided with Dave and talked the Captain into letting Jans come. The Captain didn't want to mix with that sawmill crowd any more than Shim did, but, of course, they'd both have to treat him right since he would be a guest. Mack Short was coming too, and he'd be somebody for Shim to talk to, and let Dave have his new friend.

The dogs all started barking, but quit as suddenly as

they'd started. That meant it was Dave and the other two out there now. Miss Cherry called to the kitchen, "They're here, Aggie, and all hungry, I suppose."

Shim hadn't got used to its being Henry's Aggie in the kitchen instead of Kiz. Miss Cherry wouldn't have needed to call Kiz. She'd have heard them and had biscuits in the oven and hot food on the table time they got here. Aggie was big and slow-moving. Shim stopped thinking about Kiz.

They came into the dining room, talking and laughing, Fanchie first, clattering her head off to a black-haired boy almost as tall as Dave and even better built. He had keen blue eyes, and Shim felt that even while he was smiling at Fanchie and replying to something she'd just said he still didn't miss a thing in the room, from the smoldering sticks in the fireplace to the fly thawed out from the night before buzzing against the windowpane. Dave introduced him, and they all took their places at the table, Jans acting as easy and at home as the rest of them, not a bit stiff or awkward like Shim would be in his shoes.

The Captain had stood up to shake hands with Jans and Mack, and he didn't sit back down. "If you all will excuse me," he said, "I've finished eating, and I'll go outside and smoke." He half turned, and stopped. "Dave, you boys will have to walk. I don't want to risk any of my riding stock over where you're going."

Shim and Dave looked at him in quick disappointment. Dave recovered first and said with a half grin, "You must think we're going to run up on that old cat that's been on the warpath all summer and that folks think is the one that killed Matlock."

Shim felt a little wiggle in his shoulders every time he thought about Matlock, a man from down near Mooresville who had borrowed the cabin from the Captain a couple of weeks ago. Two men Matlock took with him brought what was left of him out of the woods. He'd gone down to the lake about sundown to dip up a bucket of water, and a panther had dropped on him from a limb overhead.

The Captain half smiled, but his eyes stayed serious.

"If that's the cat you boys are after, be sure you get him and don't give him a chance to get you. Whenever anybody gets killed like Matlock, tales get started about a varmint bigger and more vicious than usual that did the devilment. In this case, I'm inclined to believe there's something to them and that there's an extra-bold panther over there. It was hardly sundown when Matlock was killed, and that's not like the average panther. Several men on hunting and fishing trips claim one makes a practice of staying around close to their camps, squalling all night and sometimes even in the daytime. And when their dogs get after him he takes time to kill one or two before he runs off. He won't tree, or, if he does, jumps out before anybody gets in shooting distance of him, and that means he's an extra-smart one."

He shoved his empty chair up to the table. "Panthers are all bad, and all dangerous, and there are plenty of them over there. You boys be careful every minute. And it's no place for riding stock."

Miss Cherry was looking up at the Captain, frowning, her mouth half open. Shim knew what was coming. For a little while after something bad happened in the woods she'd fret every time he and Dave left the house with their guns. And the Captain's talk had got her stirred up sure enough.

"Mr. Govan," she said, "are you going to let these children go down there without an older person on hand to look after them?"

"Our boys have looked after themselves in the woods for quite a while, Miss Cherry," the Captain said calmly. "I see no reason to start worrying now. It's only the careless folks who get hurt, and a careless person can blow his brains out on his own front gallery cleaning his gun. These boys can take care of themselves all right. But they'll have to walk. They can't look out for horses."

"What about my horse, Captain?" Mack said. "Papa said I could take him."

The Captain hesitated. "Judge Short knows this country about as well as I do, and he's heard these tales too. If he's willing for you to take your horse, do just as you wish." The Captain walked out of the room and down the hall.

Shim was wishing he hadn't walked so fast coming the two miles from school at Overcup Ridge—six miles more to the cabin on Lake Thursday would go a little hard on his legs—when Jans came up with just about the strangest remark Shim had ever heard.

"That's a good one." Jans laughed. "Your father is willing for you boys to go where it's too dangerous for his horses."

Silence fell around the table. Even Miss Cherry couldn't think right quick of anything to cover such bad manners. Quick as a flash, Jans covered them himself. "I say, I didn't mean that like it sounded. I was just thinking out loud." He turned to Miss Cherry. "I'm always saying the wrong thing, Mrs. Govan, and getting into hot water over it. Please excuse me. I was trying to be funny, I guess, and didn't mean a thing by it."

His eyes, the bluest blue Shim had ever seen, looked so apologetic and his smile was so honest that Miss Cherry couldn't help smiling back. "We can't expect outsiders to understand our ways," she said, "any more than we can understand theirs." The stiffness was gone from her face and everybody's, and Fanchie burst out like she'd been holding her breath.

"You see, Jans, you boys can look out for yourselves, and, besides, you'll be inside the cabin after dark, but the horses would be outside, and no way for you all to protect them from an attacking animal."

"Of course," Jans said. "If everybody would be as nice as you people about helping me, I'd learn not to make so many blunders."

Fanchie blushed and batted her long eyelashes right fast at him. Shim, through eating, asked to be excused. Fanchie made him sick. Besides, he wanted to do what had to be done before Dave had a chance to tell him to. He went through the kitchen to the back gallery. Jans Dobson sure talked easy. If he himself had put his foot in his mouth like Jans had, he'd have been so embarrassed he couldn't have said a word. But, of course, he never would say a thing like that to start with.

Taking down a big pan of cornbread cooling on a high shelf on the back gallery, he went out to the dogyard. When all the dogs were inside, he fastened the gate and began feeding them. He gave only small pieces to Rope and Music, saying to their surprised and disappointed expressions, "A lean dog for a long race. You can't have a full belly and the fun of a fight, too." He half thought they understood him the way Music's lips curled back like she was laughing, and Rope acted frisky and pleased.

By the time he and Dave had changed their clothes, Aggie and Miss Cherry had sacked up biscuits, corn meal, coffee, sugar, salt and a slab of fat bacon for grease. Mack tied the bundles to the back of his saddle and mounted. His little pony-built, dun-colored horse tossed its head and pranced off a step or two, excitedly.

"He knows we're going hunting," Mack said. "Sure am sorry you all have got to walk." He grinned down at them. "Which way, Shim?"

"The shortest way," Shim said. "The main turnrow through the field."

With Mack in the lead, Shim found himself walking beside Jans, with Dave behind them. Shim kept throwing sidelong glances at the gun Jans was carrying. It was a double-barrel shotgun, like his and Mack's, but the stock had him buffaloed. It was so carved up, with streaks of what looked like gold and mother-of-pearl in it, there was hardly any smooth wood showing except for the cheek and the grip.

"How do you like it, Shim?" Dave said. "Isn't that a beauty of a smokepole? Jans's father has an interest in the factory that makes them and got it for Jans's birthday. Costs around a thousand dollars to buy it in a store. I knew that gun would catch your eye."

Dave was wrong about that. It caught his eye, maybe, but that was all. He didn't want a gun all prettied up like that.

"It sure is fancy," he grunted politely.

Beside the turnrow, Henry, with a cotton sack hanging from his shoulder, stopped picking and looked them over. "Great stars," he said, "just look at the hunters—one town boy and one stranger. Where you all heading for? I see you is just taking the panther dogs." He glanced at Rope and Music trotting ahead.

"Lake Thursday," Dave said. "Taking this stranger from way off yonder out to show him how our part of the country looks and what big-cat hunting is like."

Laying off his half-filled cotton sack, Henry started toward home. "You all go ahead, but don't rush yourselves. I'll get my gun and catch up with you down the trail a little piece."

Shim was mighty pleased but surprised. Ever since Kiz was killed, Henry had acted broody, didn't take up any time with him—or with anybody. It flashed across Shim's mind that Miss Cherry might have had time to send Henry word to go with them. He felt better about the trip because Henry was going. His being along would help offset Jans's unwelcome company.

They walked along a little piece in silence, then Jans said, "You people beat anything I ever saw. Walk off from school without an excuse, and now a grown man just up and quits work right in the middle of the day."

"Why not?" Mack said cheerfully.

"Oh, I like it, I guess," Jans said. "I just never saw it done before, and it surprises me."

Beyond the field and in the woods, they found the trail so covered with leaf mold, freshly fallen leaves and dead brush that Shim and Dave had to go mostly by the blazes on trees to keep from losing it. On a sweet-gum ridge they found some grapevines that almost covered the saplings they clung to. Some of them, summer grapes, were dried up and weren't much good; but the possum grapes, not much bigger than duck shot, were just right for eating since the frost. They all stopped to eat a little snack.

Jans pulled off a couple of bunches and soon had his mouth so full he had to quit talking. But not for long. He turned to Shim. "I'll ask you a question they can't answer." He waved a hand at Mack and Dave. "Those boys in Mulberry are always talking away at each other as fast as they can work their jaws. What do they talk about?"

Shim was taken by surprise. Town boys did talk a heap, and not about anything much that he could see, either; but he wasn't going to let on to this outsider that he thought so. Besides, much as Jans talked himself, it was like the pot calling the kettle black. He ducked the question. "I can't tell you unless I hear them," he said politely.

Jans was ready with another question. "Well, why do they shut up like clams when I start talking?"

Shim figured he could answer that one—Jans probably insulted them every time he opened his mouth, like that remark he'd made at the table—but he just shrugged.

"You're no more good to me than Dave and Mack," Jans complained. "It bothers me. Looks like somebody could explain it to me."

Jans was so free with his questions, Shim blurted out one of his own. "Do you think your folks will buy up enough woods to bring a sawmill here?"

"Sure they will," Jans said. "You won't know that one-horse town of Mulberry a year from now."

Shim felt his cheeks drawing like he'd eaten a green persimmon. Just then Henry came in sight, stepping spry as a young goat. "You all cut yourselves some fast walking sticks, and let's get away from here," he said, and took the lead. Mack, on his horse, followed; and the rest strung out behind.

They struck a wide flat of mixed growth—pin oaks, red oaks and post oaks, elms and ironwood. The earth was black where high water had washed the leaf mold away. Walking was easier, and Henry mended his gait. With few roots to step over and overhanging limbs to duck, they were making good time when Dave saw a persimmon tree out to the right of the trail a little ways and went to pick some up.

Shim started to follow when a racket off to their right

stopped him. Rope and Music, who had been ranging out of sight, came running full tilt, with tails tucked, out of a thicket of switch cane thirty steps or so away. They crossed the trail between Henry and Mack and, with men and guns between them and what had scared them, were slowing down when Shim heard the noise of running feet and breaking sticks in the switch cane and, above it, sounds he feared more than anything else in the woods—the harsh grunting and throaty clucking of wild hogs.

Facing the thicket, he brought his gun down off his shoulder. He heard Henry call hoarsely, "Get ready and don't miss." Dave came running and stopped beside him with his pump gun.

Knocking canes and bushes aside, the wild hogs poured out of the switch cane, heads lowered, small eyes gleaming wickedly. Mouths partly open, with that horrible sound coming from their throats, they charged, more and more of them, till it looked like the woods was full.

"Take dead aim," Dave said, and jerked his gun to his shoulder.

Guns spoke, spraying buckshot. Hogs fell, but others ran over them, coming on. The guns spoke again, and more black or spotted bodies fell. Hurrying fast as his fingers could move, Shim unbreeched his gun, pulled out the empties and was trying to shove loads in when he saw hogs going both ways. Most of them had turned back, but two big razor-back boars, long tusks showing and bristles up, were coming straight at him. Dave, with three loads left in his pump gun, blazed away, made two of the prettiest shots Shim had ever seen, and the fight was over.

If anybody spoke, Shim didn't hear what they said. He was looking at Jans's high-priced hardware on the ground near his feet—and Jans wasn't with it. Shim picked it up and unbreeched it. Both loads of buckshot were still in it. He'd have given everything he owned for that gun and its loads a few seconds ago when his own was empty. If it hadn't been for Dave's pump gun . . . Shim snapped the breech shut. Just as he'd expected, Jans had shown his mettle, and it was soft as mud.

They saw him—about ten feet up a scaly-bark sapling, with one leg over a limb and a silly grin on his white face. Dave tried to grin back at him, but his lips were too trembly and stiff. "You used more sense than we did," he managed to say politely.

"Truth, too," Henry said, dropping two loaded shells into his emptied gun. "Old as I is, and went stumbling along here and like to got hit by something we couldn't handle."

Jans dropped to the ground. "I got the idea from Mack," he said. "He looked so safe up on that horse."

Mack grunted. "Lucky I had buckshot in my gun. An old boar would gut this horse with one rake of his tusks if he got to him."

Among the nine hogs dead on the ground was a little spotted shoat, weighing maybe seventy pounds. Dave started toward it. "After a close call and a hard fight, I always like some fresh, tender meat for supper," he said. Henry followed him and they began taking off the hams. Mack got busy making room at the back of his saddle to carry them. All of them but Shim had found something to do to relieve their shame for the one of them who hadn't fired a shot. So it was to Shim Jans spoke, drying his sweating face with a white handkerchief.

"I wouldn't blame any of you if you never speak to me again. I didn't know there were wild hogs this side of India, and when I saw them coming like a breaker rolling in on a beach I was scared out of my wits."

He was honest about it, and looked like he hated himself so bad that Shim couldn't help feeling sorry for him. "They're not the kind you're talking about. These are just hogs that wandered off from their owners and went wild, but they're just as dangerous. We all wanted to climb a tree, but knew there wasn't time." Wanting to end the talk, he called to Henry, "That's a mighty heap of meat we're leaving for the wolves and cats to eat."

Henry was tying the two shoat hams to Mack's saddle. "Better them get et than us," he said.

They came to Wildcat Bayou just above where it curved to run into Lake Thursday and found only a couple of feet of water in it. Mack rode straight across, and the rest of them crossed on a sapling footlog—Jans, by cooning it, on hands and hips, after Dave got down straddle of it and showed him how. None of them were as fresh as they had been, and there wasn't much talking as they walked, single file, stepping over roots and ducking low limbs that threatened their faces.

They passed a little ironwood thicket that gave way to clusters of red-oak bushes, and Henry, still in the lead, called out, "Yonder's the mansion and the Promised Land."

The little two-room cabin sat on a hickory ridge just where the land began sloping down to the lake. The yellow cypress boards of the roof and the white-oak puncheon walls looked bright and clean in the sun's slanting rays. At the front door they unloaded, laying guns on the ground near the wall, hanging hunting coats on nails in the puncheons, or on bushes, whichever was handy. Shim blew through his teeth. "My legs are hurting up to my neck."

Jans walked to the corner of the cabin and stood looking at

the stick-and-dirt chimney. "It's the neatest little house I ever saw. Looks like it just grew here, came right up out of the ground like the bushes and trees."

"Hitch that horse and everybody get to toting out bedding," Henry said, "so it will get the little sun that's left." He shoved open the door, and a damp musty smell hit their noses. "I'm fixing to start a fire in here to air things out."

Shim gathered up the mattress from the first of two bunks on the east wall and put it down again. Once he and Dave had spent the night here and failed to sun the mattresses. Next morning Dave found a small snake that had crawled in through a torn place in his mattress and he'd mashed to death lying on it. Shim didn't want to take any chances. Not finding any tear in this one, he picked it up again and carried it out.

The bedding was all hanging on low limbs or spread out on bushes in the sunshine when Shim noticed that the two dogs were straying a pretty good distance away and sniffing around like they might be trying to smell out a trail. It wouldn't do for them to strike something and start running tonight. He called them, took them into the back room and fastened the door.

Henry had a good fire in the fireplace and was putting water on to boil to wash up the cooking utensils and eating tools. Dave hung the two hams on the wall and said with a grin, "Henry, I bet you looked up in the trees good before you dipped up that water."

"You just watch things close as I does," Henry grunted, "and you'll be all right."

Mack came in the door and dropped his saddle on the floor. "Come on," Shim said, "I'll show you where to put your horse."

They led the horse a few yards west of the cabin, through

a gate and into an enclosure where there were only a couple of small trees but a good supply of switch cane and scattered bushes. Mack slipped the bridle off and, with a piece of cloth he pulled from his pocket, rubbed out all traces of head stall and saddle print in the dun-colored hair, and wound up by giving the legs a good rub. It struck Shim funny to see him working so hard and looking so serious.

"Do you always take this good care of your horses?"

"I do this one," Mack said. "Papa says I think more of this little horse than I do of my folks. Say, what about water?"

"Plenty of it. There's a ditch runs in from the lake," Shim said. "Maybe we'd better walk around the fence, though, to make sure none of the rails are down where he could get out."

They made the round and were coming out the gate when Jans and Dave came by with their guns. "Come on," Dave said. "Jans wants to see where the panther got Matlock."

A few yards from a little clear space on the lake bank used for a boat landing, Dave pointed to a leaning red-oak tree, maybe thirty inches through, its trunk slanting over the landing. "That's it," he said. They all stopped still and looked at it. Shim felt a quiver in his shoulders and wondered again how any man could have been careless enough to walk under that tree without first looking up.

"That cat didn't make more than about a twelve-foot drop," Dave said.

Jans was looking up with his mouth open. "How can you tell?" he said.

Dave pointed. "See that space above the small lower branches and before the bigger ones spread out? There's the only place he could have dropped from without hitting limbs and making a noise. That's where he was—flattened against the trunk, with a clear space for his spring."

Mack and Jans both kind of hunched their shoulders, and to get rid of the feeling in his own, Shim said, joking, "Dave, you cover us while we empty this boat. We may want to use it."

The heavy, flat-bottomed boat, chained to a tupelo-gum sapling, was half full of water. They all took a hold, pulled it out onto the bank, tipped the water out of it and slid it back. There was a whistling of many wings in the air, and, looking up, they saw a flock of wood ducks passing overhead. Across the lake, the ducks circled once and dropped below the treetops. Cupping their wings, they came down like they were being poured, hitting the shallow water among a thicket of elbow bushes and cypress trees.

"Let's go get them," Jans said excitedly.

"Wait till I get my gun," Mack said, starting for the cabin.

"Hold on," Dave said. "No sense in wasting them. We've got plenty of meat, and if we kill ducks now they'll spoil before we get them home. Wait until tomorrow."

"You are the waitingest folks I ever saw," Jans said with a grin to hide his disappointment. "I come out here to kill a lion or something, I thought, and we waste all this daylight doing nothing. Now there's a whole world full of ducks, and you've got another good reason to wait."

Henry's voice came from the cabin. "You all young'uns better rally round here and get that bedding back inside, so's you'll be ready to eat up these good victuals I done cooked."

"That's something we don't have to wait for, Jans," Dave said, and they started at a trot. The smells of fried fresh pork, hot cornbread baked in the Dutch oven, and coffee boiled with good lake water had them in a run by the time they reached the cabin.

After eating more than they needed they sat outside on blocks of wood, waiting for the last light of day to fade out and bring bedtime. Twilight was longer here than at home, because it started sooner. Here the trees hid the sun, while back home in the fields it would still be shining. Full-bellied squirrels were jumping and running on tree limbs, just out of shooting range, playing before going into their den holes for the night.

"This cabin is built right smack on the ground," Jans said. "No foundation at all. What's your floor laid on?"

Studying about the cabin, asking questions, instead of watching and listening and just resting.

"Puncheons, like the walls," Dave said, and set the coal-oil headlight he'd been cleaning on the ground.

"I thought the walls were logs," Jans said in a puzzled voice.

"Puncheons," Dave repeated, and winked at Shim. He knew Jans wasn't going to quit his questions till he was satisfied.

"Tell you the truth," Jans said, "I don't know what puncheons are."

"Well," Dave took a deep breath and said good-humoredly, "you take a big white-oak log and set wedges in it. When you hit the wedges with a maul, they run inward with the grain to the heart. You split off pieces the length of the log. They'll be six or eight inches wide at the bark side, but run in to a point, maybe less than an inch thick where the grain runs into the heart and the puncheon splits away from it." He pointed to the cabin. "Look there, at the corners. You can see they're V-shaped. You get your floor level by sinking one side of the thick edge into a trench in the ground. The walls you just notch and fit the same as you would round logs."

"The same as who would round logs?" Jans said. "I thought I knew something about carpentry, but this is hard to believe.

Why, a man who could build this cabin with just trees, his hands and a couple of crude tools—if he got hold of mill-sawed lumber and up-to-date machinery—why, he could build things folks haven't even thought of yet."

Unexpected as a flash of lightning from a clear sky, there swam before Shim's eyes pictures he'd seen in books of castles and palaces. One of them seemed to swell till it was bigger than a whole town; the sun was shining on it; it was prettier than anything he had ever seen or dreamed about, and it looked like it was made of big slabs of cypress bark, only a hundred times bigger than any he'd ever seen.

"A good man don't need all that stuff," Henry said flatly. "All us brought from home for this cabin was nails and doors." Henry didn't like Jans's bragging about what a man could do with sawmill lumber, and now that his voice had brought Shim back to himself, he didn't either.

Henry was looking Jans over right hard. "Boy, is you ever hunted panthers?"

"Mountain lions a couple of times in Washington," Jans said. "But it wasn't anything like this. We didn't sit around camp wasting daylight like we've been doing."

"Us goes here at the first bust of day in the morning," Henry said.

"I guess we do look mighty lazy to you, Jans," Dave said, "any way you look at it."

Jans thought a minute. "I guess so," he said seriously. "In Mulberry, now, I'm always asking what somebody does for a living, and he doesn't do anything. Folks down here, if they've got anything at all to live on, don't seem to work. They loaf around in stores and on the street, laughing and talking like every day was a holiday."

Shim wondered why anybody, anywhere, would work if he

already had enough to live on, when there were so many pleasant ways to pass the time—hunting and fishing and good friendly talk.

Jans must have figured from the silence that he'd said the wrong thing, because he said quickly, "Maybe you would be as awkward dodging folks on crowded streets in a city as I am in the woods."

Shim, remembering his trips to Memphis and the way folks jostled him on the streets, thought Jans was probably about half right. In the quiet, the craunching sound of Mack's horse eating cane leaves came from the pasture.

Mack shifted his hips on the block he was sitting on and frowned. "My horse sounds kind of lonesome out there. I sort of wish he had some company, but I reckon he's safe."

"He's all right," Henry said. "I ain't never heard of a panther tackling a horse except when high water had done runned the game out of the woods and he got powerful hungry. What I hopes for is that that old panther what got Matlock and what keeps pestering everybody that's comed in this section lately will come close enough here tonight so these dogs will pick up his trail first thing tomorrow morning."

"From what folks been saying, he will," Dave said. "We better lay our plans."

"I been studying about that," Henry said. "Without horses, the best thing we can go by is where we hears the most fuss tonight. You take the one horse we've got and drive, Dave. If the biggest of the squalling is west of the lake, the rest of us will be done spread out around that buckvine thicket up northwest of here, where there's buckvines ten feet high and thick as hair on a dog's back, and trees, bushes and canes so rank the sun ain't never touched the ground. If we hears most of the racket on this side tonight, we'll strike out for where Swimming Slough runs into Wildcat Bayou, and we can get a race started there."

Dave looked at Mack. "It's your horse. Is that all right with you?"

"Sure," Mack said. "You know how to make a drive and I don't. You can handle your dogs better than I could, too."

"You all will have to get up and leave ahead of me and the dogs, so you'll be on your stands before I start out," Dave said. Shim guessed that unnecessary statement was to make everything clear to Jans.

Shim noticed suddenly that the tree trunks around them were blurred and dim-looking. It was dark enough to put a man to using his mind. With their night eyes and good noses, varmints knew somehow that folks weren't a match for them after dark, and it made them bold and dangerous. If the dogs were out here, he could watch them for any sign of danger and be safe, but they were shut up inside. He began raking sticks and leaves together and started a fire.

"Now we're safe," Mack said, "because a panther won't come to a light."

"I'd hate to trust a light for protection," Henry said. "But they tells me if you covers up your head with a quilt or a tin tub or something, a panther won't tackle you."

Jans said, "All you got to do is look him in the eye and he won't jump on you."

"Who's fool enough to try it?" Shim said. "I can't look a dead one in the eye."

Dave stood up, yawning. "I'm going to bed."

The fire in the fireplace was low. Henry lighted a lamp, and the small square room seemed extra light because of the yellow color of the rived cypress strips on the walls, sealing cracks where the puncheons didn't fit close. He set the lamp on the mantel. "It's a funny thing," he said. "I haven't heard a wolf howl or a panther squall yet tonight."

"I noticed that, too," Dave said.

"You stay awake awhile and you'll hear them," Shim said.

Henry dropped a small stick on the fire. "I'm a sap-sucking son of a gun," he said. "We plumb forgot to air the bunks in the back room."

Shim yawned. "We can look through them for varmints and snakes." That was where he and Henry were going to sleep. The other boys were already stretched out on the three bunks, two on one side of the room and one on the other.

Henry was pulling quilts down from the joists overhead. "Me and you sleeps on the floor," he said. "Plenty room here for a couple of pallets."

In pitch-dark, Shim awoke and heard the dogs whining and growling low in their throats. He felt beside the wall for a lantern, lighted it and opened the door into the back room. The dogs were lying on their bellies, their eyes bright, bristles raised.

Jans jumped out of his bunk. "What is it?"

"The dogs say there's some kind of varmint outside." Shim said.

"They do?" Jans said. "How can you tell?"

Henry turned over on his pallet. "Same way you can watch another fellow and tell when the gal you're with is making eyes at him," he said. All these silly questions were beginning to bother Henry, but Jans didn't know it.

"Let's go out and get him," Jans said.

"You just as well be looking for a needle in hell's haystack as for a varmint out in that dark," Henry grumbled. "You all go to sleep. Them dogs'll be smelling something or other all night."

"Stop the racket," Dave mumbled from his bunk, "and let's get some rest."

Shim slept again, and awoke to the best smell on earth—cooking over coals in the fireplace. He raised up on an elbow. The frying pan was sizzling and the coffeepot was boiling, but there wasn't anybody watching them. In the firelight he saw the three boys were in their bunks, but Henry's pallet was empty. He reached for his shoes.

The front door opened and Henry, lantern in one hand, a shotgun in the other, came in out of the first light streaks of coming day. "I never would have believed it," he said, low and slow, shaking his head and hanging the lantern on a nail in a joist.

"Believed what," Shim said.

"That I'd lay up here and sleep like a log, whilst a devilish panther hauled off and killed that horse right under my blasted nose."

The three bunks were suddenly alive, and then empty.

"Claw cuts on his back and big teeth marks in his neck, and that neck broke like snapping off pie crust," Henry mourned.

Mack cussed and grabbed for his pants, then his gun. The others pulled their pants on and were out the door close behind him.

The meat was smoking, burned to a crisp. Henry pulled the frying pan off the coals and poured fresh water into the almost dry coffeepot. Slicing more meat to fry, he shook his head sadly and said again, "I never would have believed it. I done lost my stroke not to have thought about the smell of them fresh shoat hams on that horse's flanks running a panther crazy."

SHIM

The boys were back, Mack in the lead, still cussing, his face pale and looking long as a plow handle. "Turn the dogs out," he said. "And when they tree I want you all to help me shoot that varmint's legs off. Don't kill him, because I want to cut him up in little strips before he dies."

Dave and Jans were sitting down pulling on their shoes they hadn't taken time to put on before running to the pasture. Mack looked down at his own bare feet and dropped his gun on the bed. Grabbing up his socks, he pulled them on without sitting down. Still standing, he managed to work one shoe on, but the laces of the other one had to be loosened before it would go on his foot. He crooked a finger under the lace, pulled, and jerked a hard knot in it. "Hellit to damn," he said, gave a snatch, and the lace broke. He threw the shoe down and grabbed up his gun. "I'll go barefooted," he said through clenched teeth. "Come on. You all are slow as molasses in January."

"Take it easy, Mack," Dave said. "It's too late."

"Too late?" Mack's voice rose so high it cracked. "With those fresh tracks out there, these dogs will have him up a tree in no time."

"And where will we be when they do? Who'll keep him there? You reckon he'll wait for us to get there?" Dave tied his shoes and leaned back. "No, Mack, I know how you feel, but you know well as I do that panther can play ahead of these hounds from now till midnight tonight if he wants to. He could be twenty miles from here. And where would we be—on foot?"

"I don't care if he's forty miles from here and midnight tomorrow night," Mack jerked out angrily.

"Remember what day tomorrow is?" Dave said. "You know we can't be disgraced by being caught hunting on a

Sunday. We've got to be home by midnight tonight."

"Then what are we sitting around here gabbing for? If you all don't give a hoot about my horse being killed, I'll turn those dogs out and go by myself." He started for the door to the back room, but Henry was there ahead of him, blocking it.

"Sit down, boy, and listen to sense," Henry said. "I hates it about that devilish panther getting your horse right under my nose near about as bad as you does. I hates it so bad I ain't fixing to let you go off half cocked and ruin our sure chance to get him."

"What chance?" Mack said, sitting down on the edge of a bunk and looking like he might bust out crying any minute.

"I tracked that varmint up the lake bank a piece," Henry said. "He's headed north, right for that buckvine thicket where us was planning last night we might make a drive this morning. That's where he's laying up right now, waiting for tonight to come so he can start his devilment again."

"And we sit here like knots on a log." Mack jumped to his feet, but sat down when Henry looked at him hard.

"That's exactly how us proves us is smarter than what Mr. Panther is," Henry said. "Yesterday us was going to take a gamble on getting a panther. Today we've got a cinch."

While he talked, Henry poured coffee into cups. He pulled the frying pan off the coals; the meat in it was done to a turn. "You boys cool down. Drink some of this good coffee and eat a little snack. All panthers is smart, but this one has done set his own trap."

All of them but Mack started eating and drinking the good hot coffee. He just sat there, staring at nothing, still in one sock foot, his hands, white-knuckled, still holding his gun. Henry sat down on a chunk by the fireplace, both big hands wrapped around a steaming cup, before he went on.

"You seed the leaves and trash he covered that horse with. Well, he's coming back. Unless we act a fool and turn the dogs out and run him plumb off. What us has got to do is piddle around here today, not doing a thing out of the ordinary to make Mr. Panther suspicious. We let him think he's still kingpin, got everything his way, and he'll be back at first dark tonight, sure as God made Moses. And that's when us gets him. And that's the only sure way."

Mack laid his gun down and reached slowly for his other shoe. Shim knew he had come to his senses, and saw where Henry and Dave were right. But the look of bumfuzzlement on Jans's face hadn't changed a particle. Shim could see how crazy it must look to Jans, who didn't know the woods and the ways of varmints, not to go after that panther while the dogs would strike a hot trail. You couldn't explain anything in a million years to folks who hadn't been raised to it. You could only learn about animals from hunting them and being hunted by them. And you couldn't explain it to Jans, any more than you could explain to him why things he said made folks down here sore. Knowing folks had to grow on you with your skin, and so did knowing varmints.

Jans stood up. "If this is what you folks call big-cat hunting, I can get more action out of a game of checkers." A quick grin, and his next words, took the sting out of his rudeness. "Looks like the only hunting I'm going to see on this trip I climbed a tree and missed out on." He walked over to the frying pan and picked up another piece of the good-smelling pork. "It sure eats good, too."

It was a long day. Dave whittled out a pair of dice from a piece of second-growth ash, and they fooled around with them for a while. But they couldn't stick at anything long. They walked down to the old beaver dam, saw a deer and flushed a flock of young turkeys, but nobody got a shot. The long walk, though, took some of the wire edge off them all.

After dinner they went fishing, but the fish weren't biting much. Shim and Jans got tired of it and quit, with still a couple of hours to be killed before sundown. Shim sat down at the root of a tree on the south slope of the ridge. Jans said he believed he'd go up to the cabin and try to whittle him out some dice like Dave had made. Shim nodded and leaned his shoulders against the tree. He sucked a deep breath of air into his lungs and let it slowly out. Jans's restlessness had worn him plumb down. He settled comfortably back to enjoy a little peace.

Over near the ironwood thicket a big drove of noisy jay birds and peckerwoods were swarming over some pin-oak trees, eating acorns. He watched them idly, wondering what made folks like Jans not able to sit still and just look and wonder at what went on around them but always had to be in a strain to do something about it. He hadn't any more than got settled good when here came Jans, busting out of the cabin toward him.

"Say," Jans said, his blue eyes bright, "I just thought. I heard somewhere that people living down here in the South all have worms of some kind. Maybe that's why you're so slow."

Shim felt a swimming in his head and nearly lost his temper. Catching himself measuring Jans for size, and picking the spot he'd hit him when he came up, he looked quickly back at the birds. Jans didn't mean any harm. He just couldn't keep his mind still any more than he could his body, and whatever came into it he blurted out. Besides, if he did hit him, Jans would never in this world understand why.

SHIM

The jays he was watching suddenly flew off about fifty yards, their squawks different, longer, than just squabbling with other birds. They stopped in a white oak. White-oak acorns were too big for their throats. Something had scared them, and Shim fixed his eyes on the thicket they had flown away from, watching closely for movement.

Movement came from another direction. Dave, carrying three nice bass, and Henry and Mack were coming up from the lake, heading at a good clip toward the ironwood thicket. Shim stood up.

From the bushes Marmaduke Fredell appeared, like he'd come up out of the ground. He stopped stone-still, gun resting in the crook of his left arm. Beside him were two mean-looking animals with cold glassy eyes, half dog and half wolf. That was what had brought Henry and Dave in such a hurry. They had seen him from the lake and knew they had to get those dogs away from here before the dogs picked up that panther trail and ruined everything.

"Howdy, Mr. Swamp Man," Henry called out. "How are you fixed on an average?"

Marmaduke's clothes were dirty and torn and there was a couple weeks' growth of beard on his face, but he stood straight as an arrow and was as fine a built man as you'd ever see. Henry always called him "Mr. Swamp Man" when they met in the woods, and was the only one nervy enough to carry on foolishness with him.

"Good enough," Marmaduke replied in a quiet voice. "How are you?"

"Well," Henry said, "I'm kicking but not high, jumping but not far, weak, but I've got to go."

Marmaduke said, "Huh—I'm after that panther. He cut up one of my dogs the other night."

"You is fishing in the wrong pond," Henry said. "We ain't got him."

"He's here somewhere," Marmaduke said, "because he wasn't around my camp squalling last night."

"I wouldn't know him from the devil's work ox," Henry said, "because I don't know one panther from another, but if I sees him around anywhere I'll let him know what you said."

Marmaduke frowned like he was losing patience. "I'm going to wait here until he squalls, and then I'm going to put these dogs after him. They'll have him up a tree in no time."

Henry changed. He spoke low and slow, and his eyes were narrow. "No, Mr. Swamp Man. Not tonight you won't stay here. Take them dogs back to your own camp, and there won't be no trouble between us."

"Certainly." Marmaduke bowed, polite as a basket of chips. "I didn't aim to intrude." And he turned back the way he had come.

When he was out of hearing, Dave said, "Why did you get so rough with him?"

"That's the only way to change him when he gets his head set on something," Henry said.

"Well . . ." Jans said, and, like the word had squeezed the last breath of air out of his lungs, he took a deep breath to fill them again. "I was looking for a panther to come walking out of that thicket, and out walks as fine a looking man as you'll ever see, except for his whiskers, and with the manners and talk of an educated, highfalutin gentleman. Somebody tell me something."

"Get Shim to tell you," Dave said. "He hasn't hit a lick all evening. We've got fish to clean for supper."

The three fishermen went on to the cabin. Shim sat back down, and Jans squatted beside him.

"Nothing much to tell," Shim said. "He's an aristocrat all right. Born and raised over near Mooresville in the next county. Fine folks, with plenty of money. He was the biggest cotton buyer in the county, with a big, pretty home, a wife and a couple of children. He walked out of his office one day to be gone about fifteen minutes, and it was over two years before anybody saw or heard tell of him again. Then a couple of hunters that knew him reported seeing him in the woods with some wolf dogs. His folks tried to get hold of him and carry him home by force, but those wolf dogs were always on guard. He's been living in the woods five or six years now."

"If those were wolf dogs with him today, I don't blame anybody for letting him alone. Danged if they weren't the meanest-looking brutes I ever saw. What's a wolf dog, anyway?"

"Folks take a bitch that's in season out in the woods and chain her. The he-wolves find her, and her pups are half and half. But don't ask me why Marmaduke took to the woods, because I don't know, and far as I ever heard, nobody else knows."

Marmaduke Fredell's unexpected appearance, and cooking and eating the fish, gave them something to think and talk about besides the slow passing of daylight, and suddenly, for all their waiting, the time was up.

Dave, throwing a handful of fishbones on the fire, stepped to the open door and said in a low, excited voice, "It's first dark."

Mack stood up, shifting his gun from one hand to the other. They'd laid their plans. Mack was to be the one to do the killing, and Dave was going with him just in case anything went wrong. It was only right for Mack to get revenge for his horse, but Shim wished he was going to have a chance at that rascal himself. All the hand he and Jans would have in it was to cover Mack and Dave from behind while they watched the pasture.

Mack's eyes were narrow and bright, but his jaws looked pulled and trembly. From a tight mouth he said, "I'll soon be jerking his blasted hide off."

"You'd better kill him first," Shim said. Mack was so excited he'd forgotten you couldn't ever be dead sure what a varmint would do.

"You take care of your business and I'll take care of mine," Mack flared.

"You boys watch what you're doing out there," Henry warned, "and don't be hollering and whooping at one another when you talks. Talk low. Mr. Panther ain't no fool. I'm fixing to lay down and catch me a little nap of rest. I might have to tote one of you weak-legged young'uns in home tonight if you gives out on the trail."

Shim saw Jans's eyes widen, and laughed. "Henry can sleep anywhere, any time. But don't worry—he never misses a thing."

Dave picked up his gun and walked out. Mack followed him. They went first to the pasture gate and looked over it. Canes, bushes and trees beyond made it dark as pitch all the way across. Turning right, they followed the fence in darkness under the trees, staring across the pasture for a place where they could get enough skylight to see the dead horse.

"This is it," Dave said in a low voice, and stopped. From here they had an opening that showed a streak diagonally across the pasture, a few panels of fence to the right and on out across the lake. Bright stars overhead gave all the light they would need to see anything of size that came near the horse.

They found a couple of chunks and sat down, their guns across their knees, facing the wide cracks between the fence rails that gave them plenty of space to see through.

"Move back some," Dave whispered. "You're too close to the fence to have room to shoot."

"I'll stick my gun through that crack," Mack said.

"And break it," Dave said. "It'll fly up when it shoots and hit that next rail. You better do like I say."

"I'll be durned," Mack mumbled. "I forgot about that." He moved his chunk back a couple of feet. The muzzle of his gun now pointed directly at Dave's middle, and he lifted it quickly and stood it against a little bush almost in front of him. "When he comes," he said, "I'll open up on him, and you just be ready in case something goes wrong."

Dave nodded.

Back in the dark cabin Henry lay stretched out on the floor, his eyes closed. Shim and Jans took their guns and went quietly out. They were about halfway between the cabin and the pasture when they made out the bulks of Dave and Mack sitting still as two stumps over by the fence. Shim stopped and glanced carefully around into treetops bare enough of leaves so that any big animal in them would show up in the starlight. Then he sat down with his shoulders against a big hickory tree.

"You sit on the other side," he said in a low voice. "And don't just watch Mack and Dave. Watch the ground all around you. I'll take care of this side. That panther knows we're here. He'll see and smell us, too, and might take a notion to slip in from this way and tackle one of us. He doesn't have to come back from the same direction he left."

Jans sat down on the other side of the tree trunk, and Shim settled back to watch and listen. Across the lake two owls were hooting at each other. There were splashings in the water that meant a coon, or a mink, or both, were diving for fish. Near by a screech owl began chattering his sad tune. Birds, disturbed by something, chirped and flew, their wings rattling the dry leaves on the bushes where they had been sleeping. From down toward the beaver dam a wolf howled and was answered by another one near the lower end of the lake. It was a lonesome sound.

Jans stuck his head around the tree. "I haven't got animal eyes," he whispered.

"Look for anything moving, or any odd shape that wasn't there a minute ago," Shim said.

He could hear Jans fidgeting around and giving little grunts once in a while, and was sorry that he didn't like the stillness and the noises and just being in the woods, like anybody and everybody ought to. The way everything looked so different in the dark from what it did in the daytime; the way some animals got bold after sleeping all day, and prowled around and got into devilment, or kicked up a lot of fuss one way or another.

Jans twisted around again. "It's getting late," he said. "My legs have gone to sleep. I don't believe that panther is coming back."

Up the ridge about a hundred yards an owl hooted twice and stopped short. "Hush," Shim said, and his muscles tightened. That wasn't right. When an owl started hooting it generally hooted eight, sometimes as many as twelve, times, unless something scared it. Something unusual was going on. He widened his eyes to see better, and parted his jaws to hear better.

At the fence, Dave shifted his tired hips on the hard chunk. Mack did the same, and rubbed a hand across his heavy eyelids. He fixed his gaze back on the pasture and felt like he'd been hit a hard blow in the chest. Like something from nowhere, a long shape was sailing over the fence. It dropped inside the pasture without a sound. His eyes glued on it, Mack grabbed with both hands for his gun. His aim was bad; his right hand closed on nothing, and the knuckles of his left struck the barrel, knocking it off the bush. He lunged to get it, and his elbow hit Dave's gun stock, driving its muzzle into the spongy ground.

Dave jerked his gun up and pushed a finger into the muzzle. It was packed full of dirt—useless. "Kill him, quick!" he said. Mack, down on hands and knees, didn't move.

"Mack, what's the matter?" Dave's jaw trembled and he knew he was scared, in reach of sudden death and holding a useless weapon. He lunged, frog-fashion, grabbing Mack's gun on the ground, but two strong hands were keeping it there. "Let me have it!" Mack didn't move. Dave jerked, but Mack, crazed with fear, had frozen it. Dave lit out in a dead run for the cabin. He'd have to get another gun, or clean the dirt out of his.

Shim, on his feet, his eyes big as saucers, saw Dave passing tree trunks like a streak. When he was nearly halfway to the cabin, Mack straightened up and lit out after him. Shim's straining eyes could find nothing else moving. A couple of heartbeats changed fear and confusion to curiosity. This was his chance to see what was going on. He ran on tiptoe to the fence, looked over into the pasture and was scared so bad that he wanted to turn and run, himself, but he couldn't move.

He saw the big, long body first, then the round head, looking big as a water bucket and facing him. The terrible eyes, their glitter hidden by darkness, were aimed right at his own and might be coming on him. Two leaps would cover the distance.

He tried hard to move—a foot, a shoulder, or any part of him that would start his arms to working. He managed to move a shoulder, and his arms did work; but not right, when he tried to take aim. His gun jerked and waved around at the treetops; he was going to miss if he fired.

"Shoot before I kicks your devilish rump." Henry spoke from right behind him. Instantly Shim saw the big round head and long body lined up with his sights, and he pulled the trigger.

By lantern light they looked the dead panther over, and put away their knives. The skin was ruined. Much of the hair was gone, and in its place were ugly scars. He was a big one, but not old, because his teeth weren't worn down any. Mack opened his knife again and said the first word that had been spoken since the lantern light had fallen on the scarred body.

"I'll take one of the ears. It's got hair on it."

"I'll take the other one to Gimlet," Shim said, opening his own knife.

Henry stared down at the panther like he was studying about something. "So help me, Lord," he said. "You all done killed the rascal what killed that woman about a year ago down on the Yazoo River. There's no two ways about it. He's the only one would have a hide messed up this-a-way."

Shim and Dave knelt down for a closer look.

"Yes," Dave said, "here's shot holes. He's been carrying a heap of lead around in him besides those scars from burns."

Mack and Jans were looking questioningly at Henry.

"This woman," Henry said, "was carrying some fresh deer meat to a neighbor living on t'other side of a little skirt of woods. It was twixt sundown and dark, and she ought to have knowed better but didn't. A panther got her. Next day folks gathered up about a wagonload of bear traps and set them, then hung a piece of deer meat in a bush right amongst all them traps. That night the panther comed back and two traps got hold of him.

"Folks was so mad and heartbroke over the woman, they decided to burn that panther alive. They piled brush around him and set it afire. When Mr. Panther was about half cooked he all of a sudden got stout enough to break aloose, and he left there. Got plumb away, with all of them shooting at him. I reckon he's hated folks the worst sort since then, and that's how come him so bold he got Matlock and laid around camps bantering and disturbing folks night and day with his squalls."

"I wonder why he didn't holler last night?" Dave said.

"Varmints is smart enough to fool you, sometimes," Henry said.

The scarred-up body somehow looked different to Shim, and he didn't feel so proud that he had made the kill.

Staring down, Jans said slowly, "I guess, as he saw it, he had a right to hate people."

Shim suddenly felt a wondering, warm feeling for Jans. He had put into words a sadness that was confusing Shim for the first time in his life. He'd been raised knowing you had to kill or be killed. He still knew it; but he pulled from his pocket the ear he had cut off and tossed it to the ground. "I don't believe Gimlet wants that ear after all," he said.

"I'll take it then," Mack said, and picked it up. He was still a little low-voiced over the way he had acted.

"Go ahead," Shim said. "And if it'll make you feel any better, you killed this panther, Mack, as far as any of us will ever tell it."

Dave turned toward the cabin. "We better get to cleaning up that back room so we can leave here. We got some hard, fast traveling to do to make it home before twelve."

"Yeah, and I want a lantern in front and one behind while we do that traveling," Mack said.

chapter eleven

FIRES BURNED IN BIG FIREPLACES IN EVERY ROOM OF THE lower floor of the Beckhams' house, and light from swinging lamps and chandeliers shone on well-polished furniture and dressed-up folks. Through the open door of the room where the older women sat chatting and swapping gossip Mrs. T. Parks Early and Miss Cherry could see across the hall and into a corner of the parlor, where the dancing was going on.

One of the skipping, turning couples broke at the door and walked out into the hall, red-faced and laughing. The man was a stranger.

Mrs. Early's chin went up and she spoke deep in her throat. "I can't see what the Beckhams were thinking of, inviting such people to their Christmas party." She let her breath out like she was in misery. "Sawmill folks, and from nowhere."

"That's a Mr. Garret Askew," Miss Cherry said, "and he brought the Calhoun girl from town."

Shim hung a leg over the arm of Miss Cherry's chair and

SHIM 215

said, "All that good music, and nobody here but grown folks."

Miss Cherry reached up and pulled his ear. "Go back in there and dance, you overgrown hulk."

Cousin Salina Ferguson, sitting straight as a ramrod, said, "I don't know what the world is coming to. Some of the best families in Mulberry are associating with those—" she broke off like she couldn't find a word that suited her, and sniffed— "those people you spoke of."

"Maybe," Miss Cherry said, "they feel sorry for these strangers so far from home and it Christmastime."

Shim crossed the wide, high-ceilinged hall and stood against the wall in the parlor, sizing up the dancers and trying to protect his toes from their moving feet—especially Dave's, Uncle Ben's and Fanchie's. They were deliberately trying to step on him when they passed. Wick's father pushed by him and on to open a window, so the room wouldn't get too hot. There was a big fire in the fireplace and the night wasn't much cold to start with.

Shim figured out a round of dances for himself. First he'd dance with Jane, and then Josie, Ferguson. Anne Calhoun next, then Betty Lou. None of them were any taller than he was, and that would take care of his duty dances.

The game he liked, of flagging and being flagged, finally brought his list to the last one, Betty Lou. He waited against the wall until she came by. Mr. Garret Askew was dancing with her. Shim stepped out and tapped him on the shoulder. The music stopped and the three of them were standing in a close V—one hadn't quite turned Betty Lou loose, and the other hadn't exactly got hold of her.

Shim, holding her left hand, was embarrassed and, with a silly grin, dropped it. He started to walk away, but Mr. Askew stopped him. "We were just going for some punch.

Please join us." He said it plain and friendly, and like he was talking to somebody his own age.

Shim mumbled a "Thank you, sir" and stepped to the other side of Betty Lou.

At the door they saw J. Ney Ward going down the hall, hat in hand; his cutaway coat was unbuttoned, showing a heavy gold watch chain that reached across the front of his purple vest from one pocket to the other. He was late, and about three sheets to the wind. Wick was showing him to the room where the men left their hats and shooting irons.

In the guest dining room the long table was loaded with food—platters of wild turkey and thin-sliced ham, every kind of cake you could think of, and at either end a big cut-glass bowl filled with punch. When Shim and his two companions were served they sat down in chairs against the wall to eat and drink. In the corner near them the houseboy stood beside a small table, attending a big pewter-colored bowl. That was eggnog.

"I want you both to come to the ball we're giving in town sometime this winter," Mr. Askew said. "The music will be the best Memphis has got, and we'll dance till dawn."

Shim couldn't believe that what he heard was meant for him. He was too young for a big ball—music from the city and all-night dancing. But Betty Lou said, "It sounds delightful, Mr. Askew, and I'll be depending on you, Shim, to see that I'm not a wallflower."

J. Ney came in with Anne Calhoun and, leaving her at the long table, went to the eggnog bowl.

"Shucks," Shim said, "I can't dance well enough to go to a ball."

"Nonsense, boy," Mr. Askew said. "Don't believe that for a minute."

Betty Lou laid her cake on the plate and patted Shim's arm. "Anybody would think you were one of the grown dancers, Shim. I'd just as soon dance with you as anybody—except Ben," she whispered close to his ear.

"Mr. Dobson is going to arrange for the biggest hall in town," Mr. Askew was saying, "and of course he's taking care of all expenses, so we won't have a thing to worry about."

Shim wasn't used to hearing folks mention money, come right out with talk about expense. It made him think of Jans Dobson. All these sawmill folks just blurted things right out, never thinking about manners. Still, there was something about them that was exciting and made you feel extra important and alive. He was going to that ball, and said so.

"Fine," Mr. Askew said. "The invitations will be sent out in a few weeks."

Anne and J. Ney took seats a couple of chairs away. The idea of getting a written invitation was another pleasant thought to Shim. J. Ney took a spoonful of nog from his mug and said importantly, "I've bought new furniture and a bigger chandelier for my dining room, Miss Anne. Maybe I'll give a party sometime soon."

Mr. Askew said, "I understand this house has another dining room and kitchen across the back hall from this one. I wonder if we three could go over and see them. I never saw a house with separate ones for parties."

Betty Lou hesitated. "Well . . . the dining room maybe, but people here don't allow visitors in their kitchens."

Mr. Askew looked surprised and began apologizing.

On the other side of Shim, J. Ney was leaning forward and talking right into Anne's face. "If I had a beautiful girl like you to act as hostess, I'd give a party folks wouldn't forget."

Anne hadn't said a word, and her face looked like it was

carved out of white rock. J. Ney's trying to get thick with her didn't suit her at all. Uncomfortable at overhearing it, Shim half turned his back, sitting sideways in his chair. Standing over by the table, Wick's mother was talking to Wick and Ben. Shim guessed she had seen Anne's embarrassment and would try to do something about it; and sure enough, it wasn't but a minute till Ben, wearing a big smile, came over and began a conversation with J. Ney. Shim admired Ben for chancing it, remembering that the last time he'd seen those two together they'd been trying to kill each other. But it worked out fine. J. Ney was friendly as could be, and seemed tickled to have a bigger audience for his bragging.

Shim collected glasses and plates from Mr. Askew and Betty Lou, and while he was gone to the table with them Wick took his seat by Betty Lou. Shim drifted back to the parlor.

The music was a slow waltz, and Shim, glancing around, saw Anne Calhoun dancing with Wick. Ben and Wick between them had managed to rescue her from J. Ney. Watching her feet, he decided she was the smoothest dancer on the floor right now, and, since a boy going to a big ball pretty soon needed practice in smoothness, he started across the floor to flag her. But he was a couple of steps too slow. J. Ney was ahead of him.

At J. Ney's tap on his shoulder, Wick, of course, had to break. He did and would have walked off, but Anne caught his arm, saying, "Come back here, Wick Beckham. What do you mean by leaving me this way?" J. Ney's eyes widened, and his face turned red as a beet. Wick looked plumb blank, but Anne held onto him, and after a second he caught her and danced off.

Somebody bumped into Shim, almost knocked him off his feet, and he heard Dave say, "You must think you're out in the woods somewhere." He didn't feel like making any smart answer, because a pulse was beating pretty heavy in his stomach. He wondered who all had seen what had just taken place when J. Ney flagged Wick and Anne wouldn't dance with him. He worked his way through the dancers and went out onto the front gallery, where he backed up against the wall just outside the rays of light coming through the open hall doors. He was mighty uneasy that J. Ney was going to make trouble before the evening was out, over the insult he'd got. Anybody else would take it and keep quiet, because it was Anne who had refused to dance with him and it wasn't Wick's fault. But J. Ney didn't take insults. He was fighting mad and was going to take it out on somebody.

The Captain and some other men were standing around near the top of the steps, smoking and talking. Shim heard Mr. Askew say, "I've been hoping somebody would kindly tell me the legend for which this lovely house is famous."

T. Parks Early, leaning against the white column at the right of the steps, said, "It will be a pleasure, sir. It's one of the most baffling and tragic things that ever happened here in the Delta."

He turned and tapped his pipe against the palm of his hand. Little sparks of burning tobacco sank slowly through the darkness and were blotted out when they hit the damp ground five feet below. Wondering how much T. Parks would tell to a stranger, Shim listened closely to the tale he'd heard many times.

"It was a good many years ago," T. Parks said, "long before the Beckhams bought this place. Folks named Lorance owned it, mighty fine folks, with one child, a daughter, named Suenette. She was engaged to a young man named Brantley—another fine old family around here in those days. Time came for the wedding festivities and folks arrived from long distances to stay the week out. So the night before the wedding was to take place the house was full to overflowing with guests, good music, food and drink.

"The rehearsal for the wedding over, the music struck up and dancing started. But the betrothed couple went out on the side gallery to be by themselves for a few minutes, and in those few minutes, sir, the lives of two entire families were ruined. Nobody will ever know what took place between those two. Nobody noticed anything out of the way when they rejoined the others. They came around that corner right yonder—" he pointed to where the side gallery joined the front one—"dancing together smooth as glass, as fine-looking a couple as you'll ever see. He was looking pale, some said afterwards, but nobody thought that out of the ordinary because a man in love is always off color in some way or another, and if ever two young people were head over heels in love, Suenette and Brantley were.

"They got right about even with where we're standing now when some fellow flagged them. It seemed that was exactly what Brantley wanted, for without a word or glance at Suenette he walked down the hall. He stopped in the dining room just long enough to drink a tumbler of whisky and pour himself another one, which he took with him and disappeared through the kitchen door.

"Everybody was having a fine time. All the young blades were giving Suenette a big rush, and she, herself, was so gay and laughing that nobody missed Brantley. That is, they didn't until along about midnight, when Suenette suddenly turned up missing. Folks got to inquiring around, then, and it seemed nobody had laid eyes on Brantley since he went out the kitchen door a couple of hours before.

"They searched the house and grounds and found no sign of either of them. By that time Suenette's folks were frantic, and men got lanterns and started out. They picked up Brantley's trail in the back yard and it led across the field and into the woods. Suenette's tracks were there too, some of them right inside his. When they first noticed hers, about half the men wanted to go back, figuring the young'uns had decided to run off somewhere and get married, just for a joke or something, and they ought to let them go. On second thought that didn't hold water. If running off together was what they were up to, she wouldn't have waited a couple of hours before starting after him. It was pretty plain that she was following him the way we were now following the two of them. Their tracks led into the woods to a footlog across a bayou, half a mile or so from the house. Brantley had crossed the log and gone on. Suenette's tracks stopped at the log.

"They found her there, in the bayou, her neck broken. She had dived head first off the footlog onto an old drift of logs just under the water. A couple of days later they found Brantley's horse in a livery stable over at the depot and learned that Brantley had caught a train there, a few minutes after Suenette disappeared from the house, the night of the rehearsal. She had never overtaken him. Why he had left, why Suenette had followed him as far as the footlog and then killed herself, nobody even guessed. No word ever came from Brantley to his folks, and in a few months his family, and hers too, pulled up stakes and left here.

"Then, ten years from the day he disappeared, Brantley showed up in Mulberry. He looked twenty years older instead of ten, and the banker was the only man he talked to. He went straight to the bank and asked about his folks and the Lorances. When the banker told him they'd both left the country years ago he was surprised, said he'd heard nothing from them and seen nobody from around here since he left. He didn't tell the banker where he'd been, but evidently it was a long ways off. He never mentioned Suenette, and of course the banker didn't.

"What he did do, when he found the bank owned this place, was to buy it. That same day he hired a rig to bring him out here. He ate supper with the caretaker, who lived in a little house in the back yard, and got him to put up a bed in this big old empty house. Told him he hadn't slept in six months but knew he could sleep here and was back to stay.

"But about midnight that night he woke the caretaker and asked to borrow his gun, dogs and headlight so he could go coon hunting. Said he couldn't sleep. Before day the dogs came back, alone."

T. Parks paused and cleared his throat, and Shim wondered how anybody could be so long-winded. He would string this out for another half hour. Shim could have told it in half a dozen sentences.

"Well, sir," T. Parks went on, "they went out hunting Brantley, of course. And they found him—by the same footlog where they'd found Suenette ten years before. He'd come to his end exactly like she had. His neck was broken from diving off onto the same drift. Plenty of folks won't be caught in those woods after dark till this good day—claim he was tolled to his death by ha'nts. You see, Brantley never knew that Suenette was dead, say nothing of how she died."

Shim didn't hear any more, because J. Ney and Ben, arm in arm, came out of the hall and stopped at the opposite side of the steps from the others. J. Ney, drunk enough to be unsteady on his feet, yet cautious enough about approaching the edge of the high gallery, reached out both hands to the big column to brace himself while he turned and rested his shoulders up against it.

"I've been insulted, sir, insulted," he said to Ben. He'd been hitting the pop-skull so hard his tongue sounded thick.

Ben spoke, in the pacifying voice he used when trouble was in the air. "Maybe it was a mistake—unintentional."

"He made a mistake, you're right about that," J. Ney said. "Wick thinks he's smart. He don't know who he's fooling with." He jerked his shoulder straight. "Go get him. I'm going to mash his mouth."

"Sure, I'll go after him," Ben said without stirring. "But Wick's so hardheaded. Why don't you wait and whip him tomorrow?"

J. Ney's shoulders kept sagging, and he kept trying to straighten them. "Going to whip him now. Bring him out to the gate."

"Trouble is," Ben said, "Wick's mighty contrary and doesn't like to take a whipping. I tried him once."

Shim looked hard at J. Ney's hipline, but could see no bulge in the coat, no print of a shooting iron.

J. Ney stiffened and glared at Ben. "If you're my friend, do what I say. If you aren't, say so."

"Whatever you call for is as good as done," Ben said positively, but he still didn't go. He was doing his best to keep the conversation going and wear J. Ney down, but Shim didn't believe it was going to work much longer.

He hotfooted it back to the dining room and went straight to the eggnog bowl. The houseboy, about to serve him a glass, noticed who he was and said, "Nothing but grown folks drink here."

Shim said in a low voice, "Come show me Mr. J. Ney's hardware."

The houseboy thought that over for a second. "Is he acting up?"

"About ready to go on the warpath," Shim said.

"Then we better fix the shooting iron," the houseboy said.

In the room where hats and overcoats hung, or were piled on the bed, the houseboy pulled open the top dresser drawer. A lot of shooting irons lay in it, and Shim was glad his pepperbox wasn't among them to be laughed at by the owners of these .38s, .44s and .45s. The houseboy, who had seen them all when they were left there, pointed and said, "That's his'n." It was the same little .38 J. Ney had shot at Ben with that time on the lake.

Shim emptied the cartridges out and, holding them in his hand, counted them to make sure none were left in the cylinder. He placed the pistol carefully back where he had found it and went out.

In a corner of the parlor he found Ben and Wick, standing close together and talking. "Try to tell him," Wick was saying, "that I can't fight here at my own house—unless I have to. Tomorrow, and anywhere he says. Tomorrow I won't be his host."

Shim held his hand up before them and opened it. "I took these out of his pistol."

Ben whistled, louder than the band was playing.

Betty Lou, pale-faced and big-eyed, was beside them. "Go up in the attic, under the house, anywhere, and hide until he leaves. Please, Ben. Don't go back out there where he is." She slipped her arm in his.

Ben gave it a quick squeeze. "You're charming tonight, honey, but right now you look like a little scared fawn. Stop spying on me and worrying your pretty head about J. Ney. He's mighty fond of me tonight, and I'm in no danger at all.

Wick is the boy J. Ney's mad at tonight, and you've given me the very idea we need. Wick is going to hide out."

Betty Lou stood there looking at him, more scared than Shim had figured she would ever be, because women never did seem to get scared when men did.

"That's right, Betty Lou. I'm the one he's after," Wick said. "And when he finds out his pistol has been unloaded—by Shim here—he'll probably blame that on me, too."

Shim's face got hot as a skillet. Trying to keep down trouble, he'd just given J. Ney another excuse to jump on Wick. He looked down at the cartridges in his hand. "I'll go put them back."

"No, you won't." Betty Lou grabbed them from his hand. One dropped on the floor and she scooped that one up too. "You did exactly right, Shim. And I feel safer about you, Ben, than I have all evening. I tell you what I think. I think J. Ney is only pretending to be all that drunk, so he can get an excuse to hurt you."

Shim sidled along the wall and close to the band, feeling heavy-hearted because he had put his foot in his mouth and it was too late to straighten it up. Betty Lou had seen to that. The fiddle, mandolin, trombone and bass fiddle, loud in his ears, sort of made him forget.

The crowd was thinning out. Folks were beginning to leave. The band played "Home, Sweet Home" for a minute or two and switched it from waltz to two-step time. Dave called from the door. "Get your top piece, Shim, and let's go."

Ben was standing beside the empty surrey when Shim got there. It wasn't necessary to light the dash lamps, because a half-moon was shining brightly down from a little east of south in a clear sky. Well-loaded rigs were driving away from the fence, women calling last good-nights back and forth.

There were only two saddle horses over at the hitching rail—Ben's and J. Ney's. J. Ney was working and grunting trying to mount his.

Dave spoke in a low voice. "Thank goodness he's leaving."

"What did it?" Shim said.

"I told him Wick had gone off somewhere, but that I would arrange for them to meet and settle their differences tomorrow. He was happy as a lark, because he figures he had scared Wick away from home. Sent me after his overcoat and hat. I neglected to bring his pistol, so that's working out all right. He's plumb drunk, though, and somebody's got to see he gets home. Guess I'll have to do it."

J. Ney finally made it into the saddle and rode off, swaying from side to side. Ben got on his own horse. "Tell the Captain I'm following J. Ney," he said. "Can't let him fall off and maybe lay out all night. It's getting colder every minute, and he'd catch pneumonia."

The Captain, Miss Cherry on the front seat with him, held the horses to a walk on the rutty, moonlit road. On the back seat, Dave, Shim and Fanchie, disappointed that the frolicking was over, were silent, the sound of talking and music still in their ears and the movement of dancing in their muscles.

The Captain broke the silence. "I'm going to the city day after tomorrow."

"Which one?" Miss Cherry said.

"Get me a new suit to wear to the ball in town," Shim said.

The Captain answered Miss Cherry first. "I won't know till tomorrow whether Jackson or Memphis. Shim, have you got above the new suit I bought you in the fall?"

"I'll have to have long pants for a ball," Shim said. "I'm plenty big."

"Remind me before I leave," the Captain said, and looked sideways at Miss Cherry.

Fanchie and Dave were giggling, but Shim pretended not to notice it. The Captain would get the suit. He began humming a new piece the band had played tonight—silly words, about "a hot time in the old town tonight," but it had a good strong beat and he began patting his foot in time.

They were driving along the bank of Haphazard Bayou now, and the moonlight, coming through bare treetops, shone on the road in irregular streaks and patches. Reaching the ford, where the trees had been cut down and the road was in full moonlight, they saw J. Ney's horse standing to one side, riderless. The Captain pulled up and stopped. Shim felt a flash of uneasiness about Ben, before he saw him out in the bayou, water halfway up his horse's sides. Ahead of him, J. Ney, water up to his waist, was wading.

"Come back out of this cold water," Ben said. "It'll ruin your clothes and give you pneumonia."

J. Ney looked back over his shoulder, stumbled, caught himself and said thickly, "Come on, Ben. Cool off. I'm hot. Aren't you hot, Ben? Let's take a swim."

Ben leaned forward over the saddle horn and caught his collar. J. Ney was still arguing, but Ben, turning his horse, partly led and partly pushed him back to the bank.

J. Ney walked straight to the surrey. "Sure am glad you all showed up," he said through chattering teeth. "Come on and take a swim with me and cool off."

The Captain said quietly, "You children get out and give him the back seat."

One good thing about the mess was that everybody was so friendly. Fanchie sat in Miss Cherry's lap. Ben helped J.

Ney into the back seat and got in beside him. They spread Ben's and the Captain's overcoats over him to keep the wind off. It was already nearly cold enough to frost, and, taking the chance of breaking an axle on the rough road, the Captain put the horses to a trot. Shim and Dave came behind on the two saddle horses.

Two little carriage lamps, one on either side of the hall doors, lighted J. Ney's front gallery. The houseboy opened the outer gate at the road and trotted along beside the surrey to the yard fence. He opened the little gate and waited.

J. Ney, bedraggled in his soaking clothes and nearly too cold to talk, stood still long enough to take off his hat, bow a polite good night to Miss Cherry and Fanchie and thank them for the ride. The Captain, Ben and the houseboy went into the house with him. He needed warming up and putting to bed.

Shim and Fanchie climbed into the back seat. "Wait a minute," Miss Cherry said. "That seat must be sopping wet." Fanchie let out a squeal about ruining her dress, and Shim spread out the two damp overcoats to protect them before they sat down. Dave stood on the ground, on first one foot and then the other, his shoulders drawn up against the cold.

They waited so long that Miss Cherry finally said, "Get in, Dave, before you catch your death of cold. We'll go on. The Captain can borrow a horse and come on behind us. It's getting cold as fludgeons."

"Wait just a minute," Dave said, "and I'll go in and see what's keeping them."

He wasn't in the house but a few minutes before he and the Captain came out and climbed into the surrey. The Captain gathered up the reins and started the horses.

"Well, it looks like old sores have healed," he said. "J.

Ney shook hands with us and said he'd never had better friends." He laughed. "He's mighty thick with Ben. That's what took us so long. The houseboy couldn't do a thing with him. Nobody could, except Ben. J. Ney wouldn't take off a stitch of those sopping clothes unless Ben took off something first. Ben had to strip naked as a jay, a piece at a time, so we could get J. Ney's clothes off. He kept insisting Ben spend the night with him. But he went out like a light soon as we got him on the bed. Ben's about got his own clothes back on, and he'll be out in a minute."

The surrey had made the loop of the driveway and was heading back toward the road when Ben came down the high steps. He got as far as the gate when they heard J. Ney call his name. The Captain stopped. Ben turned.

J. Ney, pants pulled on over nightshirt, stood on the gallery with a long, black single-action horse pistol in his hand. "You dirty scoundrel," he called, his voice clear as a bell, no thick tongue, no chattering teeth. "I'll stop you from interfering with me once and for all." He pulled the hammer back with his thumb and raised the big .45 pistol.

Ben, in one movement, pulled his .38, stuck his right shoulder forward, spread his feet and bent his knees. Shim saw sparks fly out of J. Ney's .45, a little pale-blue blaze turn upward at the muzzle and vanish, and the noise of the explosion beat on his ears. It was sort of like boys in a Roman-candle fight, because Uncle Ben's small pistol, a double-action, answered with two flashes, one right after the other. J. Ney looked like he was working at the hammer of his pistol, pulling it back again, but he didn't fire; he just stood for the bat of an eye, then dropped the .45 and, slowly, like he was doing it on purpose, partly fell and partly laid back on the floor.

The Captain and Dave jumped out of the surrey, the Captain calling, "Ben, are you hurt?"

The answer, like it was squeezed out of Ben's throat, didn't sound like him at all. "No. The bullet tore a hole in my coat, though. He'd have got me if I hadn't turned sideways."

Miss Cherry gave a long sigh like she'd been holding her breath a good while, and Fanchie began to scream. Shim caught her by the shoulders and shook her till she cut the fuss down to sobbing.

Dave stopped beside Ben. The Captain went on up the walk, slowly, his shoulders extra straight, and stepping short and cautiously. He climbed the tall steps and stood looking down at J. Ney. There was no movement on the floor. He stooped, and by the way he got up and started back Shim knew it was all over, that J. Ney was dead.

The Captain spoke to Ben. "Get in the surrey and go to my house with Cherry and the children. I'll take your horse and notify the neighbors."

Ben, shoulders drooping, moved like he was too tired to walk. When he climbed in the back seat beside Fanchie, Miss Cherry reached back, trying to loop her arm around his neck, but he sat down and was out of her reach. She took a firm grip on his knee. "Drive on, Dave," she said, "but watch for the ruts."

Shim imagined he could taste a mixture of gunpowder and blood in the back of his throat. He swallowed hard.

They were a pretty good little piece down the road before Dave broke the silence. "He's been looking for a chance to get you ever since you introduced him to the sawmill men that bought his woods."

"I can't believe that," Ben puzzled slowly, in a voice that still didn't sound like his. "He knew I had nothing to do with the price they agreed on. No, I can't believe it. Not friendly as he was just a few minutes ago, begging me to stay all night with him. I thought he was asleep when I shut the door. Maybe that woke him up, and the liquor had him crazy enough to kill. Or it could have been hurt pride because I wouldn't stay. I don't know. We'll never know."

Shim remembered Betty Lou saying at the dance that she didn't believe J. Ney was as drunk as he was making out like. Suddenly Shim didn't believe it either. It was like the Captain said: easy-got money ran folks crazy with greed. J. Ney had got a big stack of money for woods he'd never expected to get anything for. He'd been bragging about fixing to quit farming and move to town, he was so rich. But he hadn't been satisfied. And now he was dead. And Ben might have been.

Ben believed J. Ney was just liquor crazy and didn't know what he was doing. When Betty Lou had insisted he was still after Ben, Shim had thought she was just like all women, harboring grudges that men forgot. But maybe J. Ney hadn't. He was mighty clear-tongued and light-footed when he came out on the gallery just now, and he was sober enough not to shoot Ben in the back. Shim's head hurt trying to figure it out.

"Do any of you all reckon he could have been just pretending to be all that drunk?" he asked uncertainly.

"You children quit worrying Ben," Miss Cherry said firmly, and squeezed Ben's knee. "He's carried out the first law of life—to defend himself—and it certainly wasn't of his choosing."

"J. Ney was always looking for trouble, drunk or sober," Dave said, "but I didn't think he'd play it so dirty. If you hadn't been quick as lightning——"

"You mustn't speak ill of the dead," Miss Cherry said

quickly, "and you can't undo what's done. Besides, I wouldn't be surprised if J. Ney isn't now getting the first rest he's had in several years."

Shim was puzzling over what she meant by that when a wheel dropped into a deep rut with a hard jolt. The surrey careened and righted itself.

Ben sort of tried to laugh, and said shakily, "You must be trying to cripple us, Dave."

Dave, following Ben's lead in trying to ease the pressure bearing down on them all, said, "When we get home, Ben, I want you to teach me that figure you cut when you found yourself looking into the barrel of that forty-five."

It didn't work. Nothing could lighten the pressure of a killing—even one like this that there had been no way on God's earth of getting around.

Miss Cherry suddenly took her hand off Ben's knee and turned around straight in her seat to hide a gush of tears.

chapter twelve

DAY BROKE ONE MORNING ON A STRANGE AND UNFAMILiar world. While folks slept, snow had covered the black loamy land with a thick layer of white. Inches of it covered housetops and the upper sides of dark, bare tree limbs. Excited children ran, whooping, outdoors, those of them who had seen snow before carrying big spoons and pans to scoop up the soft cold whiteness and carry it into the house to make snow cream.

Grown men came out on their galleries, thinking of the extra work it would take to keep animals and stock from suffering in this weather they were not prepared for. At the sight of the muffling whiteness changing completely every familiar thing, they felt wonder and excitement stir in their chests. Here and there one of them turned loose an undignified ringing yell that echoed for miles across the cold woods and fields. Inside the houses women moved around getting breakfast, their feet light and skippy like children's and their eyes extra bright.

Both big and little flakes were so thick in the air you could see hardly any distance, until well past twelve o'clock when a cold wind blew out of the north and by dusk-dark had frozen everything hard.

That night houses began to pop and boom like somebody was beating on the fourteen-inch sills or the attic rafters with a big sledge hammer, and more than one man, thinking somebody was trying to tear his house down, ran outside with his gun to stop it.

The next day it was still colder, and the next. Redbirds and blackbirds came to barns and houses to eat corn, peas or bread put out for them. Quail found the places where bushes or weeds held the snow up from the ground, and went down where they could find warmth and seeds to eat. Rabbits did the same, cutting long tunnels under the snow, searching for food. Here and there at the mouth of one of these tunnels a heap of feathers or a piece of rabbit fur told that some preying varmint had found the hide-out. In the woods, birds fell out of the trees, starved and frozen, or when somebody or something scared them would start flying away and, burning up their last spark of life, fall dead in flight. Folks had never seen such weather before.

After the first few days the newness of it wore off, and time hung heavy on Shim's hands. There wasn't any school, of course, and you wouldn't go hunting with the birds and animals half starved and freezing. You couldn't go anywhere visiting, because nobody would think of putting their unshod horses or mules out on the frozen roads, where they'd slip on the ice or, breaking through into the soft dirt underneath, would cut, or maybe even break, a leg.

All over the plantation fights began breaking out among the tenants. Housed up and with nothing to do, they fell out with one another and got into devilment. When the Captain wasn't busy trying to settle fights, he sat by the fire reading the last newspaper he'd brought from the post office before the freeze. Shim felt like he knew every word of that *Atlanta Constitution* by heart, much as he'd heard the Captain read it aloud to Miss Cherry. To Shim's way of thinking, somebody named Bill Arp wrote the best things in it. He wrote like talking instead of like writing. Shim thought about walking to the post office to get the next of the weekly papers just to hear something else Bill Arp had written, but it was too far in the cold.

Finally folks got so restless and lonesome they had to do something about it, and they started walking to visit each other. Miss Cherry and the Captain pitched out one day and walked the two miles to Cousin Salina's. Shim thought about going with them, but at the last minute decided instead to go down to Henry's house and mold some bullets and reload some more shells. By the time early dark came they had about half a bushel of shells reloaded—enough to last them all summer. When the weather broke and they could hunt again, they wouldn't have to take time out for that.

Shim went back to the house, halfheartedly running and sliding on the ice—fun that had lost its newness. Coming in the back door, he felt the good warmth of the kitchen and sniffed hungrily at the ham Aggie had on the back of the stove frying for supper. She was bending over the churn taking up the butter.

"Give me some buttermilk, Aggie," he said.

"Tain't no account," Aggie grumbled. "Tain't never thick in good cold weather like this when you have to pour hot water in the churn to make the devilish butter come. Quit pestering me whilst I gets my biscuits rolled out. Your folks going be coming home hungry any minute and supper ain't near about ready." She picked up the big churn and began pouring the buttermilk into a crock on the table. It looked sort of lumpy and Shim decided he didn't want any.

He went down the cold hall to Miss Cherry's and the Captain's bedroom, the only room besides the kitchen where a big fire was kept burning all day in cold weather. The minute he stepped in the door Fanchie squealed, "Come on, Shim, and play with me. Dave beats me every time."

Dave looked up with a shamefaced grin from the checkerboard on his and Fanchie's knees. He sure was out of something to do to be playing checkers with Fanchie. But weather like this, when you couldn't do any of the things you wanted to, you'd do most anything to pass the time. Except for the firelight the room was dark, and light from the window was fading fast. Shim lighted the lamp on the mantel and the one on Miss Cherry's sewing table.

Much as he hated checkers—even Fanchie always backed his last two kings up in a double corner and held them there—he was about to say he'd play one game with her when the dogs started barking outside. They stopped suddenly, and a minute later Miss Cherry and the Captain came in. Her cheeks pink from the cold and the walk, Miss Cherry went straight to the closet and hung up her coat and took off her hat. Shim knew from the set of her mouth that she was stirred up about something, but a quick glance at the Captain told him it wasn't anything bad. Because the Captain had the teasing look on his face he always had when Miss Cherry got all stirred up over something that didn't amount to anything.

"Did you hear any gossip, Mama?" Fanchie said. "What are Cousin Salina's folks doing to pass the time? I'm so sick of this old snow and ice. Was anybody else over there?"

Miss Cherry turned around, her cheeks flushed a deeper pink. "Your Uncle Ben slipped off and got married. He and Betty Lou are in Jackson right now on their honeymoon."

She said it like it was something terrible, and her black eyes were snapping. "If any of you children did a thing like that to your father and me . . ." She choked up and said, "My baby brother."

Fanchie jumped up, dumping the checkerboard into Dave's lap and sending checkers rolling across the floor every which way. Throwing her arms around Miss Cherry, she burst into tears. "That's the meanest thing I ever heard of. They won't get any wedding presents and no fun of a big wedding. Oh, Mama, as good as you've always been to him, how could he?"

"I thought you were both crazy about Betty Lou," Shim said, puzzled. "I thought you wanted him and Betty Lou to get married."

Miss Cherry looked at him like she was too disgusted to answer, put her arm around Fanchie and said, "Come on, Sugar, and let's go see if supper is about ready. Men!" She finished that sentence in the way she closed the door—not anywhere near slamming it, but with a sharp little click.

Standing at the fireplace, the Captain, the teasing look still on his face, went on filling his pipe. He lifted a small coal with the shovel and laid it on the tobacco. A few puffs caught it, and with a tilt of the pipe—so that the coal fell to the hearth—the Captain said, "Women, boys—you'll never know anything about them the longest day you live."

"How did Ben get away, with the roads like they are?" Dave asked.

"You know how your Uncle Ben is," the Captain said. "Whatever folks say can't be done, he'll do."

"I don't see how he got over that road to the depot," Dave said.

"Well—" the Captain grinned—"Ben rigged up a sort of slide. Put a wagon bed on wooden runners. He made it down at Alf's livery stable there in Mulberry, and nobody knew it but Alf. Then he talked Alf into hitching four well-shod horses to it, picking him and Betty Lou up at the preacher's that night and driving them to the depot to catch the midnight train south. Not a soul but Alf knew a thing about it till the next morning." He sucked on his pipe. "Your mother's mighty cut up. Feelings hurt, I reckon, because Ben didn't tell her."

The sound of the hand bell came from the back hall calling them to supper. The Captain knocked out his pipe, laid it on the mantel, and they all headed for the door. Meals were about the only thing that gave these long, cooped-up days any shape at all.

Miss Cherry and Fanchie were already in their places at the dining table. Passing Miss Cherry, the Captain winked at Dave and Shim and said, "Miss Cherry, I've just been telling your sons that their Aunt Betty Lou may have her hands full married to a Caulfield, but she'll never have a dull moment."

Miss Cherry half smiled, like she didn't really want to, and something about the way she looked at the Captain made Shim realize for the first time that they had been young once like Ben and Betty Lou. It gave him a queer feeling.

The flaky white biscuits, the ham and grits, the preserves and the good hot coffee, and all of them sitting here together around the lamplit table, was just like always, but there was something different, too. Fanchie, her questions tumbling out one on top of the other, didn't get a frown from Miss Cherry for talking too much but, instead, her undivided attention. "Why didn't Betty Lou's mother miss her when she slipped off to meet Ben at the preacher's house after supper?" Fanchie said. And Miss Cherry told her all about Betty Lou's mother thinking she was in bed and never knowing a thing about her being gone till the next morning when she was fixing to get breakfast she found a note from Betty Lou in the little drawer of the coffee grinder.

There was some new sudden understanding between Fanchie and Miss Cherry that put the rest of them off to themselves. The Captain started a conversation that men could handle. "I saw this week's newspaper today," he said to Shim and Dave. "The price of cotton is up, and soon as the weather breaks I'm going to ship some to Memphis."

The freeze lasted only a couple of days longer. Just when folks were halfway getting used to cold a rain came, the wind blew warm from the Gulf and the snow was gone so quickly it was hard to believe it had ever been there. A few pleasant days of sunshine and the ground was dry enough for work to start. It was a couple of weeks yet till plowingtime, but there was every foot of fence to be looked over and repairs made where needed—a broken post or wire down on the wire fences; in the worm-rail fences, rotted rails to be replaced by new ones. Every tenant on the place was out of firewood, and wagons were busy going to and from the woods hauling a fresh-cut supply. It was good to have the dead, dull winter weeks gone and to see folks stirring all over the place again.

Standing by the lot gate in the warm sunshine, Shim watched men loading cotton the Captain wanted hauled to the depot for shipment. Shim aimed to go with them. Looking forward to the long leisurely ride on one of the wagons, he tried to put out of his mind the nagging thought that this might be the last spring the wagons would be making that pleasant drive to the depot. By next spring, everybody said, the railroad would come clear to Mulberry, sure as shooting, with the mill there. He had given up hoping the mill wouldn't come. Already the outsiders had set up a circle saw—a little groundhog mill—over on Peterson's Ridge and were sawing lumber to be hauled to Mulberry to use in building the big mill.

Peterson's Ridge—covered with as pretty white-oak trees as you'd find anywhere, and so high that it was always above overflow water. There was a deer stand on the south end where Dave had killed his first deer. One night last spring Shim and Henry had camped over there and each had got a fine turkey gobbler the next morning. Shim rubbed his dry face and tried to get his mind on the work he was watching—men busy greasing wagon axles, others rolling big bales of cotton from the cotton shed and loading them on the wagons to have everything ready for an early start in the morning.

Henry came over and rested his shoulders against a fence post near Shim. Pewatt Hodges, a big white cloth wrapped around his head and a look on his face like he was down in the dumps, came through the gate and, crossing the lot toward the busy men, called out to them, "Don't ask me to work. I'm just here hunting company."

"One more laid up for a few days," Henry said.

Pewatt's wife, a little-bitty woman, had cut a furrow across his head with a poker iron a couple of nights ago, and suddenly Shim was curious about it. "What makes them fight so much?"

"Mostly jealous," Henry said. "But, too, folks needs to work. When there ain't no work much, they fights."

Shim found that a little too thick to see through, and asked another question. "How do these little women manage to whip these big men?"

"Well," Henry said, "the man don't want to hurt her if he can help it, so he fools around and get's careless, and that's when she half kills him with a scantling or something. Another thing is, womens is always studying out schemes for beating a man. They studies that more regular than they does religion."

"I didn't know women were that way," Shim said.

"Some womens is good like they says angels is," Henry said. "But the biggest half of them ain't."

They watched men roll a bale of cotton up the skids and place it on the wagon. "Boy," Henry said, "I've got to tell you a heap of things one of these days before long, because you don't know much. Growing up is full of misery, but there ain't no way around, if you lives."

"What do you aim to tell me about?" Shim asked curiously.

"Well," Henry said, "mostly about folks. You ain't met many but the good kind yet, but you will. Folks is so mean. Some accidentally, some on purpose. And they'll mess you up if you ain't careful."

"Miss Cherry says to always be honest and you'll be all right," Shim said.

"That's good, mighty good," Henry said. "I don't know nothing better. But the hitch is that folks won't be honest back at you." His face suddenly went smooth and blank. "Oh-oh, your hands is full now. Here comes your dandified friend what climbs trees so good when it gets dangerous on the ground."

The Captain was riding down the lane, and behind him on the horse was Jans Dobson. Shim watched, surprised. Jans had that expensive gun on his shoulder and looked like he was in high spirits. The Captain pulled up at the gate and spoke to Henry. "You can stop them from loading. The trip is called off. Water is rising."

Jans slid down, then the Captain dismounted. Thanking him for the ride, Jans opened the gate for him.

"How did you manage to get the ride?" Shim said with a wide smile. "The Captain's mighty particular about even me riding behind him."

"I started walking out here, and he came along and picked me up," Jans said. "I didn't have anything to ride because both of our saddle horses are behind the water, over on Peterson's Ridge. They're our only carriage horses, too, and we need them in Mulberry. You and I are going over to get them, if you will. Say, a man you know took them over there—a Dr. Zuey. He hired out to my father as camp doctor, and my father lent him both our horses to get out there. He rode one and a man went with him on the other one to help carry the stuff he needed—medicines and instruments and all that. The water rose, and the horses are still there."

Shim frowned, trying to imagine the dapper Dr. Zuey, who always looked like he'd just stepped out of a bandbox, in a rough woods camp.

"What kind of a windjammer is he, anyway?" Jans said. "My father says he's a fine fellow with a good reputation as a doctor, but the strangest-talking man he ever saw. Always telling about the men he's killed, saying the reason he's alive is because he's a crack shot and nobody ever beats him to the draw." Jans laughed. "I guess he's just heard timber camps are rough and is trying to get his bluff in to start with."

"He's killed seven men," Shim said evenly, the words *windjammer* and *bluff* sticking him like thorns. "One he killed with a stove leg in the Sheriff's office. Got into a fight while he was waiting there for court to open, already under arrest for having shot another man." The minute he said it he wished he'd kept his big mouth shut.

Jans turned white. "Why, he's a dangerous criminal," he blurted out.

Shim had a hard time getting words past his teeth. "It's not criminal to kill in self-defense, and he's not dangerous because he never bothers anybody unless they bother him."

He was glad to see T. Parks Early riding up the lane. The interruption would give him a chance to shake off the coldness he felt toward Jans before Jans sensed it and began apologizing and asking questions there were no answers to for an outsider. Dr. Zuey was a gentleman, a good friend of the Captain's and all of them, and Jans had as good as said he, and Mr. Dobson too, thought he was a liar.

T. Parks started talking as soon as he was in hearing distance. He said he'd seen a man in town who had just come from over on the river and brought the good news that it wasn't so terribly high; that in just a few days it would be back in its banks and able to take care of this water from the hills that was flooding them now.

T. Parks hadn't much more than stopped his horse at the lot gate when up the lane from the other direction rode Rance Lavender. This was more company than they'd had in weeks, and Shim was feeling the need of company. The men exchanged the usual greetings about how all their folks were, and then Rance said, "Gentlemen, I'm on my way to town to whip old man Moulton till one more lick would kill him."

T. Parks's bushy eyebrows went up. The Captain's expression didn't change. Shim thought that if old man Moulton was as good a fighter as his son Orland, Rance would have his hands full.

Rance went on. "You know where Moulton's land joins my folks'? Well, he's moved over and run a line to take in three quarters of a section of our woods. He's had an estimator in there. He's aiming to sell it along with his, and I'm fixing to teach him some manners." He kicked his horse and rode off.

"Keep your head cool, Rance," the Captain called. "I guess the mill company will have abstracts on all the land they buy."

T. Parks shook his head slowly. "There's going to be trouble and lots of it. Hardly anybody knows where their lines really are. Corner trees have been cut down for one reason or another, and with money flowing and folks getting greedy there'll be many a chance for an argument." He cleared his throat. "Captain, you and I both know that money is the greatest destroyer of character. . . ."

T. Parks was off on one of his long-winded sermons, and Shim turned to Jans. He hadn't much missed being rude to him awhile ago, so he said, more friendly-like, "It's nearer from town to Peterson's Ridge straight through on the ridge road. Why did you come way around this way?"

"I've got to go by boat," Jans said, "and that ridge road isn't under water except in a few places where bayous and sloughs cut it. There's too much of it out of water that I'd have to drag a boat over. I saw Dave in town and he told me that if I'd come out here, we could go in a boat all the way to Peterson's ridge, the way the bayous and lakes connect up with the low land."

Shim traveled it in his mind. Take Muleshoe Bayou and go out through Muleshoe Lake; swing a little north of west across some overflow land and hit Wildcat Bayou. Follow that into Lake Thursday. Beyond Lake Thursday overflow land again. Then the old cypress brake, where the water was pretty apt to be swift. From there on they'd have still water clear to the ridge.

"Dave's right," he said.

"I've already asked the Captain if you could go," Jans said eagerly. "He said yes, and that we could take your best boat. The foreman over there will send a man back here with it tomorrow, and you and I will ride the horses out to town by the ridge road—just have to swim them in a few places."

Shim didn't want to see those pretty woods on Peterson's Ridge messed up and ruined by that ground-hog mill; at the same time he couldn't refuse to do a friend a simple favor. Come to think about it, he'd like to see how Dr. Zuey could fit into a place of that kind. Proud and high-strung as Dr. Zuey was, Shim would have thought working for a salary for these mill folks was the last thing on earth he'd ever do. His folks had plenty of money and he didn't have to practice medicine at all for a living.

"All right, I'll go," Shim said, and stepped over to speak to the Captain. But he and T. Parks were still talking about lines and corners, the Captain saying he was collecting up iron bars, old buggy axles and such and was going to have an engineer sink an iron into the ground on every one of his corners.

Before the Captain got his last word out good, T. Parks was talking again. Shim couldn't interrupt. "Come on," he said to Jans. "I'll tell Miss Cherry and get my pepperbox. We better take a little bottle filled with matches, too, and cork it up good so they won't get wet in case we turn over. Can you use a paddle?"

"It will surprise you the way I work a paddle." Jans grinned.

On their way to the house Shim said, "What were you going to do if I didn't go with you, after you came all the way out here?"

"I knew all I had to do was get here," Jans said, "and somebody would go with me. You may be the hotheadedest folks I ever saw, but you're the most accommodating. You know, for a minute I thought I'd made you sore, though, by something I said about Dr. Zuey. I'm glad I didn't."

Shim didn't say anything.

Coming back out of the house, they met the Captain on the steps. "You all are going to have a heap of hard pulling to do," he said, "because you're going to hit some still water. There are places where it'll be swift, too. Remember to watch out and don't get slammed against a log or something and turned over."

"We'll be careful," Shim said.

On the bank of Muleshoe Bayou, Jans laid his gun in the boat and while Shim was unfastening the tie chain from a bitter-pecan bush began hauling things out of his pocket—a hand compass, and then a big blue sheet of paper that he unfolded and spread out on the ground.

"What's that?" Shim said.

"Our map—to figure our route by," Jans said.

Shim scowled down at strange markings and lines, and saw familiar names here and there. "Where'd you get it?"

"It's just a rough sketch the engineer in the office made."

Shim grunted. "A coon goes where he wants to without all that plunder, and his head is smaller than mine. All those things will do is get us lost as blind ganders. Put it in your pocket and load up and let's go."

Peterson's Ridge was almost due west. To make use of the current that was running south, Shim hit the bayous and lakes

SHIM

where it was swift, from the north or the east. He knew just how far he could let it carry him each time before he'd have to pull out again into the still water of the overflowed woods to keep on course. Jans had a fair stroke with a paddle, and with Shim managing the boat they made good time.

It was still more than an hour till sundown when the high, steady whine of a saw cutting through green logs came out over the water, making Shim's eardrums tingle painfully. A good many paddle strokes later, guiding the boat among tree trunks and around the tops of bushes sticking out of the water, Shim saw the ugly scar the mill made in the woods, and for a second his head swam like he was coming down with high fever.

He saw rough shacks, two pretty good-sized ones, tents, plank walks built up above the muddy ground, freshly sawed planks stacked high, piles of logs that had once been trees, and the sawmill steel reflecting the chilly afternoon sun.

They tied the boat to an ash bush and stepped up on the plank walk running from the bayou to the huddle of shacks and tents and the mill.

"That biggest one—" Jans pointed ahead to the bigger of the two large shacks—"is the bunkhouse. The other one is the kitchen and dining room. The tents and little shacks strung along here are where some of the men bunk—the foreman, the timekeeper and others."

They were passing the open door of a small shack when Shim slowed his steps. Dr. Zuey was in there—tall and slim and moving light and quick as a cat around a table. A man was on the table. "What's going on in there?" Shim said.

Jans looked in. "Looks like there's been somebody hurt."

Dr. Zuey laid a hypodermic needle on a shelf and glanced out the door. "Hey, come in here, boys. I need help."

They stepped into the small shack filled with smells of buckshot mud, machine grease and blood. "Well, bless me if it isn't Cap Govan's boy and Mr. Dobson's boy way down here on our island. Glad you happened along. Red's got all he can do to handle the chloroform."

"Red's the timekeeper," Jans said in a low voice to Shim as they watched the sandy-haired, red-faced man who was cutting the torn boot and sock from the mashed right foot of the man lying on the table. The man groaned. Dr. Zuey took a close look at the bloody foot and said quickly, "You boys keep the fire going in the heater and the water boiling. Yonder on that shelf is the pan of instruments, and wrapped in the towel are needles and thread. Hand them to me when I ask for them."

Red put a contraption over the man's nose and began dropping clear liquid from a bottle onto it. The rank smell of chloroform wiped out the other smells in the room. Dr. Zuey went to work.

Shim watched the strong hands and long supple fingers working on the mashed-up foot and, remembering how rough they had handled healthy folks, felt a deepening wonder. Dr. Zuey was acting as worried and gentle with the hurt man as a woman over a sick baby. It seemed a long time to Shim, and he was beginning to feel mighty dizzy, when Dr. Zuey straightened up, the job finished. With a quick look at him and Jans he said sharply, "Get outside and take in some fresh air, you two."

Out on the plank walk, Shim drew a couple of deep breaths of cold damp air and felt his spinning head clear.

Jans grinned. "Bother you in there?"

"No more than it did you," Shim said. "You're white as cotton."

"My legs got to feeling like a couple of wet dishrags," Jans admitted. "Come on and let's go down where they're handcutting."

He led the way past the mill and a little off to the right, where men were measuring and cutting lumber with hand saws. "For little shacks to be built where and when needed," Jans explained. "Over there is where they're stacking lumber to be dried and used in building the mill in Mulberry. That biggest pile is timbers and flooring for bridges to be built when the water goes down."

Shim looked at the bridge timbers, all cut and shaped and bored. "How in the world do they know what sizes and lengths to make those pieces so they'll fit?"

"That's all down on paper," Jans said. "Blueprints."

"Where do they get the blueprints? Who knows all those things, and so far ahead?"

Jans shrugged. "Oh, draftsmen and engineers work things like that out."

Shim felt his heart beating faster.

They walked farther down the ridge to the lot where the work oxen and mules were kept. "There's our two horses we're going to ride out tomorrow," Jans said. They were a black and a roan, slick and well shaped, but they looked too big to Shim for this country of woods and mud. They were probably all right for town.

The lot wasn't much above water, and, only a few yards from where they were, water stood high up on the tree trunks. Lined up outside the wire fence were big log wagons with wide tires and low wheels; there were other contraptions, too, like big slides, only the runners were bigger and longer than Shim had ever seen, and the heavy pieces holding them together across the top were curved downward in the middle instead of straight. "Mud boats," Jans said, seeing him eye them. "To haul logs on when the ground is too soft for the wagons." The mud on them was dry, so they hadn't been used the last few days since the water got high; but these folks had prepared for this too. Over by the mill was a big stack of logs, enough to keep the saw busy for a good while yet.

With the high howl of the saw beating on his eardrums, Shim wondered at the things these folks were doing and might do. They worked in snow or high water; they made things in one place to fit something somewhere else. They were a work-crazy parcel of men who could build a mill here, or anywhere else, among trees. An unexpected and unwanted excitement made him look out at the familiar, living trees. Beyond their tops the sun had gone down. There was no gap in the sky line, but he knew that if he walked through the woods in any direction from here there would be raw stumps, and the biggest, the best of the trees lay in that heap beside the mill. High up in a big oak he saw a den hole. From this distance he couldn't tell for sure, but it looked too big for a squirrel. Coons had denned there most likely. But they wouldn't this spring. Sadness and excitement together raced through him from head to foot; neither one was the stronger, and it shook him.

"Come out of that trance." Jans was pulling at his arm. "Supper. Let's go." The whine of the saw had stopped, and back at the dining room somebody was hitting one piece of iron against another, sort of knocking a tune.

"That's what's the matter with me," Shim said. "I'm half starved. This green lumber smells like watermelon."

It was the strangest meal Shim had ever eaten. Men crowded into the shack, sat on the benches nailed to the floor alongside the long rough plank tables, and, wasting no time in talk, fell to eating. There was no sound but the clatter of silverware on crockery. They ate like they worked, like killing snakes, with no time out for talk. The food and coffee were hot and he was cold and hungry. Except when he bit into a piece of cornbread and it turned out to be sweet as sugar, he'd never eaten better victuals. Long before he was through, the smell of tobacco smoke strong as horse-radish overlaid the smells of food. He'd never seen men smoke at the table before in his life.

"Where are all those men from?" he asked curiously when, supper over, Jans led the way toward the bunkhouse.

"I don't know—from everywhere," Jans said. "Just men who follow mills around. Why?"

"I don't know. They act like they don't even know each other, sort of. Not talking at the table or anything."

Jans laughed. "Sometimes it gets pretty rowdy, but not often. They go there to eat, so they eat." He opened the door to the bunkhouse and they went inside.

It was a long low building, with rooms opening off both sides of a narrow hall. In a front room they found three or four men sitting in cane-bottom chairs around a heating stove. The smell of wet clothes, green lumber and tobacco smoke was thick in the air. Shim pulled a chair close to the stove and held his feet out to get warm. Watching thin pale steam rise from his wet shoes, and listening to men talking about things and places he'd never heard of, he was getting drowsy fast when somebody down the hall started playing a mandolin and singing. Shim's ears perked up. It was a lonesome song about working on a mud-line road for a dollar and a half a day and paying six bits for board.

He was listening closely, hoping whoever it was would strike up a livelier tune, when Jans said, "There's a crap game going on around here somewhere that we can watch."

They went down the narrow hall until they found it. Six men were crowded around a wobbly iron bedstead. Red, the timekeeper he'd seen in Dr. Zuey's shack, was rolling the dice across the dark blanket and calling strong for "Little Joe that picked the cotton" to show up. Shim and Jans went in through the open door and propped their hips against the washstand.

"Bets aren't high—a nickel to four bits," Jans said. "They gamble for fun except on pay nights, and then they go strong to win big money."

Shim thought maybe he felt sorry for folks who had to call gambling fun, but he didn't have time to study about it, because a square-headed blond fellow with arms long as a baboon's grabbed the money off the bed, cussing and snorting in some kind of broken English. Shim caught enough of it to know he was claiming the dice were crooked and was blaming them on somebody he called Bull Puncher Jim—a little, round-shouldered man with bright blue eyes and a face fat and innocent-looking as a baby's. But it wasn't any baby talk coming from Bull Puncher Jim's lips. Anybody that accused him of putting crooked dice in a game was a "slop-eating, devil-loving, God-hating liar; a ridge-running, gully-jumping son of a consumptive wolf."

Red reached for the dice to look at them, and somebody said, "He's the one, and now he's trying to hide them." Red threw the dice down and started cussing too, and suddenly everybody was talking rough and cussing strong. A big rusty-looking fellow over in the corner slapped the man next to him across the mouth, and then fists were flying all over the crowded room. It looked like every man was hitting anybody he could reach, and in such close quarters reaching was easy.

It had all started so fast Shim hadn't moved from the washstand, but Jans must have got knocked aside, because he wasn't there. The way to the door was blocked solid by fighting men and waving fists, and if there was a window to the room, Shim couldn't locate it. Somebody backed against him, pushing him from his place by the washstand, and across the room somebody must have been knocked across the bed, because slats clattered to the floor, adding to the worst racket Shim had ever been caught in.

From his right he heard a whacking sound from something harder than fists on flesh, and saw the square-headed blond fellow who had started the rookus go down out of sight and stay down. A big fellow right in front of Shim fell next. Shim saw a chance to make the door and started when he saw what had felled the two men coming straight for the side of his own head. He ducked low, and the brass knuckles on Bull Puncher Jim's thick fist passed over his head. The way to the door was blocked again with fighting men, and he didn't have a chance to run. Still in the crouch, he pulled his pepperbox.

He didn't even get the hammer back before somebody snatched it out of his hand, and, off balance, he saw the brass knuckles coming at him again. The jig was up. But instead of the knuckles landing, a big white water pitcher swung into sight over Bull Puncher Jim's head, broken white crockery scattered across the room, and Bull Puncher Jim fell. Two men were on him like ducks on a June bug, taking away his brass knuckles, and across the struggling bodies Shim saw Jans, the white handle of the pitcher still in his hand.

"Anybody need sewing up?" Dr. Zuey's slow voice said from the doorway. He looked over the crowd. "Only some liniment needed, as usual, I see."

His eyes fell on Jans and Shim, and his brows went up. "You boys come with me," he said, "and I'll show you to a tent where you can sleep, away from this rowdy crowd."

"Yeah, get this young fire-eater out of here, Doc." Red, with a grin, handed Shim his pepperbox. "No occasion for you to shoot anybody, son. We were just having a friendly free-for-all. Jim thought you were in on it too, and didn't want to slight anybody."

"Well, well—" Dr. Zuey gave a sound more like a short bark than like laughter—"a chip off the old block, upholding our fine traditions." He said it like he meant it, and at the same time with an edge to his voice that Shim didn't understand and didn't exactly appreciate. He and Jans followed Dr. Zuey down the hall and outside into black darkness. There wasn't a star in the sky. They could barely see Dr. Zuey's bulk one step ahead of them, and they stayed behind him on the plank walk only by balance and careful setting of their feet. Shim wanted to tell Jans how much he admired him for having kept those brass knuckles from busting his skull open, but there was a coldness in Dr. Zuey somehow that kept him from speaking.

They were well away from the bunkhouse when Dr. Zuey said out of the darkness, "Don't ever kill a man, boys, if you can help it."

It took the surprising words a second or two to sink in, and when they did it flew all over Shim. Red's snatching his pepperbox out of his hand, and giving it back to him with talk that sounded like he was making fun of him, had been bad enough. But for Dr. Zuey to take a crack at him for reaching to defend himself from a man with brass knuckles didn't make any sense at all. It made him about half sore.

Stopping before a tent, Dr. Zuey pushed aside the flap, struck a match on his pants leg and lighted a lantern that was on a little rough table inside. Light fell on an iron bed and a stove. "Come on in," he said. Shim and Jans stepped inside onto wet, leaf-covered ground.

"Thanks for showing us here," Jans said politely.

"Thank you, sir," Shim said stiffly.

But Dr. Zuey didn't leave. He stood there, looking from one of them to the other.

"I was a shade older than you boys, eighteen to be exact, when I killed my first man. Did it with my pocket knife. I belonged to the class of folks that didn't work for other folks, nor with their hands. But there was a new courthouse being built in my home town, and I slipped up there and got a job."

He was talking sad and low, and so fast they didn't have time to say anything if they had wanted to, which they didn't. His eyes were sort of glassy, as if he didn't see them.

"I made it for four days and my folks hadn't found out yet the disgrace of my working with my hands. The fifth day started off fine because I was getting toughened up. But about the middle of the morning one of the carpenters started getting rough with me. I couldn't do anything to suit him—tote a plank right or put it down right. He hollered at me three or four times hand running, and I wasn't used to being hollered at."

He turned a cold smile on Shim. "When talk gets rough, folks raised like you and I know just one thing to do to save our hides."

Shim felt uncomfortable to be singled out this way in talk he couldn't quite catch the drift of. Dr. Zuey was looking way off again. "I took his roughness that morning until he said if I fooled with him he'd kick my hips up over my shoulders. I hadn't fooled with him, and hadn't aimed to, but when he said that, I dropped the plank I was carrying and told him to try it. He knocked me down flat on my back, and when I started getting up he reached for a piece of scantling. I figured he was aiming to kill me. I was on my feet, my knife open, when he swung. He missed, and I flew in on him."

Dr. Zuey lifted the top off the little heater, struck a match and dropped it inside. Kindling and paper caught, and the blaze roared up the pipe with a good, warming sound.

"That was the first man I killed," he said. "You boys sit down on the bed and get your feet off this wet ground before you catch your death of cold."

Shim and Jans sat down and put their feet on a block of wood. Neither of them said anything. Dr. Zuey pulled a bottle half full of clear liquid out of his pistol pocket, emptied it and tossed it into a corner.

"That was the first man I killed," he repeated.

Suddenly his eyes lost their glassiness and fixed bright and hard on first one and then the other of them. "Folks call me many different things," he said. "They call me 'mean,' 'not afraid of the devil,' 'cold-blooded,' 'hot-blooded,' 'high-tempered,' 'love to kill.' They're wrong, all of them. After you have had to kill a man to save your own hide, you're scared all the time, because you know it can happen again. You never stop dreading it, expecting it, and so it comes. Maybe half the killings I've done could have been avoided. There might have been a way around it. Maybe I could have outtalked or even outrun them. But killing that first time puts a steel spring inside you, hair trigger, that flies loose every time you see danger to yourself from another person." His voice dropped to a mumble. "And maybe you see it where it isn't. I don't know."

His face was pale, and his jaw muscles kept bunching up and smoothing out. "Govan, you belong to a mighty good family, proud as Lucifer, like all our kind. Seeing you with that pistol tonight excited me. You could so easily have made the mistake I did." He wiped his hand across his face like he was trying to wring the bunched muscles loose. "You know why I came out here? It was to see how these outsiders get along. They play rough, tangle with their fists, call each other names you and I have been taught to kill, or die, rather than take. But nine times out of ten it all blows over and nobody is dead. They kill sometimes, but not like we do, over a word spoken, or maybe unspoken. They haven't got our kind of poison pride that keeps us strung up tight as a fiddle string. I thought maybe if I came out here and lived with them, I'd learn . . ."

His voice trailed off like he was suddenly tired of talking, and, shoulders sagging, he lifted the tent flap. Standing there, he straightened, proud as a peacock, and looked back at Shim. "But don't forget, either, that you may be forced to kill sometime—like your Uncle Ben was. And in that case, make a good job of it. Good night, boys." The tent flap dropped behind him.

Shim and Jans undressed quickly and in silence. Shim blew out the lantern, and they crawled into the musty-smelling bed, under a stack of heavy blankets.

After a long while Jans spoke. "Didn't he go to jail for any of those killings?"

"Self-defense, every one of them," Shim said. He felt strange and upset, and like answering questions was a waste of breath. His eyelids felt like they were propped open with sticks and never would be sleepy again. The little sheet-iron stove had faded from red to black; the tent grew cold. The heavy blankets pressed down on him like lead, but they weren't warm. He turned on his side and drew his knees up to his chin for warmth, hoping to stop the voice of Dr. Zuey that was ringing inside his head.

"Shim."

"Thought you were asleep long ago."

"I'm not sleepy," Jans said. "I've been meaning to tell you that my folks are going to ask your folks to let you live with us and go to school in Mulberry next year."

Suddenly Shim was homesick. "I can't."

"You and I could go down to your house every week end," Jans said.

"As soon as we get your horses to town tomorrow," Shim said flatly, "I'm going home and stay there."

He pushed his pillow to one side and turned over to lie flat on his stomach. Maybe this way he could go to sleep. All these years he'd been halfway envying Dr. Zuey, admiring him for being fast as lightning, able and willing to stop any man who threatened him, a crack shot, and scared of nothing.

Shim's cheeks drew like he'd eaten a green persimmon. Tonight, right here in this tent, Dr. Zuey had said that he killed folks not because he was quick and brave but because he was just plain scared not to. It was plumb sickening to think about. Shim pulled the pillow over his head. It stopped the cold from going down his neck, and he began to get pleasantly warm.

chapter thirteen

THE NIGHT WAS MIGHTY COLD FOR APRIL, EVEN IN THE woods where the wind couldn't hit you. Flames from a big fire of dead brush lighted up the tree trunks and fluttered the young leaves overhead. A smaller cook fire between two old down logs that lay close together had burned to a good bed of coals, and over it Shim held a piece of bacon on a cane he had trimmed to a two-pronged fork. Dave and Henry sat on one of the logs eating bacon with cold biscuits they'd brought from home. Three tin cups of hot coffee, sending up wisps of pale steam now and then, were lined in a row on the log beside them. About fifteen feet away their three horses, hitched to swinging limbs, stood asleep, their rumps turned to the light.

Dave took from his pocket a caller, made out of a turkey-wing bone and a piece of cane, and, wiping the trash off it, stuck the cane end into his mouth and began to yelp like a turkey hen. "When an old gobbler hears that," he bragged, "you have to kill him to keep him from running over you."

"Shucks," Henry said. "I can put a leaf in my mouth and beat that."

"For me," Shim said, "the best idea is just before daylight to slip up under the tree he's roosting in, because every time I try to call one to me he misunderstands and goes the other way."

"If dark had just been five minutes later about coming," Dave said, "I would already have the one I've got roosted."

"If the dog hadn't stopped running, he'd have caught the rabbit," Shim said, turning the fork so the grease would run down and drip off the other end of his meat.

Henry picked up his coffee cup, took a swallow, set it back down and wiped his lips. "I've got me two big ones treed up an old dead red oak, but it's so open around there I couldn't get close enough to shoot before it got too dark to see them. While it's still pitch-dark in the morning, I'm going to ease across that open space. I'll be under that tree they're in when the first streak of light in the sky shows me their bulk to draw a bead on. What about you, Shim?"

"I heard so many big wings going 'foop, foop, foop' on the other side of Wrong Prong I nearly went crazy trying to find a footlog to cross on. I ran up and down the bayou till I about got the thumps and never did find one, but by the sound of their wings I counted four, maybe five, flying up to roost over there."

"Water's too high yet," Dave said. "Guess it's still got all the footlogs covered."

"What you needed," Henry said, "is that fancy horse you rode from Peterson's Ridge to town a few weeks back."

Shim, his meat cooked, put it between a couple of biscuits and sat down on a chunk, scowling. It made him mad every time he remembered that trip with Jans, on the biggest fool horse in the world. It was cold as a frog's belly the morning they started out from Peterson's Ridge on Mr. Dobson's two horses, and when they came to the first swimming-deep bayou the trouble started.

The big black horse Shim was on went in willingly enough —waded right out into deep water, and kept on wading. Water rose up and on up, into the saddle, over it, on over the horse's eyes, then ears. Shim, on his knees in the saddle, thought the fool horse was drowning. He couldn't see any sign of him at all, could only feel him there under him, still walking ahead. Jans, his horse swimming, hollered at him, asking what was the matter. How did he know? Till then he'd thought all animals could and would swim. The cold water got clear up to his neck, and the horse kept right on walking on the bottom.

He made it across that one, and three more, before they got to town, that crazy horse walking across on the bottom of every swimming-deep bayou they came to. If the bayous hadn't been narrow, the danged fool horse would have drowned himself sure. Shim like to froze to death before they made town.

"I'll bet I'd teach that hellion to swim if I owned him," he said.

"Sawmill folks ain't got time to do things with any sense to it," Henry said. "They is too busy studying about how to make more money."

"But they're so smart about so many things," Shim said. "You know, Henry, over there on Peterson's Ridge they were sawing up stuff all cut to fit and ready to build something out of somewhere else."

"Uh-huh," Henry grumbled. "Folks gets that smart, they outsmarts theyselves in the long run."

Shim didn't say any more. It wasn't any use trying to make Henry see any good in the sawmill folks or anything they did. He knew how Henry felt. They missed so much. What were the planks and lumber compared to the trees they cut down and the woods they spoiled to get them? And yet there was something exciting about what they did that he couldn't find words for. He felt pulled two ways—the way of the outsiders, that kept him curious and left him wondering, and Henry's way.

Out here in the woods, with the light from the fire making the trees so pretty, with thoughts of the turkeys they'd get in the morning, there seemed nothing else as good as this. But at the same time he was thinking that he wished they had got to the woods early enough so they could already have got their turkeys and now be on their way home to a big night's sleep. Because the big ball the sawmill folks had been aiming to give since way back in the winter and put off for first one reason and another was set for tomorrow night. He'd wanted to get a good night's sleep tonight because he wouldn't get any tomorrow night, and he didn't want to begin to weaken about two o'clock A.M. when the dancing would just be getting at its best.

Henry had been at the house waiting when Shim and Dave got home from school this afternoon, and nothing would do him but they come turkey hunting tonight. Shim, wanting a good night's sleep, had hinted pretty strong about putting it off, late in the afternoon as it was and cold too. Turkeys would be gobbling all this month, and they could come some other night. But Henry, dead set on coming tonight, didn't take any hints. It wasn't like him to get a notion he had to do something any particular time, so they'd let him outtalk them, and here they were.

Henry set his coffee cup down and wiped his lips with the palm and then the back of his hand. "You all don't have to fret about fresh meat even if you fails in the morning, because

I'm fixing to kill them two big ones in that red-oak tree and take one to Old Miss and one to Little Missie."

It had been years since Shim had heard Miss Cherry and Fanchie called "Old Miss" and "Little Missie," and it sounded strange. Following the bite of biscuit and bacon in his mouth with a sluice of coffee, he looked at Henry from the corner of his eyes.

Henry looked natural and like always—his face smooth and peaceful, his movements supple and easy and none wasted. His talk, joreeing them, giving them advice, was the same as always, but his calling Miss Cherry and Fanchie by the old, half-forgotten names threw Shim off balance. Of a sudden, Henry, who had been as natural a part of his life as the sun and rain, the sky and the woods, seemed separate—almost, for a second, like a stranger. Dave drained his coffee cup and, walking over to the big fire, began chunking it up.

Shim quit studying about Henry. He was in a hurry to lie down, because, before day broke in the morning, he aimed to be under the right tree when a big gobbler would begin walking along the limb he'd roosted on, and making the prettiest sounds ever heard in the woods—a turkey strutting. He'd throw the butts of his wings out from his body and a little forward and walk along the limb, his bronze wing feathers spread half downward and making a booming sound that would seem to jar the ground. He'd stop, cut loose and gobble, then turn and go into his booming strut again. Up and down the limb—strut, gobble, strut, gobble. Well, it was a sight hard to believe even when you were looking at it with your own eyes, and Shim knew he was going to get across Wrong Prong in the morning if he had to wade it. There were bound to be places where it wasn't over his head.

He walked away from the firelight so he could see the sky.

In the darkness beyond the horses he looked up at a world of stars, so many and so silver bright they seemed to be winking or flashing signals at him. "Clear as a bell," he said, coming back to the fire. "There'll be a heap of gobbling ringing in these woods in the morning."

"Only thing could worry us now would be if a east wind springs up," Henry said. "Course that wouldn't bother me and Dave, because us knows the exact tree where they is roosting. But you'd be out of luck."

It had always worried Shim about half foolish, why turkeys wouldn't gobble if there was an east wind. When Henry had first told him that, he hadn't believed it, till he'd proved for himself that if you got up to go turkey hunting and there was an east wind blowing, you might as well go back to bed because not a turkey would gobble. "It's going to be a still morning," he said.

"I hopes so," Henry said, and, going to a down treetop, he began breaking off limbs to make sure they had plenty of fuel for the night. "I been studying about all the years I has spent trying to show you two young'uns how to hunt, and until yet I don't know if you can take care of yourselves in the woods or not."

Dave yawned. "I feel like sleeping a line or two."

"I second the motion," Shim said.

"Dave," Henry said, "I think I'll tell the Captain and Old Miss about the time you kicked the coon." He was calling Miss Cherry "Old Miss" again. He dropped a big armful of limbs on top of a pile already handy to the cook fire, that they would keep burning all night, and sat down on a low chunk. Resting arms on knees, he looked at Dave and went on.

"You was about eleven years old. There was a thin covering of snow on the ground that day. Us took your two big hounds, but no guns—just my tap stick. I reckon that old coon was powerful busy with something or other there on the ground, because we walked right up on him, and he broke for a tree too late. The dogs caught him before he made it, and from the very start they had more than they wanted. That coon sort of molded hisself around the head of one of them and was biting and clawing at the other one, splitting ears and chewing noses, and the dogs outhollering stuck hogs. You got hotheaded and hauled off and kicked that coon, and that was the wrong thing. He turned go the dogs and took a hold of your foot, and was setting his long sharp teethes into your shoe, fixing to bite through foot and all, when I whammed him across the back with my tap stick. You knowed better than to kick that coon. If I hadn't been there—well, what I wonders is, would you do the same crazy thing again, and what if I wasn't there to get you out of it?"

"I didn't know a coon could whip two dogs at one time," Shim said.

"Uh-huh," Dave said.

Shim yawned. "Let's get things fixed so we can lie down and rest a little."

"Yes, and what about you?" Henry said. "Jumping over a log without ever looking on t'other side, and come close as nineteen is to twenty getting kilt by a alligator. Taking a case of paralysis within thirty feet of a big panther down there on Lake Thursday, and would have stood there and got et up if I hadn't threatened to kick you."

He reached down and threw a limb on the fire. "I brought you all down here tonight to try you out and see just what you does know about taking care of yourselves in the woods, or if frolicking around with highfalutin outsiders has done filled your heads so full of foolishment you've done forgot the important things—the things a man needs to remember to get along in this world. If there's any fumbling and fooling around in the morning, I'll know I've wasted a heap of my time for nothing." He wasn't joking them now; he was talking short and serious.

A burning cane Dave had thrown on the fire popped like a firecracker; out near the bayou a coon that had run into something a little too rough for him hollered a couple of times. Shim sat looking into the fire but not seeing it. Henry had as good as said that going to town, getting to know these outsiders and the way they did things, meant that he'd forget the woods and the main thing—hunting and his own good way of life. Anybody ought to know better than that. The worrisome thought popped up in his mind that Henry never yet had told him anything that hadn't turned out to be the gospel truth. But this time Henry was bound to be wrong. Shim's mind seesawed up and down.

To stop it he jumped up, found a strong stick and began raking the big fire to one side so they could lie down. Dave and Henry helped. Scattered, the fire would soon go out in the wet leaf mold, and where it had been would be a warm, dry place to sleep. When the heavy pieces were out of the way, they got brush to use as brooms and swept away hot ashes and the smaller live coals still there.

Dave rested the end of his brush on the ground. "I remember now where there's a log across Wrong Prong that's bound to be partly above water, and it strikes me that maybe I'd better go over there with you in the morning, Shim. That gobbler I roosted tonight will be mighty hard to find in the dark. There's a couple of thickets and a lot of slash water between here and him."

SHIM

"I wish you would show me that log," Shim said.

They put their saddles down for pillows, stretched out on the warm, dry ground and spread the saddle blankets over their middles. Henry threw a couple of branches on the cook fire, poured himself another cup of coffee and sat down on the log by the woodpile. "You all needs your rest so you can kick up your heels with the folks in town tomorrow night at that ball you is going to. But remember that right here is the prettiest place in the world, and I'm fixing to set here and watch it awhile."

All he was looking at, though, was the coffee cup in his hands, and after staring at it a minute he started talking again.

"You all ain't smart like a dirt dauber. Now he knows what he's doing. He lights on a spider web, but he don't get his feets tangled up. He kicks up a heap of fuss and fluttering around like he's stuck, and of course the spider, figuring he's done caught hisself a mess of victuals, comes strutting out to take him in. There's where the old dirt dauber goes into action. He up and lands on that spider, stings him in the back and paralyzes him and flies off with him. No dust, no stickum on Mr. Dirt Dauber's feets. They nests is just full of paralyzed gray spiders, still alive, waiting to get et up by the dirt daubers' young'uns."

"I've seen plenty of them," Shim said sleepily. "What I want to know is how come you're sitting up there mouthing about dirt daubers and wasting all this good sleeping time? I never saw you before not want to catch your rest when you had a chance."

"I sleeps when I is sleepy," Henry said. "And I ain't sleepy now. I is studying about the things you all needs to know and don't know. And you is already forgot your manners interrupting me. What I'm telling you is that you all ain't smart like dirt daubers, and when you steps into the wrong thing you going to have a hard time getting loose. Quality can't mix with trash. You go monkeying around dangerous, trashy folks from way off somewheres that you don't know nothing about, and you ain't going to be able to fly off when you gets ready. You're going to get tangled up sure as God made Moses."

"If you're talking about that ball tomorrow night," Shim said, "it's for first-class folks, and no rowdies or ill-mannered ones will be allowed."

"Trouble is, you might get fooled sometimes," Henry said. "Fine feathers don't always make fine birds."

Dave yawned. "What I'm thinking right now is that there's a fine-feathered bird on a limb across Wrong Prong that needs taking, and I'm going to accommodate him about the first break of day." He turned on his side, his face away from the firelight.

Henry was silent for a minute, and Shim closed his eyes.

Henry began talking again, but in that different, flat voice that Shim knew meant he wasn't talking to them but to something that couldn't talk back—maybe to the trees, or the fire, or even his coffee. "Us used to know who folks was in this country, but things is changing up with all these strays coming in here. It's going to be a heap of skulduggery and tricks breaking out. Jeems Yarn was the first."

This was the closest Shim had heard Henry come to mentioning Kiz since the day they'd found her in the brake. He was just studying about the past tonight, and that's how come him using the old names "Old Miss" and "Little Missie." Shim was worn out with the kind of talk he was doing. Ever since Shim and Dave had got their written invitations to the

SHIM

ball, Miss Cherry or Henry, one or the other, had been hammering at him about manners and the right and wrong kind of folks. They acted like he'd never been away from home.

A feeling that he was being stared at made him open his eyes. Henry's face, turned full toward him and Dave, caught the firelight some strange way so that it looked carved out of hard, smooth rock, and the deep sockets of his eyes looked empty. Shim rose on an elbow. Quick as lightning, Henry's face came alive, his shoulders straightened like he was shucking off a weight, and he stood up. "Boy, catch your rest whilst you can. Pretty soon you going to be running after the gals so hard you'll fall over something and cripple yourself."

Shim lay back down. A panther squalled from across Beaver Lake. Henry put more wood on the fire and sat down again. Close by an owl hooted like he was making fun of somebody. The last thing Shim heard before sleep got him was a wolf way off somewhere, howling. Henry still sat on the log.

It was full light and the sun would soon be up when Shim got back to Wrong Prong Bayou, laid his turkey on the ground and sat down on an exposed tree root to wait for Dave. For the first time he could see the log they had crossed on in the black dark before daylight. It was a cypress, and not very big. At about the middle, water lacked only an inch of covering it. The long green stick Dave had used to feel their way across it in the dark was lying there on the ground.

Hot from excitement and exercise, Shim took in long deep breaths of the damp, chilly air, still and thick with the pleasant smells of both green and moldy leaves. He figured they had four turkeys to take home. The gobbling of this one had led him straight to a tall bushy red oak where it was roosting. Slipping up under it, he had waited. At the first hint of light in the sky he was trying to get a bead on it through the thick leaves when he'd heard Henry's two shots boom out, just a second apart. That meant Henry had two, because shooting from under the tree, he wouldn't have missed. A second later, Shim had got a bead on his, pulled the trigger, and it came tumbling down. Standing there, waiting and listening, he had heard Dave's shot.

And now Dave was coming, walking flat-footed and careless of noise. He carried something across his shoulder, but it wasn't bronze feathers. Grinning all over his face, he dropped a big black wolf almost on Shim's feet and blew out a deep breath. "I take the cake this morning," he said.

"Well, I swear," Shim said.

"I was working my caller trying to call a gobbler that was roosting over water with no chance for me to get to him without making enough fuss to scare him off. I was backed up against a big elm, with a cluster of palmettos in front of me. This smart aleck—" he touched the wolf with his toe—"thought I was a turkey hen he'd have for breakfast and was slipping up on me from right straight out in front when I saw him."

With a little stick Shim pushed the wolf's mouth open and looked at a set of white teeth hard to believe in length and sharpness, even in a wolf. The hair too was slick and shiny, without the dusty look most wolfhides had.

"I want the hide," Shim said. "I want to have it mounted with the head on." He hoped Dave wouldn't ask him why, because he had no idea why. It just hit him that he did.

Dave looked at him in surprise, then down at the wolf. "It is the nicest wolfhide I ever saw. I may want it myself. Let's be getting across. We'll have to make two trips." He slung

SHIM 271

the wolf over his shoulder again. "You bring one gun. The next trip we'll take your turkey and the other gun."

On the second trip, Dave, carrying the turkey, was almost across and Shim was near the bayou's middle when, quick as the wink of a cat's eye, Shim's feet flew out to one side, and he was falling. Cold water rushed up his body and, when it hit his chest, knocked the breath out of him so hard he grunted loud as a mule's cough. Water closed over his head. He came up fighting for air and threw an arm over the log. He could hear Dave, on the bank, laughing and hollering like a maniac, but Shim didn't have anything to laugh about in the cold water. He made it out onto the bank, disgusted, shivering and embarrassed. His gun was on the bottom of the bayou, and his hat was floating about ten feet from where he went under.

Dave wrung some dry wood out of a hollow log and had a good fire going by the time Shim got his clothes off. They squeezed as much water out of them as they could and hung them on bushes near the fire to dry. Shim was trying to get warm without burning his bare skin when Henry, walking fast and proud and careless of kicking up leaf mold, came through the trees. He had two turkeys over his shoulder. At sight of Shim he let out a ringing whoop of laughter.

"Oh, yes, you little devil. Went stumbling around like a clumsy cow and done fell in the bayou. I been telling you all these years to watch where you puts your feets, and now look at you. Oh-oh, Lord help the world, somebody done kilt a devilish old wolf."

In spite of his embarrassment and the ragging Henry was giving him, Shim felt relieved. All Henry's strangeness of last night was gone. He was acting natural and like himself.

"I been telling you all along," Dave said, "that when I call, something always comes. This time the wolf beat the gobbler to me." Dave wouldn't have taken a pretty for this proof of the expertness of his calling, but, proof or not, Henry wasn't going to admit it.

"Huh," he said, "old wolf have to be mighty hungry to be fool enough to think you is a turkey hen and come to your calling. He sure is a fat rascal, though." He prodded the wolf with his foot. Then, laying gun and turkeys at the root of a tree, he picked up a long stick and started out on the footlog.

"Get out your knife," Dave said, "and let's get the hide off this varmint. I'm going to take it home."

"Let me get this devilish hat before it floats plumb out of reach," Henry grumbled. Coming back with it, he pushed the end of the stick into the soft ground near the fire and hung the dripping hat on it to dry. He got out his knife.

Shim fidgeted by the fire. Henry hadn't missed Shim's gun yet, and he sure hated to have to tell him it was out there at the bottom of the bayou. Dave broke the news for him when they had the wolf about skinned. With a side glance at Shim he said, "Lucky you didn't bring Jans Dobson's high-priced hardware yesterday evening, like you started to," and added to Henry, "He lost his gun out there, too."

Henry settled back on his hunkers, and Shim expected to see his face go blank and cold like it did whenever Jans or any of the sawmill folks were mentioned. But Henry was in extra-fine spirits this morning, because all he said was "I just wish to the good Lord he had brought that primped-up mess of foolishness. If it was at the bottom of this bayou I'd be tickled green, because we'd just naturally leave it there." He stood up and began taking off his clothes, without a word to Shim about carelessness.

"Give me some wood to stand on," Shim said to Dave, "so my feet will be off the ground. And see if my underwear and socks are dry."

"Still sopping," Dave said. "Henry, how do you feel now about the time you spent training him?"

"Just throwed away. I might as well spent that time playing mumble-peg," Henry said cheerfully. Buck-naked, he walked out to where wetness across the log showed him where Shim had fallen off, and eased himself into the water feet first. He was out of sight for a few seconds, and came up puffing and grunting. "I had my foot on it," he said. He took a deep breath of air and dived, duck-fashion. This time he brought it up.

When he got his dry clothes on, and Shim his half-dry ones, Henry gathered up the wolfhide, his two turkeys and his gun, and they started for camp.

"You ought to make Shim carry that hide," Dave said. "He's trying to outtalk me for it and get it mounted."

"Oh-oh," Henry said. "He about wants to give it to some gal, and that means he's a goner."

Shim wished Henry would joke about something that had some sense to it. Why would he give a wolfhide or anything else to a girl?

They went through the woods single file. The sun was high enough to get through the treetops, here and there, and shine on the ground. When they came to one of these sunny patches, Shim would stop a second to get the sun's warmth on his damp clothes, then run to catch up with the others.

"How do you all feel after your baths?" Dave said.

"Well," Henry said, "if I lives through the month of January, I ingenerally lives that year out, and January has done come and gone."

Shim, thinking about the warm bath and dry clothes he

would get at home, didn't bother to answer Dave's ragging.

"One thing," Henry said, "the Captain and Miss Cherry can't say I didn't bring them a plenty of meat. You all can eat turkey meat to a fare-you-well."

The dance was in a big new store building Mr. Calhoun had just built on the northeast corner of the Square in Mulberry. He hadn't put his stock of goods into it yet, and Mr. Dobson had rented it for this big dance. Bracket lamps on the walls added their light to that of the three that hung from the ceiling, and somebody had decorated the bare walls with branches of redbud. The back wall was near about covered with branches of dogwood. Somebody had had to go plumb to the hills to get that, and it made a mighty pretty background for the six-piece band.

A row of posts ran down the center of the long room, and that was where the stags were lined up. Standing there, leaning against one of the posts and resting his legs while he looked over the crowd to decide who he'd flag next, Shim watched the couples go around him, up one side of the big room and down the other. Women, dressed up, primped and powdered to the last notch; men, shaved and slicked, with clothes looking like they'd just come out of a bandbox; everybody straight and proper, but moving about mighty supple to the good music.

The band was playing the song Uncle Ben liked so well, the one they'd been singing the night the wolves got after them. They were playing it in waltz time, and there, passing Shim, was Ben. His head thrown back, he was singing with the music—"Come where my love lies dreaming—" and spinning Betty Lou around like he owned the place. Of a sudden his foot slipped and he almost fell. The floor was mighty

SHIM 275

slick with all the white powder they'd sprinkled around on it. Ben's singing stopped, and some of the starch went out of his dancing. Shim, laughing at him, glanced down at his own dark clothes, his first long pants, and made up his mind to be extra careful from now on. Anybody that fell on this floor would come up looking like he'd been dipped in a flour barrel.

There were a lot of folks here he didn't know—some older ones, others just good and grown, and, what pleased him most, half a dozen boys and girls about his own age. The boys he'd grown up with—the Calhoun twins, Mack and the others—wouldn't go to a dance.

Jans spoke in his ear. "Break Emmy. That guy she's with can't dance worth a whoop."

He'd met Jans's cousin Emmy a time or two and figured he needn't worry about getting stuck with her. He located her chestnut-colored curls, and, stepping out among the moving couples, broke her.

Right straight he knew he'd never had hold of such a dancer before. He thought maybe it was because he'd never danced with a girl so much shorter than he was that she seemed so light in his arms. He tried a little gliding side step, and when her feet followed his like they were his own he looked down at her and smiled. She smiled back in a way that made him know she knew he had tried her out, but she didn't say a word.

The music stopped, and, instead of leaving him to go over and sit down near the chaperones the way most of the girls and women did, she slipped her arm in his and they started walking around the floor like he liked to do. She didn't start clattering away and giggling—just walked along beside him acting natural, and looking like everything her eyes fell on made her happy.

Directly she did giggle, but so short and soft that all it

did was make him think she might be a good singer, until the words that followed it got through his head.

"It must have been an awful shock falling in that cold water this morning," she said.

Shim felt like cold water was hitting him again, in the face. She was laughing at him.

"I guess Dave won't rest till he tells everybody," he said, stiff and proper.

"Oh, don't feel that way," she said quickly. "I didn't mean to make you mad. It's just such a good joke."

Her eyes, clear and deep blue, were so surprisingly pleasant to look at that he kept looking. Studying the rest of her face for the first time, he found everything about it plumb all right. She lowered the longest lashes he'd ever seen, and when she raised them again and that straight, friendly look met his he felt sort of like when you shoot through swift water in a boat.

"Shucks," he said. "I don't care who knows it. I reckon it was funny."

She pressed his arm with her fingers, and he glanced down at her small white hand on his dark sleeve. It didn't have a ring of any kind breaking its whiteness, and he liked that. He didn't remember ever seeing a young girl or a grown woman before without at least one ring on, if not a diamond, then a birthstone.

"Say—" the words blurted out of him without his even thinking—"I'm trying to talk Dave out of a wolfhide he got this morning. If he gives it to me, would you like to have it for a rug?"

Instead of letting out a squeal and acting put-on and silly, she just looked at him and said real low, "I'd like it better than anything in the world." Suddenly he felt grown up and tall as the Captain.

They were passing the musicians' chairs, empty except for the instruments lying across them. "The band's out taking a smoke," he said. "There they come back now." It was on the tip of his tongue to tell her they had probably had a quick drink, too, and that the music would be even more lively when they started playing again. He caught himself in time. He didn't know what had got into him to make him feel so natural and easy with a girl that he like to have forgotten his manners and mentioned liquor in front of her.

"You know I've been wanting to ask somebody something," she said slowly. "I've heard that some of these people here call us 'mill trash.' What do they mean?"

He was glad she wasn't looking at him, because he felt his face getting hot and wondered for a second if she knew he had been guilty of exactly that. He wanted more than he'd ever wanted anything to explain it to her. It would take a mighty long time, but he had a crazy notion that he could. She wasn't sore or anything, just puzzled, and really wanted to know. The music started up again, so loud, close to them like it was, that he didn't have to answer. Right now he didn't want to miss a minute of dancing with her.

Jans tapped him on the shoulder, flagging, and he was so off in another world that his arms were a shade slow about turning her loose. Neither Jans nor Emmy seemed to notice it, but it embarrassed Shim, and to shake off his funny, light-headed feeling he flagged the first girl that came by. It was Betty Lou, and beaming like she had the world by the tail and a downhill drag.

"Just because I'm your old aunt now you needn't think you

can get by without dancing with me, Shim Govan. Or is it your long trousers that are making you act so uppity? Why haven't you been over to see us? Ben said the other day he didn't know where you were keeping yourself. He says you and that Dobson boy have got to be real good friends. I'm so glad, because Ben says a lot of these outsiders coming in are the finest folks in the world once you get to know them, and Mulberry sure is a heap more lively already."

Betty Lou rattled on, and he didn't have to answer her. Just so her words didn't tangle her feet up it was all right with him, and they didn't. Everybody seemed to dance extra good tonight, and the music was the best he'd ever heard. He didn't dance with Emmy again. He knew where she was in the room every minute without ever having to look, but he didn't dance with her again.

The first light of coming day showed on the courthouse dome when Shim and Dave stood on the sidewalk watching dancers climb into waiting carriages or walk off, numb-legged, toward their homes.

"I'm going over to Harvey Beckham's and sleep until schooltime," Dave said. "What are you going to do?"

"Reckon I'll saddle my horse and go home and change clothes for school," Shim said with a yawn. "I've been missing a mighty heap lately, and if I'm coming here to this one next year, I better not get too far behind so close to the end of the term."

"Good idea," Dave said. "You'll find this is a lot harder than that one-horse school at Overcup Ridge."

By the time Shim led his horse out of the Calhouns' barn where he'd left him, it was full daylight. He was climbing into the saddle when unexpected sounds no more than a couple of blocks away broke the early-morning stillness.

"Haw, haw, Jack. Whoa-hoooo—aaaaark—haw, Ben. Haw, Nig." A loud strong voice was calling on oxen to straighten up in the road and pull hard. Other drivers were calling to oxen; whips popped loud and keen. So many of them and at this time of day meant something odd was afoot. Puzzled, he sat listening. It was time for him to be heading for home. But curiosity proved too strong, and he rode toward the sounds.

Beyond the last houses he came to the road that led east to the depot, and saw there more than his fuzzy-feeling eyes could take in right at first. Oxen—black, red, white, spotted, brindle, every color ox he had ever seen—filled the road as far up it as he could see. They were pulling wagons into town. In the lead, ten pairs were yoked to one big wagon. Straining hard against their yokes and bows, they were inching over the road what must be the biggest iron thing in the world. Higher than a man is tall, and so long he could hardly believe it, it looked like some kind of boiler. Even with the driver walking beside them watching closely, hollering out in a loud voice and popping a long whip at any that didn't pull just right, the straining oxen moved almost at a creep. Behind that wagon more oxen came, hitched to another wagonload of iron, and behind that one, others. Slowly as they were moving, they must have been on the road from the depot all night.

Shim, loose in his saddle, sat motionless. This was the machinery for the big mill. He felt like he ought to whirl his horse around and get out of sight and sound of it; he felt like the ground was about to be snatched out from under him while he sat there acting paralyzed, doing nothing about it. But something held him there.

A long gangling driver, walking so slow his feet looked

like they were dragging in the brown dirt, waved to him and hollered in a friendly voice, "Time ain't long as it has been." Shim lifted a hand in reply, and, in a flash, the spell of gloom was broken. Excitement was running through him so fast and hard he wanted to follow these men and this machinery. Once when he was just a chap a clown in a circus parade had waved and hollered to him, and the same crazy desire to follow had hit him then—a craving not to miss a minute of the wonderful sights hinted at and promised.

The sun, extra bright, came up over the treetops. It stung his tired eyes and dry face and brought him back to himself. Something the Captain had said came to him. "Nothing is free in this life, son. One way or another you always have to pay for what you get." He saw it plain as day. Last night had been about the best night he'd ever had—dancing to more good music than he'd ever heard, talking to Emmy, who felt like he did about things. And now, this morning, here was the mill machinery, coming in to ruin the woods, to change his whole good world. What he needed was to see the Captain, or Henry. They knew something about the big things of the world and could straighten out the mixed-up feelings of excitement and sadness packed up inside him. He turned his horse and headed at a quick fox trot back through town and toward home.

He passed the cotton gin, crossed Platinum Bayou bridge and was in the lane between fields before he slowed his horse to a jog trot. Off to his right a man was quarreling with his contrary plow mule in a deep baritone. "Come up there, mule, gee, geeeee." The sound drove both last night's blaring of horns and whine of strings and this morning's slow creaking of ox-drawn wagons from his ears.

He drew in deep breaths of the rich damp smell of freshly plowed ground, and the mixture of stale perfumes still in his clothes from the dresses of the women he'd danced with faded from his nose. The slanting sun was bright on rows of tender green leaves of cotton and corn that had broken through the earth on the ridges. Suddenly he knew he wasn't going to school today. He was going to see Henry. They'd go to the woods and stay all day.

Reaching the forks, he took the road that led around by Henry's. Just the sight of Henry's house, shaded by chinaberry trees, the yard clean-swept, the smoke of breakfast fire coming from the chimney, would make him feel better. A house always took life from the folks that lived in it. Lively folks had a lively-looking house, sad folks a sad-looking house, and when nobody lived in one it was just a ramshack, hollow place that the tenants believed ha'nts lived in. Henry's house was like Henry and Aggie—clean as a whistle, strong, shaded from the hot sun, and everything plumb happy; hens singing, hogs wallowing and grunting, the children rolling and tussling or already at work in the field.

He was a hundred yards or so from Henry's house when he raised his tired eyes into the sunlight, and his first sight of it hit him like a sledge hammer. It looked too still. The house and everything around it reminded him of a burned-out campfire. Getting closer, he saw the front yard that Aggie always kept swept spick-and-span was littered and dirty. No chickens moved about there. A glance at the lot told him the hogs were gone. No one was in sight. Looking across Henry's field, he saw nobody working there.

Lifting the gate latch with a foot, he rode into the yard. Through the open front door he saw the back door standing open too, and nothing between but emptiness. The walls and floor, that Aggie kept as clean as boiling water and lye soap could make them, looked dirty and dingy the way they always looked in an empty house.

The litter around him in the yard was straw. It had been emptied from mattresses, and for only one reason—to make the load smaller. Wagons had come in the night from somewhere, and Henry had loaded up his folks and his belongings and gone.

Not Henry. It was a dream, a bad one, and it looked so real he didn't see much chance of coming out of it.

Something different about the worn top step caught Shim's eye. He rode closer and looked down at it. Fresh-carved letters, shaped about as neat as any in his copybook at school, ran almost the full width and length of the rough plank. Henry had carved them. All these years he had never known Henry could read or write. But Henry had carved these letters: I LEAVES IT WITH YOU.

Suddenly the fresh morning air was choking to breathe. Henry was gone, and there was no mistake about it. He had known he was going, and that's why he had been so set on the three of them going on that turkey hunt, why he had acted like he did that night. He knew it would be their last hunt together.

Henry was gone, and they would never know where. All they would ever know was that it was somewhere way off, farther back in the woods, far away from outsiders. Away from the very outsiders Shim had been in Mulberry kicking up his heels with last night while Henry sat here carving his good-by.

Shim's horse moved restlessly, lifted his head and neighed.

Answering brays came from plow mules in different parts of the field, and Shim jerked his shoulders straight. Folks in the field could see him sitting here, still wearing his dance clothes. He rode out the gate and down the turnrow toward home.